STALIN'S SPEAR

ALSO BY BRENT TOWNS

Team Reaper Thrillers

Fear the Reaper Series

The MI6 Files

Talon Series

Mark Hayes Series

Dave Nash Thrillers

Treasure Series

The Gods of War Series

Genocide

Congo Ice

STALIN'S SPEAR

THE GODS OF WAR
BOOK 3

BRENT TOWNS

ROUGH
EDGES
PRESS

Stalin's Spear
Paperback Edition
Copyright © 2024 Brent Towns

Rough Edges Press
An Imprint of Wolfpack Publishing
1707 E. Diana Street
Tampa, FL 33610

roughedgespress.com

Paperback ISBN 978-1-68549-361-5
eBook ISBN 978-1-68549-360-8
LCCN 2024941375

STALIN'S SPEAR

MI6 INTERROGATION SITE, LONDON

WE FOUND OURSELVES ONCE MORE IN THIS FAMILIAR BOARDROOM, *the third day of questioning by the latest generation of politicians from the intelligence committee. Christine Ryan, her short dark hair framing her face and her eyes set with the intensity of burnished copper, had walked the clandestine halls of intelligence before. The two other gentlemen, both graying at the temples, sat beside her. But unlike their female colleague, they were newcomers to the world of classified information and covert operations.*

Charles German, Jack Holland, and Christine Ryan were our interrogators.

We sat across from them. John Reaper Kane, Holly Smith, and Raymond Knocker Jensen. We were the focal point of the investigation, not the infamous Russian generals known as The Gods of War, despite their reputation as ruthless killers. At least that's how it appeared to us.

I had gained the moniker Reaper, a name that originated from the intricate tattoo across my back. While I bore others, that was the most significant one, apart from the odd bullet scar.

Like Knocker, I had darker hair, and our faces bore the ruggedness of many days without a razor.

Although Holly's skin would have looked good with tattoos, it remained unadorned. Her short, sun-kissed blonde hair framed her face, and her athletic build was testament to her disciplined life-style. On this covert operation, she had been our handler.

German stared at us. "Welcome back, gentlemen...and lady."

He was that type of guy, and I wanted to punch him in the face.

"Another day of mining for the truth and getting to the bottom of your shitshow of an operation."

Yeah, really wanted to punch him in the face. However, Knocker did it verbally. "Fuck you."

Short and sweet.

"I see your intention to be openly hostile toward us today is an ongoing thing, Mr. Jensen. It is becoming tiresome." German sighed.

"Only to people I don't like," he growled. "You just happen to be one of them. Miss Ryan, on the other hand, I respect because she's lived the life, has been in our shoes before, so to speak."

"Thank you, Mr. Jensen."

"Even if she is a bitch."

I glanced at Knocker. "You done?"

"Just getting warmed up, Reaper."

Jack Holland narrowed his eyes and said, "Miss Smith, will you keep your attack dog under control?"

"You'll have to forgive Mr. Jensen. He's a little under the weather this morning."

"I think hungover is the word you're looking for," Christine Ryan said with a smirk.

"Bollocks," Knocker snapped. "If anything, I'm still bloody pissed."

She glared at him. I just shook my head. I recall him bumbling around at about four in the morning. Now it was nine, and he was feeling the effects. I didn't blame him. The witch hunt they were on was bullshit.

"Now, where were we up to?" German asked.

Where?

The five generals—now down to four—had committed heinous acts: they'd massacred a village to secure oil, orchestrated a coup in the Democratic Republic of Congo to gain access to the country's diamonds, and ruthlessly eliminated their own politicians to over-

throw the president and install a puppet leader. We knew who two of them were. Mikhail Shatov and Lazar Noskov. A third general we'd had on our radar, Misha Durov, had been killed by the betrayal of his own associates in Antwerp. Then there arose the first mention of Stalin's Spear.

And that was just the beginning.

German continued, "I believe we were going to examine the Berlin operation today."

Berlin was something else entirely.

Berlin was complex.

"I read in the report that you were all brought back from an operation in Mexico to fly to Berlin. Is that correct?" German asked.

I nodded. "We were recalled and given a mission to perform an extraction."

"The extraction of someone you personally knew."

"That's right."

"I understand he was, however, bait to get you there."

"Yes, and we fell for it. Hook, line, and sinker."

KANE AND JENSEN

HOOK, LINE, AND SINKER

On a damp and chilly night in Warsaw, Mark Stevens trod along the rain-slicked sidewalk. The street held puddles that reflected the nocturnal glow. His destination was a rendezvous arranged just the previous day. The MI6 officer moved with purpose, slipping beneath a street lamp adorned with a half-raised lampshade, its colored globes casting an eerie illumination. Along the sidewalk, sturdy concrete bollards separated the pedestrian realm from the vehicular lane—a precaution necessitated by the ghosts of lone-wolf terrorist threats.

Stevens's damp shoes crunched on the gritty ground with each step. Ahead of him, two lovers strolled, wrapped up in long dark coats and each other. The MI6 man was nervous, his heart racing. This was his first meeting with someone from the other side, a person with the potential to prove valuable beyond expectation.

The contact's name was Andrey Popov. He was a serving general in the Russian army—sorry, the Army of the United Soviet Socialist Republic, since Sergey Lash had changed it back to its former name.

The MI6 man surveyed both directions before stepping off the curb and crossing the road. As he moved up onto the sidewalk, his eyes caught sight of an illuminated tattoo parlor. Through the large front window, he glimpsed the artist at work—a young woman lay on a custom-designed bed, her bare back exposed. The artist's needle danced across her skin, her flesh relating the permanent story being etched there. There was an air of secrecy about the scene, where art and pain intertwined, indelible marks being left on both canvas and soul.

"You wanna buy some gear, man?"

Stevens did a sidestep, his intake of breath audible as he was dragged from the scene before him. A young man stepped out of a shadowed doorway toward him. Pushing past, the operative kept going, picking up his pace.

"No?" the man called after him, throwing an inquiring hand in the air.

Continuing past the next intersection toward the park, Stevens took in the narrow street giving way to a winding path. This led through a picturesque landscape of meticulously tended green grass that looked soft underfoot. The leaves of towering trees rustled in the breeze, and flower beds were full of vibrant colors. At the heart of the idyllic scene stood a majestic marble fountain, its waters dancing and sparkling in the ambient light. This was a place of respite from the bustle and noise of the city surrounding it.

When he reached it, Stevens stopped and waited. He looked around. There was a couple seated on a bench seat and a woman jogging. Somewhere in the distance, a vehicle backfired, putting Stevens on edge.

Ten minutes passed before Popov appeared, emerging from the shadows, looking around nervously. He wore a long dark coat and a black hat. "Mark? Are you Mark Stevens?"

"Andrey?"

"Yes."

"Good. I cannot stay long. I think they tried to follow me."

Stevens peered into the surrounding vegetation as

though searching for something or someone. "Come with me, Andrey. I can get you out of Warsaw."

"No. There is one man, and only one man that I trust. He is called The Reaper. He is an American working for your MI6. I will come in with him."

"I've never heard of him," Stevens said.

Popov took a step forward, and Stevens glimpsed the terror in the man's eyes as his face came into the dim light of a park lamp.

"It must be him. Only him. I will meet him in Berlin. Wonderland. One week from today. Do you understand?"

Stevens nodded. "I understand, Andrey. But we have many men you can trust."

Andrey shook his head. "No, it must be him. He is an old friend. He is the only one I trust completely."

"Okay. I will get him."

"Thank you. Now, I must go. Remember, one week, Wonderland Berlin."

"Wait, what time?"

"Night like this. Ten o'clock."

"Okay. I'll pass it on."

The meeting over, each man went their separate way, Stevens retracing his steps and Andrey Popov blending into the shadows of the trees once more.

When Popov emerged from the park a short time later, he climbed into the back seat of a Mercedes sedan. Closing the door, he turned to the man beside him. "It is done."

Without giving Popov a glance, the man replied, "You did well."

"What now?"

"You still have to finish what you started, Sergey."

"And then?"

"And then I won't need you anymore," the man replied.

CHAPTER 1

WE WERE IN MEXICO. KNOCKER, HOLLY, AND I. WE WERE sunbathing by the pool among all the other hotel guests. Some wore rather skimpy bathing suits, others tried. We were doing surveillance on Luis Govea. Cartel kingpin for most of Mexico. Killer extraordinaire. Peddler of drugs into the UK, responsible for ninety percent of all drug deaths in the Kingdom.

The man had sinister methods of dealing with rivals. He would decapitate them, sending a gruesome parcel to their families. The remaining body parts were fed to the pigs on his farms. When dealing with judges and politicians, his brutality escalated. He had a surgeon amputate their limbs without the benefit of anesthesia. These unfortunate souls suffered a horrifying ordeal as they were fed alive to his pigs.

The man was evil incarnate, and our mission bore a singular purpose: we were there to kill him. And at that moment he was wearing aviator sunglasses and a deep tan, looking relaxed on a sun lounger across the pool. Beside him lay a woman. His fiancée, Andrea, was a news reporter for a local television station.

"Reaper, I think I'm looking at a million-dollar set of titties," Knocker said.

"You think he paid that much for them?" I asked him.

"Sure. What do you think, boss?"

"Don't ask me," Holly said. "I wasn't blessed in that department when I hit adolescence."

"I don't know," Knocker replied. "You seem to fill that black bikini out rather well."

"Eyes on the prize, Raymond."

"I have, boss. Both of them."

"It's like going on holiday to Ibiza with a bloody teenager."

"Reaper?"

"I kind of have to agree," I replied. "You don't see a pair like that every day."

"Christ, two of you."

"Hey, Reaper, she's looking at me," Knocker said.

"Sure."

"I got a smile."

Rising from her sunbed, Andrea spoke briefly to our target before walking around the pool. I tracked her movements while pretending to watch the revelry in the crystal-clear waters of the hotel pool. As she walked past us, she made hard eye contact with Knocker. He shrugged at us then got to his feet and began to follow a discreet distance behind her.

"I hope you know what you're doing, Knocker," I said in a low voice.

I could hear the grin in his voice. "It's called gathering intel."

"Christ."

Holly said, "He's going to get himself killed, isn't he?"

"More than likely."

Picking up my beer, I took a sip. A drop of condensation from the bottle dripped onto the bare skin of my abdomen. It was cold and the sensation felt shocking on my hot flesh. I stared across the pool. Luis Govea hadn't moved.

Through my earwig I could hear Knocker's voice. I glanced over at Holly, and the look on her face told me she could hear it too. Apparently, he'd caught up with the reporter by the time she'd reached the elevator. When the bell dinged at the level she was to get off at, things had become rather steamy. I heard him say, "So this is your room. Nice."

Then I heard her say, "Shut up. We don't have much time."

"Oh shit, you're getting undressed."

I rolled my eyes.

"Did you not want to fuck me?"

"Well—"

I took the earwig out, not willing to eavesdrop on the mating of donkeys. Holly was doing the same. Looking at me, her face was etched in annoyance. There was, however, nothing I could do about it. So, I sat there studying the target.

"Would you like another drink, sir?"

I looked up and saw a young poolside waitress staring down at me. Her eyes, like her hair, were dark, her smile sultry. "Sure."

Handing her my card, she placed it on her tray. Several minutes later she was back, passing me the uncapped beer and my card along with a small slip of paper. With a seductive smile, she turned and walked away, the swing of her hips issuing an invitation.

"Please tell me that isn't what I think it is," Holly said softly, shaking her head and rolling her eyes.

She meant the phone number I'd just been handed. "Okay, I won't."

Now there was movement across the pool. Govea sat up and spoke to one of his tattooed bodyguards. The man nodded and started walking toward the hotel. "Ah, shit."

I reached for my earwig and put it back in. "Knocker, can you hear me?"

All I got was silence.

"Knocker, you've got a bodyguard on his way up. Get out of there."

Still nothing. Holly tried and got the same response.

"He's got his earwig out," I said.

"Damn it, go and fix this."

"On my way, boss."

Following the bodyguard, I entered the elevator car behind him. He selected a floor and I pretended to do the same, indicating that I was going to the same floor. "We're both going the same direction," I said.

He glared at me as though to say *shut the fuck up*.

The door dinged, and as it slid open, I waited for him to step out onto the red-carpeted hallway, then followed him.

He moved with purpose, traveling to halfway along the corridor before stopping outside the door to Govea's room. He used the electronic key provided by his boss, and the door snicked open. Then I struck.

Having no weapon, the strength contained in my six-four solidly built frame was all I had to neutralize him. I put him into a powerful chokehold and waited for the lights to go out. There was no getting loose, but he fought it to the end.

With him still in my grip, I pushed the door open and dragged him into the suite. I put him into the bathroom and closed the door. Then I went into the suite looking for my wayward friend.

It was obvious where they were by the noises I could hear emanating through the bedroom door. And yes, it sounded like two donkeys hammering each other.

"*Really, Reaper? I didn't think it was that bad.*"

"*It was pretty bad.*"

"*You sure?*"

"*I said so, didn't I?*"

The three people across the table gave me an impatient look.

The trick was getting Knocker's attention without causing too much fuss. So I opened the door and walked in.

"Shit, what the fuck?" Knocker snapped when he saw me standing there.

He was splayed out on the bed while Andrea rode him like he was her last hope in the Kentucky Derby. She let out a yelp and dove under the covers. I must say, Knocker did well not to use my name. "We need to get out of here. Now."

"What? Now?"

"I don't have fucking time for this. Maybe you would like to tell the bodyguard when he wakes up in the bathroom."

He rolled off the bed and got dressed. I saw him slip his earwig in and said, "Great, now you fucking have it in."

"We wanted some privacy."

"Idiot."

"What are we going to do with her?" he asked.

"Nothing. What's she going to say? Hey, I was in our bed fucking some guy I met, and another guy walked in on us?"

"Yeah, I see your point." He lifted the covers. "Bye, sweetheart."

She came out of her bed hurling insults our way. When we exited the room, she was standing on the carpet, no clothes on, chest thrust out, threatening us with death.

"You were right," I said to Knocker.

"About what?"

"I reckon he did pay a million for them."

"Told you."

———

Ten minutes later, we were back in our room and dressed in jeans and T-shirts. A knock on the door had us drawing our Glock 19 handguns. I walked over to it and stood to one side while saying, "Who is it?"

"Holly. Let me in."

Opening the door to her, I stepped back as she entered. She stopped in the center of the room and stared at Knocker. "You bloody stupid bastard. You could have cocked the whole thing up, you fucking pillock."

"I managed to get some intel."

"Like what? Her tits aren't real? She bucks like a horse while you're riding her?"

"Govea is going to a football game tomorrow in Mexico City. It will be a good chance to nail his ass."

"Instead of his fiancée's?"

"Something like that," Knocker replied with a stupid grin.

"You seem to have forgotten something, Raymond. John had to get your ass out of there. What's stopping Govea from heading back to his place in the desert instead of going to Mexico City?"

"She won't tell," I said. "That leaves the bodyguard."

"And he won't want to tell Govea he fucked up," Knocker added.

"I hope you're right, because if you are wrong, this whole thing will be one big cockup."

We were partly right as it turned out. He did nothing about his bodyguard. Andrea was a different story.

Room service knocked on our door the following morning with a package. Knocker was in the shower, and I was downing my first coffee of the day. It was strong and bitter and tasted good.

The knock on the door was loud and clear. "Room service. I have a delivery."

"Who for?" I asked through the door, my Glock in my hand.

"It does not say, senor," the man answered.

"Leave it there and I'll grab it."

"Outside the door?"

"Yes, outside the door."

He put it down and went away.

Slowly I eased the door open until I was sure it was clear. Looking down I noted a cooler and knew right away it was bad. The only good thing that comes in a cooler is beer, and it was too early for that.

Using the plastic handle, I picked it up, looking each way down the corridor before backing into the room and closing the door. I set it down on the table. Knocker appeared. He had a towel wrapped around his waist. "Who was that?"

I pointed at the cooler. "Room service."

He stared at the object. "Too early for beer."

"Yeah."

"This isn't good, Reaper," he said to me.

"No."

For at least a full minute we contemplated what to do. Did we open it or not? I looked at my friend. "You want to do it?"

"You're in command."

I sighed. Reaching out slowly, I moved the handle so I could take the lid off. My fingers rested on the lid as I looked at Knocker. He took a step backward. "Thanks a lot, buddy."

He glanced at me and shrugged.

The lid came away and I wished it hadn't. After looking down into the void I closed my eyes. I heard Knocker say, "Motherfucker."

My eyes opened again and locked with those in the head at the bottom of the cooler. "I guess he knows."

"What are we going to do with it?" Knocker asked.

"How the hell should I know."

Knocker put the lid back on and said, "Leave it with me."

I shook my head. "No, I'll do it."

What I did next was typical Knocker Jensen. Maybe I'd been around him too long. It was just crazy shit. I knocked on Govea's door, the cooler in one hand, suppressed Glock in the other. A bodyguard opened the door and I hit him with a rock-hard gun barrel between the eyes.

He staggered back and fell to the floor. Stepping over his body, I walked into the suite proper. Govea was drinking a coffee, sitting at the table.

"I believe this belongs to you, asshole," I growled.

To his right, another bodyguard moved, coming up off the sofa. The Glock came around and I shot him. "Sit the fuck down."

Govea remained unmoved. He stared at me and said, "Who are you, Gringo?"

"Ever heard of that prick who rides a white horse?" I asked.

"What?"

I shot him in the head, the bullet blowing out the back of his skull and splattering the floor with blood and brains. Before I left the room, I policed my brass and closed the door behind me. The cooler came with me. Andrea didn't deserve to be left in the company of that asshole.

"What did you do with the head?" Holland asked.

"Disposed of it appropriately," I replied.

"How?"

This prick didn't need to know that I'd thrown it in a river.

"Maybe I'll tell you one day. Just not today."

CHAPTER 2

WE FLEW INTO BRIZE NORTON AND WERE DRIVEN TO LONDON through a drab gray day under a heavy overcast. The streets were wet, and as normal, the traffic was chaotic. We were greeted by Lisa Goodall. She was wearing her usual pantsuit, her hair cut short.

She gave us a look like we were children about to be chastised by a teacher for their inappropriate actions. "Well, well, if it isn't my little band of fuckups."

"We got the job done," I pointed out.

"It was a bloody mess," Lisa snapped. "You walk into the target's suite holding a head and shoot him."

"Like I said, we got the job done."

Her steely gaze switched to Knocker. "And you. Of all the stupid, cocked-up, idiotic moves you have made," she held up his file. "And there have been numerous ones. You sleep with the target's fiancée."

I waited for Knocker to say something in his usual fashion, something like no sleeping was done, but he said nothing. He just sat there and took the berating, which was very unlike him.

The next and last person in the firing line was Holly. "Do I need to replace you?"

The question was short and sweet. "No, ma'am."

"Because I can. Maybe I should. Give these miscreants over to someone who can control them."

"It wasn't Holly's fault," I said, coming to her defense.

"I wasn't asking you, Mr. Kane."

We were in a small conference room, and before Lisa could continue, there was a knock on the door, and it opened. A woman's face appeared.

"What?" Lisa snarled.

The woman just backed out, pulling the door closed behind her.

The MI6 officer returned her glare to us and continued her tirade. "I'm trying hard to find a reason why I shouldn't throw all three of your asses out of the building permanently."

"Because we're good at what we do," Knocker said.

"Oh, you're good at something, all right. And I would be kicking you all out, except something has come up."

She waited for us to ask what but none of us said a word.

"You're being sent to Berlin, where you are to extract a Russian general. Supposedly he has a host of information our government intends to utilize. He has asked for you personally, Mr. Kane."

"Me?"

"Yes. His name is Andrey Popov. I gather you know him?"

Popov. I hadn't heard that name for a long time. I'd come across him on an operation in Syria. He was one of the good guys, even for a Russian. "He asked for me?"

"Yes. He wants you to meet him in Wonderland, Berlin."

"What's Wonderland?" I asked.

"Abandoned amusement park. It's due for demolition."

I nodded.

"It doesn't mean you can just go off and destroy it yourself."

"Why would we do that?"

"Why would you do a lot of things?" Her face changed.

"Now, seriously, our man in Warsaw said the general was scared that he was being watched."

"By whom?" Holly asked.

"Whoever is suspicious, I suppose. I don't know. Word is that since Lash has taken over, the FSB is to be disbanded and the KGB reinstated."

"I thought they were pretty much the same thing," Knocker said.

"Maybe he likes the name."

"When do we leave?" Holly asked.

"Tomorrow. Until then, I want you all to write reports on the operation in Mexico."

Christine Ryan opened the folder in front of her and took out some sheets of paper. She held up the first two and I recognized my writing, and I guessed the other was Holly's. Then she placed them on the table and picked up the remaining three.

I stifled a grin.

"Stick figures, Mr. Jensen?"

"Writing reports never was my strong suit, ma'am."

"Neither is drawing by the look of it."

"No, ma'am."

"I do not see the point of all this," Holland growled. "Can we just get on with it? We're wasting time."

Finishing our reports, we made preparations for the mission in Berlin. Holly had the intelligence crowd get us all she could on the area where the meet was meant to take place.

The Wonderland was a former amusement park which had opened in 1967. At the time, it had been West German territory, and between East and West it was one of only two such parks built. Later, after Germany and Berlin were unified, the park changed, including new attractions and management like the park in East Germany.

They must have spent too much money because around 2001, their admission prices were raised substantially. By the time 2003 arrived, they were insolvent. Things went from bad to worse after that, with the park closing its gates after 2004. The same fate was suffered by the Spreepark.

I studied an old map of the former tourist attraction. Wonderland was set among trees, more so now after it had been left derelict for so many years. It had a lake, old roller-coaster, train line, different rides, and a couple of water-slides. Like all amusement parks, it had the obligatory carousel and a Ferris wheel.

"Where the hell is this meeting supposed to take place?" Knocker asked.

"In the park, ten p.m.," Holly said.

"It's a bloody big park. Depending on where you meet him, limits where I can set up overwatch."

"We," said Holly. "I'll be with you."

He shrugged. "We."

"I need to get a closer look at the perimeter," I said.

Holly passed me another picture. Looking it over, I muttered under my breath. She raised her gaze. "What is it, John?"

I tossed the photo in front of her. "There is only one way in and out of the park. A high fence has been placed around it to keep people out. The place is a damn enclosure."

"What do you want to do?"

"Nothing we can do. Suck it and see."

"Do you want me to put a fireteam together?"

I thought about it for a long time before shaking my head. "No, he might get spooked and run if he thinks something is off."

"I can have them standing by in a helicopter five minutes away if you think that might be a better solution."

"Okay, we'll do that."

So, that's what we did. The next day, we went to Berlin.

————

Our small team was met in Berlin by an MI6 officer named Michaelson. Arthur A. He'd been there two years and was ready to go home to London. The man was in his forties and operated with his team out of the UK Embassy.

For our backup, Holly had managed to secure a team of freelance mercs. They were private contractors who were based in Berlin, which would work out well if things went to shit.

A black SUV took us to the embassy. From the front seat, I heard Michaelson say, "I can't understand why we couldn't have just done what needed to be done. It's not like we're useless."

"All I know is that John was specifically requested," Holly replied.

"Have you seen the weather report? There is a large storm front moving in. Looks like snow is going to shut down the airport and God knows whatever else."

"We saw something about it."

"Do you know who Popov is?" Michaelson asked.

"Russian general."

"No, really is?"

"How about you tell me."

"The last few years he's been working on the development of newer rocket motors for nuclear weapons for the Red Army. Supersonic ones that are much faster than what we've seen. If the west gets their hands on the tech that he can provide, then we'll be on a level playing field."

"How do you know that it's Popov who has been running the program?"

"We've had someone on the inside."

"Then why can't you get the stuff you need through them?"

"Not that simple I'm afraid. However, I still think we could have got him and his wife and child out."

"What was that?" I asked. "Popov's wife and kid died in a car wreck years ago."

Michaelson shook his head. "According to intel, he got remarried. Younger woman who brought the kid with her."

Holly glanced over her shoulder at me. My response was

a WTF expression. Michaelson caught it from the driver's
seat. "They didn't tell you?"

"We had no idea," Holly replied. "As far as we knew, it
was just him."

"Well, someone made a cockup."

"Obviously."

"Weapons?" I asked.

"We have them," Michaelson said.

"I'll need a DMR," Knocker told him, meaning a Designated Marksman Rifle.

"Four Seventeen good enough?"

"Copy that."

———

Upon reaching the embassy, we were shown to our
accommodation. After settling in, we went over the plan
once more. In, out, and if anything went wrong, we had the
mercs on standby. Given that the meet was the following
night, I decided to look for myself.

Supplied with a Mercedes SUV by the embassy, we took
it that afternoon and went to scout the amusement park.

From the outside, it looked like the city had been slashed
by a giant hand, the remaining scar visible but long forgotten. It reminded me of pictures I'd seen of Chernobyl. There
was a tall fence and chain across where the entrance had
been, a large keep out sign attached to it.

We parked on the opposite side of the street and
absorbed the scene.

Knocker mused, "If I can get on that rollercoaster scaf-
fold, I should get good line of sight for the whole park."

Holly said, "According to this old park map, the only
decent open area is on the other side of the entrance. If I set
up in this building here, I should be able to cover you as
well."

Looking down at the map I saw where she was pointing.
Nodding, I said, "Looks good."

"Is it just me, or did you pick up that tail we had, Reaper?" Knocker asked.

I looked in the rearview mirror and saw the Audi sedan. "Audi R8?"

"That's him."

I stared at the vehicle through the mirror. "Two occupants."

"Not sure."

My cell rang. "Yeah, Kane."

"Hello, Mr. Kane. It's been a while since we last talked."

Mikhail Shatov. One of the Gods of War, all-round asshole. "Hello, Mikhail."

"I see you're in Berlin."

"You don't miss much," I replied. "Why don't you come on over and we can catch up?"

"Sorry, I'm a little busy."

"What about Noskov? Send him. I'm sure Durov would like to see a friendly face."

"Now, Mr. Kane, one shouldn't speak ill of the dead."

"What do I owe the pleasure, Mikhail?" I asked him.

"Just wanted you to know I was still around, and to expect a visit sometime soon."

"Are they your people tailing us?"

"No, Mr. Kane. Do you expect me to blatantly show my hand?" Shatov said. "Although I did hear that a certain cartel from Mexico had sent a team to Berlin. I think the Syrians too. But more about that later. Goodbye."

I stared at my cell.

"What was that all about?" Knocker asked.

I stared through the windscreen. Snow was starting to fall. "I have no idea, but whatever it was, you can bet it won't be good. Let's get out of here."

"What did you think the call was about, Mr. Kane?" German asked.

"I had no idea. He was talking in riddles. He had a habit of turning everything into a game."

"Did you have any indication of what was about to happen?" Christine Ryan asked.

"No, ma'am. We had an inkling that there would be dire consequences, but not to the severity that unfolded. As I mentioned yesterday during our wrap-up, they launched a significant offensive."

"They declared war on us, ma'am," Holly said. *"I doubt Berlin has seen the likes of it for a long time."*

Christine Ryan's face turned grim. *"Yes, I doubt it had."*

By the time we made it back to the embassy the snow had intensified. The remainder of the day was spent going over our equipment and the plan. The people at the embassy had thought of everything. We'd been issued with Glock 19s and suppressed C8 carbines. Knocker got his Heckler and Koch 417, which fired a 7.62 round, and we all got NVGs. Body armor was also issued, as well as stun and fragmentation grenades. We even had spare ammo and batteries for our comms.

"Hi, guys."

Turning as one, we saw Sam Swift standing in the basement doorway. The color of his red hair seemed more intense than when I'd last seen him. The ultimate geek, I'd sent out an SOS for his help on this mission. He would remain at the embassy running observations and anything else we needed.

"Hey, Slick, you made good time," I said.

"Never let a friend in need down," he replied. "How can I help?"

I briefed him on the requirements and expressed my concerns. He nodded slowly and said, "I can do that. I'm most apprehensive about the incoming stormfront. It has the capacity to shut down the entire city, and you'll be out among it."

"How's it looking out, Slick?" Knocker asked.

"Getting heavy."

"We'll have to deal with it once we're out there. Is there anything you need?"

He slapped the laptop case at his side. "I have everything I need here. If I can't do it with that, then it can't be done."

"Hello, Sam," Holly said.

"Hey, Holly. It's been a while." He grinned.

She returned his smile. "Yes, a whole couple of weeks."

"We're just checking our gear," I said to him. "Give us a few minutes and we'll get you the intel to go over."

"All good, I can wait. I might have a coffee though."

While Swift made himself an instant coffee, we finished up, and Holly found the intel he would need. We also informed him of the plan of what we intended to do.

As evening fell, we sat around talking and watching television. We tried to make a ritual of relaxing the night before embarking on a mission. Preparation for the challenge ahead required more than just physical readiness. Mental fatigue could creep in like a stealthy adversary. I made a point to unwind, if only briefly. I never truly powered down. My mind remained vigilant. Those stolen moments gave me an opportunity to recalibrate, charge my mental batteries.

Slick appeared while we were deep in an episode of Strike Back. Knocker and I were discussing the finer points of fiction versus reality, with him trying to explain that it was created for entertainment, not a bloody documentary. He looked over my shoulder and said, "This looks like trouble."

I turned and Holly looked up from her book about an MI6 officer in West Berlin. "You look like you're about to bust, Slick," I said. "What's got you so excited?"

"He's here in Berlin."

"Who?"

"Mikhail Shatov. I got some feed of him entering a hotel with another man I've never seen before."

My mind reeled. Our number one target here in Berlin? Why on earth would he be here?

Knocker asked, "Do we go after him in his hotel, Reaper?"

I wanted to. Oh, how that appealed to me. However,

common sense warned me to slow my roll. "No. If he isn't worried about being picked up, it means there's something in the wind. We could be walking into a trap."

"Weirdly, he's here at the same time," Holly mused.

"Not weird, planned."

"You figure he's tied into this whole thing somehow?" Knocker asked.

"You know what he's like. Would it surprise you if he was?"

"Not in the bloody slightest."

"Slick, can you trawl through camera footage to see if there's anyone of interest with him? Maybe Noskov?"

"Sure."

"Also, run facial rec on passengers coming through the local airports over the past few days to see if anything pops."

"Roger that. Anyone in particular?"

"No, just those parameters."

"I'll see what I can dig up."

Slick disappeared and left the three of us to it. Holly looked at me and said, "You figure this is all tied together, don't you?"

"I hope it isn't, but two and two makes four every time. It can't mean anything but."

Knocker rose and stretched then began to walk from the room. "Where are you going?" I asked.

"To get more guns."

I looked at Holly. "I need a new phone."

CHAPTER 3

THE SNOW FELL RELENTLESSLY THROUGH THE NIGHT, continuing into the following day. Airports across Germany succumbed to its icy grip, shutting down operations. Traffic on the roads was on the brink of chaos. Most of the U-Bahn trains persevered with eighty percent of their routes subterranean.

While we made preparations to leave that morning, Slick came to us with what he'd found. "I don't think you're going to like this."

"Hit us with it, Sam, old chap," Knocker said. "If we didn't get bad news, we'd get none at all."

"There is a whole team of Shatov's operators in Berlin with him. I saw them getting off a transport outside of Berlin."

"Who was the guy with him?" Holly asked.

"No idea. If he's in the system, he's buried deep. But that's not all. I've picked out Mexican Cartel shooters and Syrians as well. All flew in before the airports were shut down."

"Is that everything?" I asked.

He stared at me.

I nodded. "No, it's not. It never is."

"I've also identified Albanian hit teams as well as Georgians. Then throw in Triad hitmen and Yakuza."

"You chaps seem to draw a whole heap of excrement down upon you, don't you?" German said.

"It's what you get for doing your job well," I replied. *"But even for us, it was a new level of attention."*

"This was their attempt at stopping us in our tracks," Holly supplied.

"The report never stated that it was this bad," Christine Ryan pointed out, lifting a sheet of paper as though searching for what wasn't there.

"That's because we never put it in," I replied. *"Who would believe that so much firepower was sent after us. Then there was the bounty."*

"What bounty?"

"They've put a fifty-million-dollar bounty on your heads, Reaper," Slick said.

"Good Lord in heaven," Knocker said calmly. "The whole mission is screaming *can me*."

"We can't," I said. "Andrey is counting on us."

"But what if it's a trap?" Knocker asked. "Everything points to it. I'm not averse to bucking the odds, but I'd like to be prepared."

"You know what I do. I'm not asking you to come. If need be, I'll go on my own. But I considered this man a friend, and I intend to get him out."

"Shit, you know I'm not going to let you go alone."

I looked at Holly. "It might be better if you sit this one out."

"No, John, I'm in."

"We're going to need someone to coordinate things on the off-chance it all goes pear-shaped," I pointed out.

"John—"

"What he's trying to say in his own sweet way, Holly, is that he doesn't want you out there," Knocker spelled it out. "He just doesn't want to hurt your feelings. You will be more valuable here with Slick."

"Is that what you're trying to say?" she asked.

I nodded. "Pretty much, but you're the boss. The final call is yours."

"Okay, I'll stay."

"Thank you. I have a feeling you just made a wise choice."

The snow that night was reminiscent of another not so long ago when we were transporting a terrorist through the UK at Christmas. But that's a story for another time.

The snow was becoming deeper, and we passed little traffic during our travels to the old amusement park. The only ones out in this inclement weather were the dumb and the desperate. I wasn't quite sure which category we fell into. The trains, however, were still running, some of them almost empty.

Knocker and I had donned battle attire, our forms swathed in warm layers. Our faces were partially concealed by snug masks, a defense against the biting cold. Woolen ski hats embraced our heads, solace from the chill. Beneath them, we wore head mounts for our night vision goggles. Our weapons were in the back, alongside other essentials. As we embarked on this mission, I hoped we wouldn't need to wield them.

Arriving well ahead of the scheduled rendezvous, Knocker cut the chain to let us in. Once the van was parked, we moved into the back between the seats and got ready. Knocker had his 417 as well as a Milkor MGL six-round grenade launcher. I, on the other hand, had gone with one slung under my C8 carbine.

"Slick, copy?"

"Lima Charlie, Reaper."

"Radio check," Knocker said.

"Good copy, Knocker."

"Holly with you?" I asked.

"I'm here, John," she replied.

"Okay, what's your ISR feed like?"

"Spotty," Slick replied.

Not what I wanted to hear. "Roger that, do what you can."

I looked at Knocker. "You ready?"

He nodded. "Let's do this."

Carrying our gear, we left the van. Knocker disappeared into the darkness, and five minutes later, I heard his voice over comms, "In position."

"All right, now we wait."

The frigid wind took my breath away, the thick snow-covered landscape taking on surreal shapes. Ice was forming in patches which could prove treacherous later. I lowered my NVGs and scanned around the immediate area. It was dark but not pitch. "Slick, anything?"

"Nothing."

I gently cradled the C8 even though it dangled from a strap. My gloved hands sought warmth, the right one with a trigger finger cutout. I tucked that hand into my pocket, preserving its heat against the chill.

"Knocker, sitrep?"

"I swear, Reaper, if I have to move too fast, my bollocks will hit together and shatter. Bloody hell it's cold."

I was hearing him. "Getting soft, old chap?"

"Been hanging out with you too long."

I walked another lap around the van. Something nearby crashed loudly as a sudden gust of wind tore through the park. A loose shutter, maybe. An open door? I looked at the illuminated face of my watch. It was just after ten and still no sign.

An additional fifteen minutes elapsed before Holly said, "John, can you hear me?"

"Yeah, go ahead."

"Give it another ten minutes, and then call it a night."

"Roger that."

Halfway through the extra time, Slick said, "Reaper, I have three vehicles inbound."

"Roger that. Knocker, head on a swivel."

I could imagine him settling down all businesslike. His experience on ops like this was irreplaceable.

Headlights appeared and the three vehicles pulled in behind the van. I held the C8 ready just in case. Nine armed men alighted from the SUVs, three who weren't. The headlights illuminated the three. Only one was unfamiliar. He was bald. Mikhail Shatov and Andrey Popov were the others.

"I am sorry, John," Popov apologized.

"It's okay, Andrey."

The man I'd never seen before raised his weapon and shot Popov in the head. My friend dropped into the snow, his blood staining it red. I took half a step forward, and the man aimed his weapon at me. I froze.

"Reaper, just say the fucking word," Knocker said.

I remained silent, knowing that had they wanted me dead, I already would be. There was more to the situation. My eyes narrowed, but I said nothing.

"Now, Mr. Kane, let's get down to business. As much as I would really like to kill you, I have something else in mind."

"You're a fucking asshole, Shatov."

"Come now, I'm sure you can be more original than that."

I nodded at the red dot on his chest. Shatov looked down. "I see your friend is with us this evening."

"Yeah. He's got an itchy trigger finger, so don't sneeze."

"Let me shoot the fucker, Reaper."

"Before you do anything hasty, Mr. Kane, I have something you might like to hear. Besides, even if your friend does in fact kill me, my people will do the same to you. So you see, nobody wins."

"All right, speak."

"Somewhere in the city are the wife and child of your

friend. You have twenty-four hours to find them. If you are one minute late, they will both die. The task is simple."

There was a smug smile on his wrinkled face. Nothing was ever that simple. "How is it simple?"

"Okay, maybe it isn't that simple. But I'm sure you will do your best."

So, that was it. We were pawns in his game of chess. But why? "Twenty-four hours?"

He looked at his watch. "I tell you what, Mr. Kane. I'll give you a little extra time. You have until eleven p.m. tomorrow night."

"An extra twenty minutes, you're so fucking generous."

"Reaper, you've got five SUVs inbound your pos. ETA, two minutes."

Shatov gave me a sympathetic wave. "Anyway, I must be off. Good luck, Mr. Kane. You're going to need it."

The group climbed back into their vehicles, the last one in was the Russian with Shatov. "Slick, see if you can find something on that bald prick."

"Copy. Incoming one mike out."

"Copy that. Also, find the woman and the kid. What about our QRF?"

"Nothing is flying in this."

With that, the five SUVs came into view. By the time their headlights swept across the area where I'd been standing, there was nothing for them to see.

From the shadows, I watched the SUVs disgorge their loads of four per vehicle. Twenty to two. Not the best odds but we had faced worse in the past. As soon as they began talking, I could tell who they were. Mexican Cartel. Pulling my NVGs down, I slipped even further into the park. "Knocker, put them down."

I heard two rounds crack as they passed over me. The sound of automatic gunfire ripped through the night as the cartel shooters panicked. Knocker said, "That's two down, Reaper. The rest have scattered."

"Copy that. Just don't shoot me."

Through the green haze of my NVGs, a large building appeared. I hurried toward it and stepped up onto a long porch. It had large windows along the front and a tired sign above the door that told me it was the gift shop.

The door was unlocked so I slipped silently inside. A thick coating of dust and bird shit covered the floor, showing the detritus of age. Shelves still held souvenir items even after all these years. Footsteps sounded from the veranda outside, and I crouched down, watching the front door.

At first there was nothing, not a movement or sound, then a figure appeared in the doorway. He was armed with what looked to be an MP7. The laser sight attached to the C8 in my hands centered on the would-be killer just before I caressed the trigger. The 5.56 round punched into his chest, and he staggered. To make sure, I fired again, and the Mexican dropped to the dirty floor.

Gunfire ripped through the night and windows at the front of the building shattered violently. I ducked down behind shelves as bullets hammered into them, making their items dance wildly.

A stuffed bear fell and hit my shoulder. Other items rained around me as I crawled along the aisle to avoid getting shot.

"Reaper, are you all right?" Knocker asked.

"Bit busy, Knocker."

"At least you're breathing. Who are these cocks?"

"Cartel," I said.

"Cool, I was starting to think they were people I didn't like."

More bullets hammered through the broken windows. "Slick, tell me what you see."

"Not a lot. This snowstorm is making things difficult. I suggest you get out of there."

"Yes. Knocker, I'm moving."

"Copy. Head toward my position. I'll see if I can pick a few more off before I'm—"

The rattle of something hard bouncing across the shop

floor blocked out the rest of what he was saying. The sound was all too familiar and caused me to leap into action.

GRENADE!

I was running toward the back of the store when it detonated. The blast seemed to slap me on the back and propel me even faster. Landing heavily, face down, the air was forced from my lungs. Heat from the explosion washed over me, singeing the odd hair.

My arms and legs worked furiously as they took me across the floor into the rear room of the store.

Knocker's voice burrowed deep into my ear. "Reaper, was that you? Talk to me."

"I'm good. My bell's rung, but I'm still in the fight."

"That's something. I got another guy out the front of the store. He might have been the one who threw the grenade."

I stood and straightened myself out, finding my way to the rear door. It was unlocked and just took a good shove to get it open. A blast of cold air hit me in the face. Not that it wasn't cold in the store. I cleared the immediate area and started across the open ground toward what looked to be an old rocketship-type carousel.

Somewhere behind me, gunfire sounded, but not in my direction. I jogged past the carousel and along a path. A shadow emerged from the green haze of my NVGs, taking me by surprise. The impact of the incoming round smacked into the cartel shooter, spinning him around before he fell to the snow-covered ground.

Knocker's voice sounded in my ear. "Thank you, Ray. No worries, John."

"Shut the fuck up and get some more of the bastards."

"No can do. The snow is getting too heavy."

"I'll meet you near the bridge."

"Roger that."

"Slick, I need to know what is going on," I said into my comms.

"I'm trying to get a better picture, Reaper. At the moment, all I'm getting is snow."

"Trying being in my shoes for a minute and you'll know about snow."

Voices calling to my right drew my attention, and I crouched down behind a low wall, waiting to see what would happen next. At first there was nothing to see, but then two figures emerged from behind some bushes.

They had stopped calling out and began to move cautiously along the path. I lowered the C8 and brought up the suppressed Glock. It too had a laser sight fitted, which looked like a lance in my NVGs.

The handgun fired twice as my finger applied pressure, released, and then applied again. I shifted my aim and fired twice more. Both men dropped. One was silent, the other crying out in pain. I left my hiding position and strode forward. When I was standing over him, I put another round into his brain.

Then, like a silent and deadly wraith from a horror movie, I melted back into the shadows.

Knocker was waiting for me at the bridge.

"You all right?"

He nodded. "Yeah. Prick of a night for it."

"Yeah."

"Well, it was a trap," Knocker said.

"It was."

"Remind you of anything?"

"That time when we were transporting that terrorist?"

"Yes," he said. "Except we had more people."

"More bodies dropped too," I pointed out.

"We're not done yet, Reaper."

He was right. Whenever we got in the shit together, bodies seemed to rain like a monsoon in Thailand. There was a never-ending stream of bad guys coming out of the woodwork, all with a common goal. Our demise.

"Let's go," I said.

"Where?"

"Water slide," I replied.

"Might be a bit cold to be playing in the water."

"You're a goose."

We moved deeper into the decrepit park. Weeds turned into long grass, shrubs turned into uncontrolled hedges, and bushes were now trees. However, they all had one thing in common, they were covered in a blanket of white snow, their shapes giving the landscape an eerie look.

Puffs of mist came from our mouths with every breath. The waterslide loomed out of the darkness, looking like a thick python curling and twisting in on itself. Around the pool at the bottom were large rocks which would offer us some protection. The pool was empty, its bottom lined with cracks and junk. Someone had dumped an old bicycle with one wheel in the bottom beside a mannequin.

"You figure she came undone around that last turn?" Knocker asked me.

"Might be the fact she only had one arm," I pointed out.

"Eh? Oh, yeah, so she has. Silly cow, fancy that."

Knocker and I settled down among the rocks and waited. "Slick, you got anything?"

"Not a damn thing, Reaper. This snow is a bitch."

"What about thermal?"

"I'm doing the best with what I have. If there was a military satellite in the area it might be a different story."

"What about Popov's wife and child?"

"No. I'm still trying to find out their names."

"Ask Michaelson."

"Reaper, I've got movement," Knocker whispered.

Through my NVGs, I could see a group of five shooters. Knocker moved and said, "Hold onto your panties, old mate."

Instead of using the 417, he brought up the grenade launcher. It fired twice, each time marked by a throaty THUNK.

The explosions split the wintery night with a savage orange ferocity. The five Mexicans were torn to shreds in the blast and the snow around them painted red and black. A leg here, an arm there.

"That stopped them," Knocker growled.

"John, what was that explosion?" Holly asked.

"You saw that?" I asked hopefully.

"Blind Billy could have seen it from the moon," she replied.

"How about the feed?"

"No, we only saw it because it was big."

Typical of Knocker, never did things by halves. "Roger that. What about the QRF?"

"Forget them, they're not coming."

"Shit. All right, we do it ourselves." I looked over at Knocker. "Come on, time to leave."

Just then, out of the night came a rocket-propelled grenade with each of our names written on it.

My left fist filled with Knocker's thick coat as I flung myself back, taking him with me. The rocks where we'd been hiding bore the brunt of the impact. The base of the pool might have been cracked, but it was unforgiving on impact, and the air rushed from my lungs. Pain shot through my ribs as I landed on something hard. Knocker crashed down beside me. "Motherfucker, Reaper, what did you do that for?"

"You're welcome," I told him, dragging him to his feet. "Come on."

Climbing from the far side of the shallow pool, we ran toward a large structure. I knew what it had been for, the map ingrained in my mind. It was where the dodgem cars had been set up. Beside it was something called the Gopher Theater.

Cutting through the dodgem car area, we looked for a way into the theater. There was a door around the side which stood ajar, and Knocker pushed it open. I followed him in, and we took shelter on the stage.

It wasn't large, but sufficient to accommodate a few families who would have come to watch the shows.

"Slick, Holly, copy?"

"We're here," Holly replied.

"Is that ISR working any better?"

"No. Yes. Maybe."

"Which is it?"

"There looks to be a small break coming," Slick said. "Wait. Oh shit. You've got another four SUVs incoming, Reaper."

"Damn it. Holly, I don't care how you do it, but get that fucking helicopter up. Now, before these pricks kill us."

"I'll see what I can do."

CHAPTER 4

A COLOSSAL EXPLOSION REVERBERATED THROUGH THE AIR, banishing the darkness for a short while. Knocker and I had discreetly left the theater but had planted a surprise for anyone who might inadvertently stumble across it. And someone had. The snowfall had abated slightly, and we got the call that the helicopter was on the way in. But fate had delivered the next slap to our faces in the form of a new batch of shooters to the unfolding drama.

"Reaper, the helicopter is three mikes out. It's going to put down near the fountain and they'll start from there."

"Roger that, Slick." I turned to Knocker. "Helicopter is three mikes out."

Magic Mountain loomed behind us, its silhouette reminiscent of a miniature rollercoaster that once spiraled in and out from the summit. I dropped out my almost spent magazine, executing a tactical reload, muscle memory guiding my movements. With Knocker by my side, we slipped into the cover of the surrounding trees, our footsteps muffled by fallen leaves and snow. Our destination was the weathered fountain, waiting silently for our arrival.

I could hear the helicopter in the distance, its WHOP-WHOP-WHOP reaching out through the abating storm.

Holly came back to me saying, "They'll only get one shot at this, John. Things are about to pick up again."

"Is there any radio traffic from the Berlin police?"

"Nothing as yet. The last thing we want is for police to step into a firefight like this."

As the helicopter neared, we could see the snow swirling around with the beat of the rotors as well as the down wash. The bird seemed to hover for a moment, suspended from an invisible string, then exploded in midair.

"Shit, Reaper, did you see that?"

"I would have to be blind to miss that. Someone just fired a fucking rocket. Holly, did you get that?"

"What happened, John?"

"Someone just shot the damn helicopter down. We're moving to the crash site."

"Do you want me to notify medical services?" she asked.

"Yes, but warn them we have an active shooter situation. The same with the police. There's no containing this now."

"Copy."

Knocker led the way to the site of the downed helicopter. It was near an attraction called The Gold Mine. The wreckage was burning, and while I held security, Knocked looked over the debris for survivors. He came back and knelt beside me. "There's no one alive in there, Reaper."

"Right, I've had a gut full. Time to show these assholes what real fighters can do."

Slinking off into the surrounding darkness, we waited. Like moths to a candle, they appeared. The chatter was in Spanish, which meant that the new arrivals were cartel too. They stood around, staring at the flames.

Big mistake.

The pin slid out of the fragmentation grenade in my right hand. I said in a low voice, "Now."

The grenade arced through the air and landed among them. A moment before it detonated, Knocker fired his grenade launcher and continued working it until the last cylinder was empty.

I'm not sure how many were killed, but it was more than a handful. Others who had escaped the holocaust were quickly taken down by our rifles. When we finished, there were corpses and body parts littering the snow-covered ground.

"What you did constituted a slaughter," German said. He removed a sheet of paper from the folder in front of him and waved it in front of us. "You killed a dozen people. It says so right here."

"It must be right then," I replied.

"Is that all you have to say?"

"You seem to be forgetting something, Mr. German." The last two words came from my mouth as though I was spitting out something vile. "They were there to kill us. They were the tip of the spear. This...this was just the fucking beginning."

"I think we'll take a break," Christine Ryan said.

"We've only just started," Holland pointed out.

"And I say we need a break." She looked across the table at us. "Go, get coffee, and calm down."

Knocker opened his mouth to speak but Holly's hand on his arm made him close it. Instead, we got to our feet and went to get that coffee.

I feel like going to the pub," Knocker said.

"You always feel like going to the pub," Holly replied with a shake of her head.

"He's just pushing buttons to see what type of reaction he can get," I said. "And I lost my cool."

"Exactly, Mr. Kane. It was unforgivable."

We turned to see Christine Ryan standing behind us.

Knocker said, "Check my back, Reaper, I think she still has her claws in it."

She rolled her eyes.

"What can we do for you, Christine?" I asked.

"Control your emotions, Mr. Kane. I'm not the enemy. The other two would like to see you hung up by your balls and dressed like a side of beef."

"We'll see what we can do," I replied.

Her cell buzzed as a message came through. She looked at it

and shook her head in frustration. "For crying out fucking loud. I have to go. Be back in the room in five minutes."

———

We finished our coffees and were back by the end of the fifth minute. However, things had changed. Instead of three sitting across the table from us, there were four. The addition was a man we all knew. CIA Director, Ken Newman.

He and I locked stares. I knew why he was here. He wanted to look into the eyes of the man he'd ordered killed. I felt Holly's hand on my thigh under the table, warning against me leaping across the table and choking the living shit out of him.

German started, "Mr. Newman will be sitting in as an observer for the rest of the proceedings, given that he has a vested interest."

"He'll have to get in line like the rest of you," Knocker replied.

The words brought forth the rage bubbling just beneath the surface. Newman's gaze switched to me, and he said, "I'm not leaving London until I get answers. And when I do, you're coming with me, asshole."

"That will do," Christine Ryan snapped. "Let's continue."

After we were done with the cartel shooters, we left the amusement park. We climbed—

"Wait," said Newman. "When are we getting to the part about Cuba?"

German picked up his itinerary. "The day after tomorrow."

"I have to wait around for two days before—"

"Yes, Mr. Newman, you do. However, should you choose to stay, you may learn something enlightening," snapped Christine Ryan.

"Like what?"

She looked at her other panel members who nodded. She then spent the next fifteen minutes catching him up. Once she was done, I continued.

Climbing into the van we started back to the embassy. We managed to get away before anyone else.

"Slick, have you come up with anything about the woman and child?"

"Nothing."

"Names?"

"Yes," Holly answered. "Kira and Polina is what Michaelson said. Kira is the mother."

I thought for a moment while Knocker drove. "We'll check out the hotel. I need a room number."

"Four-twenty," Holly replied. "You're about four blocks east of it. There are twenty-three hours and change left, John."

"Roger, that. Out."

"Reaper, how the fuck do we find a needle in a haystack?" Knocker asked.

"By lifting one piece of straw at a time."

"Yeah, I was afraid—"

WHAM!

The back of the van took most of the impact from the truck slamming into us. If it had hit closer to Knocker, his candle would have been snuffed. As it was, we were bashed around a bit.

The van performed a spin then stopped. I shook my head to banish the stars and cobwebs. "Knocker, you with me?"

"Who was that prick?" he asked, still not quite with it.

Suddenly the van was hammered by gunfire. Bullets punched through the thin exterior. My hand shot out and started dragging Knocker toward me. "Come on, get the fuck out."

Somehow, he managed to grab his 417 on the way through before spilling onto the snow-covered asphalt where I had already fallen. In my hands was the C8 carbine.

We hunkered down to avoid the unrelenting fusillade from the shooters.

"John, Raymond, talk to me," Holly said.

"Wait one, Holly. We're taking fire. Some prick rammed our van."

I leaned around the front of the van and saw the vehicle

in question. It was what appeared to be an enclosed delivery truck. With only three shooters visible, I wasn't fooled into thinking that there weren't more.

"Knocker, I've got three shooters near the truck."

My friend scooted across the asphalt and looked around the rear of the van. "Two more this side, Reaper."

I opened fire and saw one of the shooters duck. His friends increased their fire and forced me back into cover, bullets spanging off the van's exterior. Knocker was firing too, but having little effect. He ducked back and pressed his back against the van.

"Time to get serious, Reaper," he grated.

With a nod, I agreed. "Go at them hard, Knocker. Press forward."

"Roger that."

We came clear of cover, our weapons up. The C8 in my hands fired and the first target fell. Fire and move was the order of the day—or night. Drop one, pick another, and shoot again. A bullet picked at my coat, tearing the heavy fabric. I had two down and the third was starting to panic. A long burst fixed him good. I glanced at Knocker, who looked at me. "What took you so long?"

"I had more."

"Mine was taller."

"We need to get to the hotel," I said to him and checked one of the shooters. "We'll need to ditch everything except the handguns."

"We can't just leave them here."

I glanced around the immediate vicinity. In the gutter, I saw what resembled a grate. "Dump the ammo down there and set the van on fire."

"Who do you figure these guys are?"

"No idea."

Moving with purpose, we disposed of our gear, keeping the Glocks with the spare magazines. We even ditched the body armor because wearing it would draw attention.

Knocker and I jogged the four blocks to the hotel, which

served a dual purpose. We were warm upon arriving at our destination, slowing to a walk before heading through the front door. The foyer was virtually empty. There was a young male receptionist behind the desk, a bellhop standing in the corner, and that was it. "Talk to me, Slick."

"He's booked in under the name Volkov, Reaper."

I walked confidently up to the front desk, taking a punt that he wouldn't know who I was. He looked up from his computer keyboard and asked, "Can I help you, sir?"

"I lost my card," I said to him in German.

"What room?"

"Volkov. Room four-twenty."

"Give me a moment, please, Mr. Volkov. Ah, do you have some identification, please?"

I gave him an embarrassed look. "It is in my room with the keycard in it."

He gave me a wan smile. "Oh, dear. Never mind, I'll just be a moment."

The clerk selected a blank keycard before programming it for the room that Shatov was booked in. Once he was done, he handed it over and said, "There you go. Have a good night."

"Thank you."

As Knocker and I walked toward the elevator bank, he said to me, "That was easy."

"I had a lot of practice lying when I was a kid."

"What? Mrs. Kane's little boy was a habitual liar?"

"No, I just did it to keep myself out of trouble," I replied. "And I was in trouble a lot."

He chuckled, pressing the call button on the elevator. It dinged almost immediately, and the stainless-steel doors slid open. We climbed in and I pressed the button for the floor we needed.

When the doors opened, we stepped out into the hallway, the carpet a mass of red and brown swirls beneath our feet. The suite we were looking for was down to the left on the right side of the hallway.

Knocker took his Glock out and got ready to enter. I opened the door with the keycard and pushed it wide. Following Knocker in, my Glock was raised just like his. When we were in the suite proper, he went right, and I went left. The room took no time to clear, as well as the bathroom. That left the bedroom.

Using my spare hand, I pointed toward it. Knocker nodded and moved toward the door. He stood to one side and grabbed the handle. I nodded and he opened the door.

Of all the things I could miss as I entered, the tripwire was the one that would cause us grief. By the time I noticed it, it was too late. I heard a beep and looked to my right. There on the floor was a timer counting down.

"Bomb!"

I dived toward the doorway, Knocker close behind. The explosion followed almost immediately and rocked the hotel savagely. Alarms began to shriek and wail immediately, their whine ear-piercing.

Dust and debris rained down upon us. I rolled over and said, "Not again. Knocker?"

"I'm here."

"Let's get the hell out of here."

By the time we made it outside using the stairs, the first of the emergency services were arriving on-site.

———

Figuring that we should regroup, Knocker and I went underground to catch a train. The meet with Popov had obviously been a trap, there was a bounty on our heads, and the room where Shatov had been was designed to kill us when we came looking.

The U-Bahn station we arrived at was almost vacant. With only three other people waiting there, should have alerted me but didn't. Two were men, one was a woman. The men were wrapped in long coats which went down to their ankles, and considering the weather outside, was not unusual in itself. The woman was similarly garbed, however, she had a hand-drawn trolley, not unlike a two-wheeled thing you see with senior citizens at the store.

The trains were running late or not at all, so we were prepared for a lengthy wait for the next one to arrive. Knocker and I sat on a bench and waited, keeping an eye on our surroundings.

The reception on comms was still spotty, but at our last contact, Holly and Slick were still digging deep to find Popov's family.

Knocker said, "Something is off about this whole thing. Why would they put a bounty on our heads?"

"Because they want us dead."

"But they could do it—or try to do it themselves."

"I don't know, Knocker. It's a game to him."

"It's like they're trying to keep us busy for some reason."

I nodded. "Let's just stick to the mission and worry about that later."

A fourth person appeared on the platform. This man too wore a large coat. For some reason he drew my attention. I stared at him. A bigger guy with a beard. He glanced sideways at me.

I stared at him.

He stared back.

My gaze was steady.

He flinched and pulled his coat back.

"Shit."

The man was carrying an MP7 and trying to bring it into action. My hand went for my Glock and the scene became a modern setting for an old western movie where the fastest gun won.

"Knocker!"

My Glock came up and I started firing way too early, but the intention was to put the guy off his aim. My first bullet missed, the second hit him in the leg, the third in the stomach, and my fourth finally in the chest. He flailed his arms and fell to the hard tiled surface of the train platform with a shout of alarm and pain.

Meanwhile, his friends were moving too. The ones that hadn't tripped any mental alarms but should have.

The two men swept their coats aside to reveal their weapons. Heckler and Koch Umps. As they started to spray the platform with 9mm rounds, I took cover behind a column. Bullets smashed into it, shattering the tile encasing it. Knocker had drawn his own weapon and, before he could fire, was also forced into cover.

Meanwhile, the woman had stuffed a hand into her trolley and pulled her weapon. It was a compact grenade launcher. Things had just ratcheted up a notch.

Our awareness came abruptly as a massive explosion reverberated nearby, just short of the protection of our refuge. The stout columns bore the brunt of the blast, their forms fracturing under the impact, splintering tiles into lethal shards that sliced through the air at velocity.

"Shit, Reaper, the crazy cow has got a fucking grenade launcher."

Suddenly over the gunfire, I could hear a crazed cackling.

I said, "You're right about one thing, she's fucking crazy."

Additional rounds whistled through the air, ushing in yet another explosion. This time, it was dangerously close, and Knocker and I found ourselves caught in the storm of debris, the impact buffeting me relentlessly. My primal instincts kicked in, and I let out a guttural growl, my fingers tightening on the grip of my weapon. Peering around the corner, I locked eyes with our female adversary wielding the grenade launcher. With the stakes so high, I knew I had to act swiftly.

Firing four shots, I ducked back. She was struck in the arm and let go of the launcher, releasing its weight and letting it fall to the tiled platform. A loud screech of wild rage emanated from her throat as she produced a handgun. I heard Knocker say over my comms, "Silly cow."

He fired three shots at her, each one finding flesh. She dropped to the platform and a large pool of blood began to form around her still form.

That left the final two shooters, however, and I couldn't decide who was more perilous. The crazy woman with the launcher or the calm firing effect from the guys. No, definitely the woman.

I sent another fusillade of bullets their way until the magazine ran dry, dropping out the spent one and slapping home a new one in one fluid motion.

Knocker fired another burst and then called out, "Reloading!"

I commenced my steady rate of fire and was soon rewarded with a hit. The shooter lurched to one side, and I was able to get a better look at him. Snapping off another shot, I hit him in the head. Then there was one. At least we had him outnumbered.

Until more shooters came thundering down the stairs.

"Bollocks," I heard Knocker say as more rounds came buzzing in our direction.

The newcomers opened fire and we were soon the ones outnumbered and in dire straits. They were all using assault weapons, and before long, we were suppressed and they were trying to flank us. If that were to happen, we were screwed.

As luck would have it, the train, due to arrive five minutes earlier, arrived at the station. It looked to be vacant. "Knocker, the train."

"Oh, right. You go first, mate. I want to see how many times you get shot by these cocks before you get there."

The carriage doors slid open across from me. I sucked in a lungful of air and sprinted. Bullets sliced through the atmosphere, a deadly symphony. I lunged inside just in time, the angry swarm of hornets that had pursued me slamming into the carriage's exterior like vengeful sprites. "Come on, Knocker, or I'll go without you."

"You get me killed, Reaper, and I'll fucking haunt you."

Then he ran too.

My Glock sprang into action and emptied a full maga-zine at the assailants—perhaps more for my own release than anything else. As the doors slid shut, Knocker brushed past me and collapsed into a nearby seat. His eyes met mine, and a mischievous grin played on his lips.

"Get a load of us, Reaper, we look like shit."

He was right. We were dirty, bleeding from various cuts and abrasions, and battered like fried chicken.

But we weren't done yet.

"Who were the shooters in the train station?" German asked.

"Albanians," Holly said.

"Were they tracking you?" German asked me.

"They had a central hub that was feeding them information," I replied. *"It was set up by the generals."*

"By Shatov?"

"Yes."

"You hinted before that, at the time, you thought the Russians were up to something. Was that true?" Holland asked.

My head bobbed up and down. "Yes."

"What was it?"

"I'll get to that."

CHAPTER 5

WE GOT OFF THE TRAIN AT THE NEXT STOP AND MANAGED TO get our comms back up. "Holly, Slick, you got ears on?"

"Damn, John, it's good to hear your voice," Holly said. "Where are you?"

While we walked, I gave her our position and told her what had happened. "Have you had any luck with Popov's family?"

"I'll let Slick tell you."

"Reaper, we found them getting off a private jet outside of Berlin two days ago. I managed to track them to a café in the city called—get this—Ivans. It's run by a guy named Ivan Petrov. The place is a front for the Russian mafia. Michaelson is on his way over there now."

It was a stupid thing to do. "Roger that. Send me the address."

"It's about two blocks from where you are."

"We might have to drop in there."

"John, be careful. We can't get eyes on you from here."

"Have you got a name for that bald Russian yet?" I asked.

"We're still working on it."

"Copy, I'll let you know how we get on."

Twenty minutes elapsed, and we stood outside the café,

our eyes scanning the surroundings for a trace of Michaelson. However, there was no sign of him.

"Holly, have you heard from Michaelson at all?"

"No. He's not there?"

"Not outside, anyway."

"I don't understand, he should be there by now," she replied.

"We're going in," I told her as I drew my weapon.

The unlocked door should have been an immediate red flag, but I brushed it aside. Consequently, what unfolded next was undoubtedly my own doing. As we stepped inside, the dining area lay deserted, illuminated solely by the soft glow of night lights strategically placed to discourage potential intruders.

I said to Knocker, "Let's go to the kitchen."

We had covered half the distance when a formidable group of armed men materialized. They seemed to emerge simultaneously from both the rear and the front door—the very one we had just passed through. Futility hung in the air. Attempting to shoot our way out would have been a swift death sentence. So, with resignation, Knocker and I raised our hands in surrender, allowing ourselves to be disarmed by our captors.

"Ah, bollocks," Knocker growled.

"John, what's going on?" Holly asked. "John, speak to me. John!"

Ignoring her voice in my ear, I waited for our weapons to be taken. Disarmed, we were escorted through to the rear of the building into a large kitchen. There to greet us was the bald man who'd been with Shatov. He looked us over and said, "I'm impressed. We did not expect you to get this far, yet here you are."

"We've always been good at hide and seek," I told him.

In that moment, my attention was drawn to Michaelson, securely bound to the chair, a cloth muffling his voice. The signs of a struggle were evident—bruises and cuts—but he remained conscious, albeit barely.

The Russian said, "I believe you know Mr. Michaelson."

I nodded. "Yeah, but who are you?"

"While the details may not be crucial, what truly matters is that you find yourself facing a decision."

The Russian nodded, and in response, two of his men vanished momentarily, only to reappear with a woman and child. These were none other than Popov's family. The little girl, her eyes wide with fear, fought against the man who gripped her. His hand met her cheek in a cruel slap, and at that very moment, Knocker, fueled by rage, lunged forward. But his progress was short-lived. A swift, calculated blow landed behind his ear, sending him crashing to the floor. The room echoed with his frustrated grunt as he crumpled, defeated. The air hung heavy with tension, and the fate of Popov's loved ones remained uncertain.

"Son of a bitch," I growled.

"Tie the woman to the chair," snapped the bald man angrily.

Kira found herself pushed into a chair, movement prevented as she was restrained next to Michaelson. My gaze remained fixed as I witnessed the last round being removed from my Glock, with only a single round left in the chamber. The weapon was then handed to me, its safety engaged. Meanwhile, the bald Russian drew his own firearm, the tension in the room palpable.

"Now, Mr. Kane, pick."

"Pick what?"

"Which one you will choose to kill."

Kira burst instantly into tears. "Oh, God no."

"I'm not killing either of them," I replied.

"Oh, but you will, or I will shoot the little girl." His arm extended and his weapon was pointed straight at Polina's head. "Now, let's try again. Choose!"

"Shoot the fucker, Reaper," Knocker rumbled from where he lay.

His words provoked a brutal kick from the man towering above him, and a cry of agony escaped his lips. My gaze shifted from the cold steel of the Glock clutched in my hand to the bald Russian before me. Holly's desperate pleas echoed in my ear, urging me to reconsider, but my vision remained fixed on the frightened child and the anguished expression etched onto her mother's face. It was the same look that haunted Michaelson—a blend of regret, fear, and a lifetime of choices made leading to this pivotal moment. The weight of the gun pressed against my palm, and I knew that whatever decision I made would change their lives forever.

Unable to face the condemned, I walked around behind them. I glanced at the man inflicting the torment on us all.

"Make a choice, Mr. Kane. You are running out of time."

Standing there in silence, my eyes focused on the wall opposite. Perhaps this was all a dream and I would wake in a few moments.

"Five…"

My head snapped around and I stared at the Russian. "You're fucking counting down?"

"Four…"

"Three…"

"Two…"

"One…"

BANG!

"John? Are you there, John? What just happened? Damn it, John." Holly's calls fell on deaf ears.

I lowered the gun and turned to face the Russian. "You're so lucky there was only one fucking bullet in this thing."

The prick smiled. "Get the ladies to escort them out. Leave these two with their dead friend. You still have twenty-one hours, Mr. Kane. Make the most of it. Oh, take his weapon. Let's make it even more interesting."

The group's departure left us standing in the almost empty café, staring down at Michaelson.

"You shot—no, murdered Michaelson?" German asked, *astounded.*

"I did."

"Oh, my lord."

"I did what I had to do," I said.

"What you did was murder an innocent man," Holland snarled.

"Seems to be a lot of it going around," Newman said.

"What would you have him do?" Holly demanded.

"Yes, what?" asked Christine Ryan. "Had I been in his shoes, I would have done the same thing."

"Preposterous. Why weren't charges laid for this heinous act?"

"Because luckily, there are people in this country with more bloody sense than you. But it didn't mean that they didn't try." Christine Ryan reached for the phone on the table. "Bring it in."

We sat and waited, and moments later, a television was brought in on wheels and placed at the head of the table. Christine Ryan turned it on while those responsible left. She said, "This is a recording that was released five minutes—that's right—five minutes later."

The screen came to life. There was no sound. On it, claiming center stage was me and Michaelson. The camera had been positioned to show only us. As we watched, I started living it all over again. Then, toward the end, the weapon in my hand came up and showed me shooting Michaelson in the head. The video stopped.

Christine Ryan said, "There was no sound, so we, or whoever watched it, could not hear what was going on in the background. One thing we can be sure of was that Mr. Kane and Mr. Jensen did not record this and put it out there for the world to see. This was carefully orchestrated, and you will be enlightened by the time we finish today."

I was starting to gain a whole new respect for the woman opposite me. She might be known around the traps as The Assassin, but apparently, she was a good ally to have.

"Continue, Mr. Kane," she said with a nod.

Like Ms. Ryan said, the recording was released on the internet five minutes after Michaelson's demise. Quite by accident, Slick stumbled across it. The whys and wherefores don't matter. When he discovered it, his first reaction was shock, and then he showed Holly. At two in the morning, her initial thought was that she was dreaming. She wasn't.

"John, are you there?"

"Yes."

We were making our way back to the embassy, still trying to reconcile what had happened.

"John, don't come back here. They have released a video of you shooting Michaelson onto the internet. It's going viral."

"Damn it. See if you can track where they went."

"Oh, no. That didn't take long," Holly said, her voice aghast.

"What didn't?"

"MI6 have just issued a kill order on you."

"Slick, Emergency Alpha."

"What is that?" Holly asked.

"Slick?"

"Roger, Reaper. Emergency Alpha."

Then we were gone.

"Bugger it, Reaper. This is getting worse by the hour."

"Yeah, come on, we have somewhere to be."

Emergency Alpha related to our days with Global. It was a signal to make our way to a Berlin safehouse we'd utilized while deployed on ops. It would be vacant because it, as the name suggested, was only to be used in case of an emergency. Slick would meet us there, and Holly too if she went along with him. From there, we would recommence operations and get on top of the predicament that the Gods had placed us in.

Once more, we boarded a train. Fortunately, there were no other passengers, nor anyone lying in wait for us. The journey lasted twenty minutes, transporting us to our destination. Outside the station, the snow continued to fall, blanketing the empty street. Curiously, a lone vehicle sat parked by the curb, its hood unfettered by snow. I reached out and touched it, surprised to find it still warm despite the wintery chill.

"They're here."

We climbed the steps of the old-style terraced apartment block, our weapons drawn just in case. Reaching out, I pressed the bell, and the buzzer sounded, releasing the door. We entered the front vestibule, shaking off our boots before climbing the stairs to be greeted by Holly.

"I'm certainly glad to see you. Even if you are a bit battered."

"No problems?" I asked.

Holly shook her head. "No. Are you okay, Raymond?"

"I'm fine, ma'am."

"This has gotten way out of control."

"Where is Slick?"

"Comms room."

We went up another set of stairs to the second room. The comms room was sequestered behind a closet off a bedroom. Slick was inside working at a computer. "Slick."

"Reaper, good to see you in one piece." He glanced at us momentarily before returning to his screen.

"You reach out to our friends?"

"Yes, they'll help any way they can."

"Great. I knew I could count on them."

Turning to Holly, I said, "What do we know?"

"I know you're in deep shit. I tried to reach out to Lisa Goodall, but her answer was for you to turn yourself in and they'll investigate."

"Bollocks they will," Knocker said, holding up a large box.

He placed the on-site medical kit onto a desk and opened it, pawing through its contents for antiseptic and gauze. For the next few minutes, we patched up our cuts and scrapes while Slick searched. Holly said to me, "John, we need to debrief about what happened."

"Talk," I replied.

"You shot Michaelson."

"I did. It was him or the woman or the girl. I'm not one to murder women and children."

"So it had to be Michaelson? That was alright?"

I sighed. "Slick, bring the video up."

"Are you sure, Reaper?"

"Yes. I need for you all to see something."

"I've seen it enough."

"Like I said, I need you all to see it."

Slick's fingers worked his mouse, locating the file containing the damning video, and we all stood around watching the proceedings with dread, knowing that the outcome would be no different from the first. Right up to the point where I shot Michaelson. "Did you see it?"

"I did," said Knocker. I knew he would, but I needed Slick and Holly to.

"See what?" Holly asked.

"I'm sorry, Reaper, I didn't see it."

"Okay, run it again. Watch Michaelson just before I shoot him."

They watched it again, and when it stopped, Holly turned to me wide-eyed and said, "He nodded."

"I saw it too," Slick agreed.

I said, "He knew there was only one way out and communicated as much."

"I have to inform MI6," Holly said.

"Good luck getting them to listen," Knocker said. "Slick, our priority is to find the woman and kid."

"And the Russian," I added.

"And Shatov," Holly joined in.

"Great Scott. It's a good thing I'm part computer database."

"How about weatherman?" Knocker asked.

"Yeah, that's another story. We're stuck with it for a good while yet."

"We can't sit about doing nothing until you find us some actionable intel," I told him.

"In that case, I'd better find you some."

While Slick dug, Knocker and I got some sleep. It wasn't long, maybe two hours, but it recharged some battery cells, and by 4.30, I was making preparations to head back out. There was, however, still nothing for us to go on.

I made a fresh pot of coffee and had poured one for myself when Knocker emerged and groaned. "I hurt."

"Know how you feel. Did you catch the number of the damn bus that hit me?"

Slick and Holly appeared from the comms room. "I think we might have something."

"What?"

"Stefan Kaltz."

"Who is he?"

"He's meant to know where all the bodies are buried," Holly informed us.

"How can he help?" Knocker asked.

"He's former Stasi turned criminal mastermind. He's someone who supposedly knows everything that happens on his turf."

"And you want us to go and talk to him, us with a bounty on our heads?" I asked.

"The way I see it, you don't have anything to lose. As they say, damned if you do and damned if you don't."

"Where do we find him?"

"This time of day, he'll be at the wholesale markets taking his cut from the sellers."

A sigh escaped my lips. "All right. Knocker, let's put some things together."

The arms cache was a giant safe in the wall hidden behind a sideboard. I used an old code to access it and the door swung wide. Inside was a variety of weapons and other items we could use. Knocker and I grabbed a couple of MP5SDs and G36Cs. Fragmentation and stun grenades, as well as body armor and ammo, were next on our list. Then we were ready to go out once more.

Looking around the vault, I saw the last item I would

need. There were four sets of automobile keys. I grabbed a set and said to Slick, "Send the address to me."

"On its way, Reaper."

After saying goodbye, we headed back out into the chill. Stopping on the sidewalk, I pressed the button on the key-fob, and almost instantly, an orange flash of indicators revealed that our motor was a Mercedes Benz G550 4X4.

"That's our ride," I said to Knocker, tossing him the keys.

We piled into the vehicle, anticipation thick in the air. Glancing at my phone, I traced the path Slick had meticulously mapped out for us to reach the markets. I couldn't shake the feeling that it would be a treacherous journey, akin to venturing into the lion's den. Yet, we had no other leads, no alternative routes. The fate of two innocent lives hung in the balance, and every choice we made carried immense weight.

CHAPTER 6

DUE TO THE WEATHER THAT MORNING, THE BUSTLING MARKET was surprising. The air hummed with activity, people swarming, their livelihoods hinging on securing the finest and freshest produce available.

A closed-in market such as this one was not the place for automatic weapons. So, once again, Knocker and I had to settle for our handguns, a pair of SIG Sauer P226s supplied by the vault.

"Comms check."

"Read you, Lima Charlie, Reaper," Slick said. "For once."

"Slick, copy?" Knocker said.

"Roger."

"What about the feed, Slick?" I asked.

"It's not the best, but it's better than what it was."

"Say the word, boss."

"Proceed on mission, John," Holly said stoically. "Good luck."

We entered the market and were instantly assaulted by the scent of fish, seafood, fresh fruit, and vegetables, as well as the associated sounds of vendors touting their wares.

Slick said, "Reaper, you need to proceed north about fifty meters."

"Copy."

We made our way through the market, taking it all in. There was a lot of activity, most of it from buyers and sellers haggling about price and quality. Knocker and I continued walking north.

"Reaper, on your left," Knocker said.

I glanced left without staring at the guy Knocker had pointed out. Big, dressed in a suit, looked out of place in a market such as this. An obvious bulge under his coat indicated that he was packing heat. "Got him."

"There's another on the right."

"Got him too."

We kept walking. Slick said, "Ahead of you should be an office."

"The one with the big guys standing either side of the door?" I asked.

"That would be it."

"Okay."

Outside the office door, the guards stepped protectively into our path, stopping us dead. I said to the guards, "We're here to see Kaltz."

They stared at us, their heavy brows creating a glower. It seemed like we weren't worthy of a reply. Even though I spoke in German.

There was a camera above the door. Looking straight down the lens, I mouthed the words, *open up*.

Then we waited.

And waited.

And waited.

Knocker looked at me and said, "I'm starting to think he doesn't want to see us, Reaper."

"Maybe he needs convincing," I replied.

Drawing our SIGs, we pointed them straight at the two guards. Thirty seconds later, a man with gray hair and a lined face opened the door. "Who are you?"

"You speak English?" I asked him, hoping to make things easier.

"Yes."

"If you are Kaltz, we need to talk to you."

He stared at us for a while, deciding whether to listen to the crazy foreigners, before stepping aside. "Come in."

We followed him into the office. Sparsely furnished, it held only a large desk, a filing cabinet, and a picture of someone important I didn't know on the wall. Knocker and I sat down, followed by Kaltz. "You never said who you were."

"Kane and Jensen."

"What do I owe the honor of your presence?"

"They tell us that if something happens in the city, you know about it," I said. "Is that true?"

He shrugged, his reply laconic. "Eventually."

"Then you'll know about the incident last night at the old amusement park."

"If that was you, then I'm truly impressed."

"And the one at the train station."

He nodded slowly.

I waited for a moment and said, "You will also know about the bounty on our heads. Which is why there was a delay. Who did you call?"

He lied. I could see it in his eyes when he said, "No one."

Knocker drew his SIG and pointed it at him. "Now, Mr. Kaltz, we came here with the plan of having a peaceful meeting. All we want is a couple of answers and we'll be on our way. The lives of a woman and child depend on said answers. And your own, of course."

Staring at the gun he remained unfazed. He'd seen it all before.

"Kaltz, we've been killing people most of the night," I said to him. "We're going to keep on doing it until we get the woman and child. If you become a statistic along that path, I don't give two fucks. You choose. But choose wisely."

He sighed. "You have maybe five minutes before they arrive."

"Who?"

"I don't know. Whoever they send."

"The woman and child? Where are they?"

"I don't know. They asked me for a place they could set up in. I provided them with one not far from here," Kaltz said. "Also, they saw Willi."

"Who?"

"Willi Lehner."

"You know they won't let you live, don't you, Kaltz?" Knocker said. "These guys don't leave loose ends. We've been fighting them for weeks now, and every loose end they have has been tied up neatly. The only way you stay alive is to tell us what you know so we can take them out."

"On the outskirts of the city, there is a wrecking yard for cars. They are there."

"Who is in command?"

"Gennady Morozov."

"How do you know his name?" I asked.

"We met him when we worked for the KGB," Kaltz explained. "He was a military liaison linked to the KGB. I haven't seen him for years."

"Who is we?"

"Me and Willi."

"Then he just turns up out of nowhere?"

"Yes. He appears and says he needs somewhere for him and his men for a few days while they run a couple of operations. I—"

"Wait...a couple of operations. Did he say what they were?"

"No."

"Think of the overnight occurrences, is there anything that stands out to you?" I pushed.

"You mean apart from what you did?"

"There must be something. Nothing gets past you."

Again, the sigh. "There was an incident at a research facility last night in the city."

"What incident?"

"An engineer was kidnapped."

I had a bad feeling. "What did he do?"

Kaltz said, "He specialized in rocket propulsion systems. At the time of the Cold War, he was working for the Soviet Ballistic Missile program."

"Which ones?"

"The R-12 system."

I stared hard at him. "The same missiles in the Cuban Missile Crisis?"

"Yes."

"What do they want with him?"

Kaltz shook his head. "I don't know."

"Holly, can you hear me?"

"Yes, John."

Kaltz just informed me that Shatov's people possibly kidnapped a rocket scientist last night. He specializes in R-12 ballistic missile rocket motors."

"Did he say what they were doing?" Holly asked.

"No. Also, I have a name for our bald Russian friend. Gennady Morozov."

"Copy that. Why would they want a German rocket scientist? Especially since they don't make them anymore?"

"No idea."

"Roger that. We'll dig it up."

"Knocker and I are on our way to a facility that Kaltz has made available for Morozov's use. I'm hoping we'll find Popov's wife and child there. Check out a name, Willi Lehner. Kaltz said Morozov talked to him too."

"Will do, good luck."

My stare focused on Kaltz. "Right, tell me everything else you know before they get here."

It was at that time that gunfire ripped through the markets.

The Chinese Golden Dragon Triad had arrived.

Knocker and I pulled our weapons. "How many men do you have?"

"Why should I worry? It's not me—" He stopped, suddenly realizing what he was saying and what he'd been told by us. "Five."

"Slick, I need to know how many tangos are in the market."

"Give me a moment."

"Cameras?" Knocker asked.

Kaltz turned the computer monitor. It took only a moment to see the activity outside the office. I saw one of the German's men appear and then fall, shot by two shooters. They looked to be armed with QCW-05 Bullpup submachine guns.

I looked down at my SIG. "You got anything better than this?"

Kaltz got off his seat and hurried over to a cabinet. He used a key to get it open and stepped aside to reveal a couple of HK G36s. I didn't care for the details of their origins, but we sure as shit were going to use them. I tossed one to Knocker and some spare ammo. Then I grabbed a weapon for myself and loaded it.

"Slick, I need numbers." My voice was urgent.

"Don't quote me, but somewhere between ten and fifteen."

"Oh nice," Knocker growled. "Let's make the pricks earn it."

"What do you want me to do?" Kaltz asked.

As I walked toward the office door, I called back over my shoulder, "Stay the fuck out of the way."

Silently I signaled Knocker. The warehouse was a dimly lit labyrinth of stacked crates and hanging tarps, concealing secrets and danger. Adrenaline surged, setting my pulse racing as I guided Knocker to the adjacent aisle, one over from my position.

Both of us gripped our weapons, fingers steady despite the chaos erupting around us. The staccato rhythm of gunfire reverberated around the warehouse, drawing ominously nearer like a storm.

I heard the echo of footsteps, a countdown to confrontation that bore a man racing toward me. Was he friend or foe? My instincts screamed caution, but his eyes held no malice. Not a threat I decided, my finger easing off the trigger.

Yet fate had other plans. Behind the runner, a second figure materialized, sinister and unyielding. His eyes bore the guilt of countless sins, his weapon prepared for bloodshed. No debate required, I squeezed the trigger of my G36 twice, the recoil jolting through my arms. The Triad shooter crumpled, his life extinguished by two rounds to his chest.

Amid the scent of gunpowder and the fading echoes of violence, I wondered how many more shadows lurked in this maze. Knocker's eyes met mine, and we pressed forward, our silent pact unbroken. The crates threw shadows, and the fruit aisle seemed to hold its breath, waiting for the next move in this deadly dance.

"Knocker, one coming your way," I called as a figure moved past the end of the aisle.

The shooter appeared and Knocker's weapon spoke, bringing the would-be killer down. There was no respite, however, as another took his place and the G36 in Knocker's hands rattled to life again, and the shooter dropped, squeezing his trigger as he went.

Fruit and vegetables were shredded on impact, spraying sweet and sticky confetti across the floor.

Then I heard Knocker say, "Fucking bollocks."

"Are you all right?"

"Bullet just clipped me. I'll be fine."

I pressed forward toward the end of the aisle. Somewhere to my right I could hear an intense gunbattle. My guess was a firefight involving Kaltz's guys.

Reaching the end of the aisle, Knocker and I were reunited. I saw his bloody sleeve and said, "You need to tend that?"

"Not yet. Keep moving."

With the sudden appearance of three more shooters, Knocker threw himself behind some display shelves while I took the option of a forklift truck. Bullets hammered at it, some ricocheting away. I waited for a pause before showing myself to open fire. The short burst from my weapon hit a shooter who reeled away, injured but not fatally. He fell to the hard floor and dragged himself into cover.

Meanwhile, I could hear Knocker firing as well. Then Slick said, "Reaper, you've got four of them trying to flank you."

"Roger that. Knocker, you got these bastards?"

"All over it, Reaper."

"Copy. I'll be right back."

Sprinting along the aisle in the direction I had traveled earlier, I was two-thirds of the way along when a shooter appeared in front of me and opened fire. Throwing myself onto the smooth concrete, I slid along on my shoulder. The G36 came around and I sprayed bullets in the shooter's general direction.

More from luck than good management, some of the rounds caught him in the chest, eliciting a cry of pain. He fell back and died in position.

Two more figures materialized, their weapons blazing. I dove to my right, seeking refuge beneath the low shelving. The air crackled with the deafening staccato of gunfire, and bullets ricocheted off the metal. It was a dance with death, and somehow fate spared me. I slid through the narrow gap, emerging on the other side, my knees hitting the cold floor. The adrenaline was pumping and my vision blurred as I contemplated how much longer my luck would hold.

The shooters realized what had happened and changed position. But this time, I was waiting for them, and as soon as the first appeared, I opened fire with the G36.

My assailant recoiled, as did his companion when he appeared. The last of the quartet thrust his firearm around the shelving, discharging it without a glance. Bullets were sprayed erratically along the aisle, and it hung in the balance —a single well-placed round could spell the end of all involved.

That round emanated from my weapon.

"Slick, what have we—"

BOOM!

A massive explosion shook the market, dust and debris falling all about. It was close by and knocked me down. "Knocker, what the fuck was that?"

"Some pillock just threw a bloody grenade."

"Are you all right?"

"Yeah. Just wish I could return the favor."

"Slick, where are they?"

"All around you, Reaper. You need to get out."

"Copy. Knocker, fall back on me."

"Roger that. Coming your way."

Moments later he joined me. "Slick, where is the nearest exit?"

"To your east."

"Copy."

I led and Knocker brought up the rear. We ran past a couple of aisles and were about to pass a third, where a man lay dead on the floor, when a shooter appeared directly in front of me. With little time for reaction, I dipped my shoulder and hit him in the middle of his chest, knocking him aside. The impact of my weight made him stumble, and he fell onto his back.

While he was down, I drew my handgun and fired. His head snapped back, and his brains painted the floor.

Meanwhile, Knocker had taken the lead and was continuing toward the door we needed to escape.

In an instant, his weapon snapped up and the room erupted in gunfire. My eyes flickered to another Triad shooter crumpling to the ground. The rounds Knocker had unleashed were the final salvos. He discarded the G36, swiftly drawing his SIG. A new assailant materialized, but Knocker dispatched him without hesitation.

Yet another Triad killer emerged behind us. My fingers tightened around the G36, its cold metal reassuring. I aimed and fired. The room echoed with the sharp report, and the assailant staggered, a guttural cry escaping his lips as he collapsed.

"These bastards are like kicking a bloody ant nest, Reaper," Knocker said.

"Slick, talk to me."

"Keep moving in that direction. You should see the door any moment."

Then it was there. "Got it."

The door burst open as I hit it with my shoulder. On the other side, there was nothing but empty space and lorry parking. Dawn was breaking over a gray morning and the ground was covered with snow.

"I've lost visual," Slick said. "All external cameras are off-line. Looks like they are jammed."

"Copy. We're making our way to our ride."

Our near success was abruptly halted by an unforeseen obstacle: six Triad operatives, each brandishing automatic weapons, stood resolutely in our path.

Knocker said, "I don't think we can go this way."

"Tell them we're lost."

"You tell them."

I sighed. "Fine. We're lost."

They remained unmoved.

"It didn't work, Reaper."

"No shit."

The men in front of us raised their weapons to fire.

Before we could react, the morning was shattered by the staccato rhythm of gunfire. The Triad assailants staggered, their bodies convulsing, and collapsed onto the pristine snow. The once-blank canvas of white now bore crimson stains, marking the violent end of their ill-fated mission.

Startled by the sudden turn of events, Knocker and I exchanged wide-eyed glances, grateful that we'd been spared. Our attention was drawn to two mysterious figures that seemingly materialized from the misty gray surroundings.

"Son of a bitch," said Knocker.

"Double," I replied.

One of the men I recognized instantly. He was an old

friend now employed in the private sector. The second I wasn't as familiar with, but Knocker knew him immediately. He was six-four, unshaven, and in his midthirties.

Former Senior Chief Borden Hunt and Former SAS operator Jacob Hawk. The latter was an operative with the Global operations team, Talon, under the command of Anja Meyer.

"Someone said you guys needed some help," Hunt—codename: Scimitar—said as he reloaded his HK 416.

I took his offered hand. "Good to see you, Bord."

"Looks like we were just in the nick of time," Hawk said to Knocker.

"Nah, we had it all under control. Was just about to take these fuckers out."

"Maybe we could talk later while we're on the move," I suggested.

Hunt nodded. "Sure."

Sprinting toward our Mercedes we all climbed in. "Slick, we need a route to the wrecker. Preferably one that doesn't have people trying to kill us. Especially MI6."

"Wait," said Hawk. "MI6 is trying to kill you?"

"Yes."

"Maybe I need to steal my own ride and meet you there."

Knocker floored the pedal. "Where's your sense of adventure, Jake?"

"Anja took it."

"What are you doing here, Bord?" I asked.

"We happened to be in the area and heard you were in trouble."

"Slick called you, didn't he?"

"Something like that."

"Slick—"

"Turn right at the intersection ahead," he said, cutting me off.

"Slick?"

"Bit busy."

Letting it go, we navigated the frigid streets of Berlin, venturing toward the outskirts where a desolate wrecking yard awaited. The entrance loomed before us, fortified by imposing steel gates crowned with razor wire. A crude hand-painted sign warned, *KEEP OUT!* The perimeters were further secured by a chain-link fence enclosing towering stacks of crushed vehicles.

Knocker and I donned our protective body armor, the weight settling comfortably on our shoulders. We reached for our trusted weapons—the G36C rifles—ready to explore the secrets of the rusted metal graveyard.

Once we were ready, I said, "Bord, you're with me. We'll let the two limeys hold hands."

"Roger that."

Knocker snorted. "Limeys, he says. Such a great friend he is. Come on, Jake, let's go around the back. Show these assholes how real soldiers operate."

"Lead out."

I said into my comms, "Slick, what do you have inside?"

"Surprisingly, I am not getting any signatures whatsoever. It looks like there is no one at home."

"Was Kaltz lying to us?"

"It appears that way. Or—"

"Or it was a trap to draw us in to keep us busy, or attempt to kill us again."

"Again?" Slick asked.

"You know what I mean."

The narrow space beneath the gates allowed us access, and we squeezed through and into the yard beyond. Knocker and Hawk utilized a gap in the back fence, making their entry through that. Hunt and I worked our way toward the main office while Knocker and Hawk cleared two large sheds.

The office bore the disheveled appearance of a place that had been ransacked, with items strewn about haphazardly. However, the thick layer of dirt and grime coating every surface hinted at a prolonged period of having been abandoned.

Hunt said, "This smells."

"Reaper, copy?" Knocker asked.

"Go ahead."

"The sheds are clear. No one has been here for a while. I'm thinking we've been set up again."

"Seems to be happening everywhere we go," I replied. "Something is very wrong with this picture. Regroup on the main office, Knocker."

"Roger that."

Hunt stared at me and said, "Talk to me, Reaper."

I filled him in quickly about what we'd been facing since our arrival in Berlin. Then I told him of my suspicions.

"It does sound like they want to keep you busy. I mean, they had the chance to kill you, but they didn't do it. Why?"

I thought for a moment. "To keep everyone looking one way while on the periphery, they're going another. Everyone is looking in instead of out."

"So, what if you look out?" Hunt asked.

"There's only one thing that popped. Someone kidnapped a scientist who worked on R-12 rockets."

"Why would they want a scientist who worked on R-12 rocket systems?"

"That is the question."

Hunt nodded. "That's where you need to look."

"What about the woman and the girl?"

"You may have to forgo them to get to the bigger picture."

"Shit."

"Forgo?" German asked. "Did he mean let them die at the hands of the Russians?"

"That's what he meant," I replied. "Sometimes, as they say, you can't see the forest for the trees. And we couldn't see the forest."

"So, what did you do?" Holland asked.

"We got a big chainsaw."

"What do you mean?"

"It'll become clearer shortly."

"Reaper, trucks incoming your position. Estimate three minutes out."

"How many, Slick?"

"Four."

I looked at Hunt and the others. "This is what happens, everywhere we go."

"Are they tracking you?" Hawk asked.

"If they are, I don't know how," I replied.

"Is there anything on you that you didn't have when you arrived in the city?"

Knocker said, "The embassy issued us with everything. What about your phone, Reaper?"

"I got a new one."

Hunt frowned.

I said, "The prick was calling me."

"You got everything from the embassy?"

"That's right."

"Ditch your comms and your cell."

"We need them."

"The easiest place to locate a tracker is in your comms. Get rid of them, Reaper. Better still, put them in the middle of the yard. You'll know for sure then."

"Shit. Slick, we're going off-channel. If you need me, call Hunt's cell."

"Ahh, copy."

With a sense of dread, Knocker and I removed our comms, placing them on the ground in the center of the small open space. The four of us turned and took cover, waiting for the incoming vehicles.

Not that it took long. The trucks punched through the gates and roared into the yard. The drivers brought their vehicles to an abrupt stop, armed men leaping from the back of each truck. There were at least thirty adversaries.

"This is fucking crazy," Knocker hissed beside me.

We watched and a single man, one who looked to be the commander, walked over to where our comms had been discarded and stared down at them.

I heard Hunt say, "Bingo."

Inwardly I cursed myself. Borrowing Hunt's phone, I dialed. "Holly, they were using our comms to track us. The stuff came from the embassy. Also, get Slick to look deeper into the disappearance of the rocket scientist. Then talk to Willi Lehner. Bugger pussyfooting around. Find out what he knows about Morozov."

"What about the woman and child?"

I said two words. "Big picture."

"All right, John. Good luck."

Looking at the multitude of armed men, I said, "Yeah."

"Pick a target," I said in a low voice. "Once it kicks off, we split up."

"Ready," Knocker said.

"Got mine," Hunt replied.

"Give me a moment," Hawk said.

"What the fuck are you waiting for?" Knocker whispered harshly.

"For a couple of heads to line up," he informed us.

"You have to be shitting me."

"Anytime you're ready, Jake," I said.

Then he stroked the trigger and two men dropped.

"Smartass," Knocker growled and opened fire.

The rest of us were only a fraction behind him. Our first magazines emptied swiftly, the crackling discharge echoing through the chaos. Bodies crumpled under the relentless barrage we unleashed, and then they dissipated like smoke in the wind. A rough calculation suggested that we had neutralized at least ten of them with that initial fusillade.

After reloading, I slipped back into the maze of crushed vehicles and motor parts. The downside of it all was that we were without comms and had no way of communicating.

An assailant materialized from behind a stack, buckling at the knees as I opened fire with the G36C. He tried to return fire at me, so I shot again, and he died instantly.

A second man stepped in behind his fallen comrade and opened fire. Bullets ricocheted off a stack of wrecks beside me and I threw myself flat. Once on the icy ground, I gathered myself and returned fire.

My bullets went low, hitting the shooter's legs. He screeched in pain as he fell, his finger reflexively squeezing the trigger and the weapon discharged until the magazine emptied.

The firefight intensified and the ranks of the attackers thinned.

I'll spare you the intricate particulars, but suffice it to say that these were no seasoned professionals. Their actions lacked the finesse of true warriors. Instead, they seemed hurled at us, mere pawns in a larger game designed to keep us busy.

We reconvened at the office, the pale dawn casting a somber veil upon us. The muted light seemed to weigh down our spirits, enveloping the room in a sense of quiet contemplation until Knocker asked, "What now?"

I looked at my watch. There were fourteen hours remaining in the countdown to free the hostages. But like I said, there were other things in play now.

"We go and look into the rocket scientist," I said.

"We'll come with you," Hunt said to me.

"I agree," replied Hawk.

I nodded. "Fine, let's do it."

HOLLY

CHAPTER 7

"MISS SMITH, WHAT WERE YOU DOING AT THIS TIME?" GERMAN asked. "I think we should concentrate on you for a while as it seems you were running an operation in conjunction with this one."

"Only out of necessity, sir. You wanted to know about what happened to the woman and child, this should clear up at least some of your questions."

"How so?"

"We called in another team who were in Potsdam. They were working an operation to do with a kidnapped bank executive. Their operation had just wrapped up."

"How convenient," Holland said.

"Who were these people?" German asked.

"It is in the report, sir."

He looked at the piece of paper in front of him. His head rose. "Odin?"

"Yes, sir, Odin. They were specialists in hostage extraction."

I watched his gaze as he grew confused. "Then, Miss Smith, you'd better explain what happened."

Christine Ryan said, "The following is the report and statement explained to us by Holly Smith spoken in her words. Present is John Kane, Raymond Jensen, Christine Ryan, Charles German,

Jack Holland, and director of the Central Intelligence Agency, Ken Newman. Proceed, Miss Smith."

Slick made the call. He turned and looked at me and said, "Ma'am, I have a solution to our kidnapping problem."

"I'm listening."

"There is another team in Potsdam who have just wrapped up an operation. I've worked with them before. They specialize in extractions."

"Who are they?"

"Codename Odin."

"Odin?"

"Yes, ma'am."

"Seems I should have heard of them."

"Yes, ma'am."

"All right," I said. "Do it. Call them in."

After an hour, they arrived at our base of operations. I met the initial two members: their commander, Ian Groves and his second-in-command, Helen Smith. Their presence marked the beginning of a critical phase in our mission.

Holland raised his eyebrows. "Smith?"

"That's right."

The team consisted of Groves, a stalwart figure who hails from the Special Boat Service, SBS. His commanding presence, coupled with a mane of dark hair, left an indelible impression on me during our interactions with him. Now he plies his expertise at Global, where his leadership skills continue to shine.

Helen Smith is a seasoned professional with roots that trace back to the Royal Anglian Regiment. Her disciplined background and unwavering commitment make her an asset wherever she serves.

Of the others, I knew Rose Holden, a former MI6 operative who operates in the shadows. Her intelligence and resourcefulness have earned her a place among the elite.

Paul Cross is a man of action who once belonged to the SBS. His battle-tested experience and unwavering loyalty make him a force to be reckoned with.

Last but not least was Evan Norris. Hailing from The Rifles Regiment, Evan Norris embodies resilience and adaptability. His dedication to duty is matched only by his unyielding spirit.

These individuals, each with their unique backgrounds and skills, form a formidable ensemble in the world of covert operations.

I shook hands with Groves and Helen Smith as they came through the door.

"Slick said you needed some help from us. What can we do?"

"Thank you for coming, sir—"

"Ian, please."

"Ian. Our mission is time-sensitive."

He nodded. "They usually are. Time-sensitive is what we do."

"We have a Russian national and her daughter who need to be located and extracted alive. John and Raymond—"

"Kane and Jensen?"

"Yes."

"Kane has an MI6 kill order on him."

"At the moment, he has a lot of people trying to kill him," I replied. Then I filled him in on the situation.

Groves sighed. "Bloody hell, what a cock up."

"Indeed. At this very moment, they are pursuing an alternative approach. We require your assistance with the other aspect. I will accompany you while Slick will manage coordination from this location."

"What do we have?"

"We must visit an address in Berlin to interview a company executive who had connections with a man named Gennady Morozov. Unfortunately, the company is closed today due to the weather. However, we do have his home address. The executive's name is Willi Lehner."

"Then let's go see him."

"Ma'am," Slick interrupted.

"What is it?" I asked.

"I came across something through chatter. It might be nothing, but then again..."

"Tell me."

"Just a word. Dolos."

"What does it have to do with anything?"

"Nothing until you delve a little deeper. Dolos was said to be a Greek mythological spirit that was involved in trickery."

I didn't have time for it. "File it and come back to it later, Slick. For now, we concentrate on the task at hand."

"Yes, ma'am."

"Was that a mistake on your behalf, Miss Smith?" German asked.

"Looking back, maybe. But I wouldn't have changed my decision because we had too many balls in the air. Adding another wasn't necessary."

"I see."

We departed from operational base in a blue Mercedes van, the very one utilized by the ODIN team. The van's interior was meticulously designed for electronic surveillance and covert operations. It was within these confines that I had my initial encounter with the rest of the team. Positioned up the front, I shared the space with Groves.

"This is some kind of mess you're mixed up in, ma'am," he said to me.

"Call me Holly, Ian. I don't stand on ceremony. But, yes, you're right. I have a team in the field that everyone wants a piece of, and right now, it's a hodge podge of shit."

"What do you expect to learn from Lehner?"

"I hope, something. In actuality, possibly nothing."

"So Morozov is part of this conglomerate of generals led by Shatov. Is that right?"

I nodded. "Yes."

"And he has these two—"

"I've explained this, Ian." I was abrupt. It was unforgivable. "I'm sorry, yes."

"It's okay. I'm just trying to get a clearer picture. We don't normally go into operations like this without a good deal of intel to rely on."

"We believe that the kidnapping, the time limit, the bounty, and the murder of Popov and Arthur Michaelson is designed to keep us looking inward instead of outward. Hence John is trying to get a lead on the missing scientist."

"Bollocks."

"Yes. So far, every move that they have made has been orchestrated. Hopefully we can break that by bringing you and your people in."

"And if it doesn't?" he asked me.

"Then hang onto whatever you can, Ian. It promises to be one hell of a ride."

———

We arrived at Lehner's, and as I expected, it bespoke the trappings of someone successful in the corporate world. We pulled into his driveway, stopping near the gates. With anticipation, I pressed the call button on the intercom box.

"Yes?"

It was a woman's voice. I said, "Excuse me, ma'am, I'm here to see Mr. Lehner."

"In this weather?"

"It is important, ma'am."

There was a buzz and the gates opened. "Here we go," Groves said. "Let's get a couple of wires up, and I need a bug as well."

In the rear of the vehicle, his people went to work, and by the time we reached the turnaround in front of the house, it was ready for operation.

Groves and I emerged from the vehicle, our breath visible in the frigid air. The steps leading to the front door were treacherous, coated with a thin layer of ice. I nearly lost my footing, arms flailing as I regained balance. The doorbell echoed through the stillness, and to my surprise, it was not the woman who answered but a man in his sixties. His gray hair framed a weathered face, etched with lines that told stories of years gone by.

"Who are you?"

"Sir, my name is Holly Smith. This is—"

"Len Barnes," Groves said, not using his real name.

"What do you want?"

"We'd like to speak to you, sir. It is about an old friend of yours named Gennady Morozov."

He frowned at us. "That is a name I haven't heard in years."

"Sir, if we could? It is rather cold on your doorstep."

He stepped aside, sweeping an arm back to admit us. "Please, come in."

Lehner took us into the living room where a fire was devouring a dry log in a large stone fireplace. "Would you like a coffee?"

"No, thank you," I said. "We won't keep you long."

He sat down across from us. I brought up a picture of Morozov on my cell and turned it around. "Is that Gennady Morozov?"

Lehner looked at me. "Miss Smith, I don't see how I can help you with a man I haven't seen for years."

"Did you not work for the East German Police, Mr. Lehner?"

"Yes, but that was a long time ago. I mean, the man is dead."

From a technical standpoint, Lehner's statement held true. After we'd dug into him, we'd found that, like the others, Gennady Morozov had also perished—this time in yet another tragic plane crash. The grim reality became evident: numerous innocent lives had been sacrificed to provide concealment for these individuals.

"No, that picture is less than twenty-four hours old."

"I-I don't understand. How can a dead man be..." his

voice trailed away as he looked at the photo then at each of us, trying to comprehend what we'd just told him.

"Obviously he isn't dead," Groves said.

"Yes."

I said, "Do you have any idea where he might be?"

Lehner shook his head. "No, no."

"He hasn't tried to contact you?"

"No."

"My people talked to Stefan Kaltz," I said and saw the flicker in his eyes.

"Yes, Stefan was friendlier with Gennady than I was. He would know."

"But you don't?"

"No."

Groves said, "Thank you for your time, Mr. Lehner."

I threw an annoyed glance at Groves, wondering at the abruptness of the termination. However, I let it go and said, "Thank you, Mr. Lehner."

Emerging from the warmth, we stepped back out into the biting cold, the door swinging shut behind us. In that moment, my head swiveled, and a fire ignited in my eyes.

"What was that?"

"He wasn't going to tell us anything straight up. He was lying. Let's see what happens now that we're gone."

We climbed into the van and Rose Holden said, "He's making a call."

As we drove away from the luxury property, we listened in.

"I had people here asking questions about you, Gennady."

"What did they want to know?" Morozov asked.

"If I had been in contact with you."

"And?"

"I told them nothing."

"Good. Our items?"

"They are at the facility under guard."

I looked at Groves.

"Good. Keep them there until I get back to you. Well done, Willi."

"No, they need to be gone, Gennady. If they are found, then…"

"Fine, I will see to it."

The call disconnected. I said to Groves, "We need to go back."

"No. If they get wind we're onto them, they will shift our targets. We need to keep that as a last resort."

"What do you suggest?" I asked.

"Rose, find out what facilities Lehner has up his sleeve and we'll break them down. Slick, are you there?"

"Roger."

"Can you work it on your end and coordinate with Rose?"

"Sure can."

"What do you propose we do, Ian?" I asked again.

"What would you do?"

"Slick, I need warehouses attached to Lehner's companies."

"On it." I could tell his fingers were working furiously on his keyboard. "I have something off Kisselnallee. It looks to be a warehouse complex with underground parking."

"Send what you have to Rose, she can guide us in. Keep looking."

"Yes, ma'am."

I looked at Ian. "Well?"

He shrugged. "As good a place as any to start."

Picking up my phone, I hit speed dial. "Hunt."

"I need John."

"Ma'am."

"Kane."

"John, what's your situation?"

"Holly, we're moving on the facility from which the scientist was kidnapped. I am hopeful we will find something useful."

"Good luck."

I hung up the phone, severing the connection. Our vehicle wove through the city streets, the sun inching toward its zenith. Surprisingly, the usually bustling thoroughfares lay deserted, a consequence of the inclement weather.

Yet what caught us off guard was the adaptability of the generals. They shifted tactics seamlessly, demonstrating an uncanny ability to thrive in adversity. Their resourcefulness was nothing short of remarkable.

"We have a problem," Rose said.

"What kind of a problem?" Helen Smith asked.

"I'm picking up a strange signal nearby."

Groves looked in the side mirror and I did the same. Everything looked clear. "I have nothing," I said.

"Same here," Groves replied.

"Then where is it? Rose, is it stronger or weaker?"

"The same. Like it's keeping pace with us."

Oh no. "Slick, I need an immediate scan of the airspace above us."

"What am I looking for, ma'am?" he asked.

"Anything that doesn't belong."

"Are you thinking a drone?" Groves asked.

"Yes."

That was enough for him. "Gear up, people. Just in case."

There was a flurry of movement in the back as they prepared their equipment.

"Here, ma'am, you might need this," Helen said.

An MP5 was passed forward to me with some body armor and spare ammunition.

After I had shrugged into mine, Groves said to me, "Take the wheel." Then he did the same while driving.

"Ma'am, you're right. There is something in the air. It looks like a drone and it's tracking your movements."

"Copy, Slick."

Ahead of us, the traffic lights changed to red, and we rolled to a stop. After waiting for more than forty seconds, the light remained red, and we realized something was wrong. As an SUV pulled up beside us, I looked at it through the side window of the van.

The windows were tinted dark, and I couldn't see inside. Snow was starting to fall lightly again, and it began to settle gently on the SUV.

When one of the windows rolled down and a figure appeared framed in the opening, it dawned on me.

"Oh, shit. Get down!"

CHAPTER 8

GENNADY MOROZOV BARKED OUT THE COMMAND, AND HIS henchmen unleashed a hail of bullets upon our van. The fusillade tore through the flimsy exterior, leaving behind a constellation of holes reminiscent of Swiss cheese.

The van shuddered as Groves jammed the accelerator, but fate had other plans. Instead of surging forward, the vehicle lurched in reverse, colliding with a second SUV. The impact reverberated through the metal frames, leaving us exposed in a chaotic tangle of wreckage.

"Everyone out," Groves ordered. This was his show, because he and his people were experts under fire in like situations. I, on the other hand, had been shot at, but had not experienced anything like this.

We bailed out of the van. Paul Cross and Norris had already assumed the position and were laying down covering fire. The rest of us sought cover. Out of the corner of my eye, I saw Cross roll something under the rear SUV. He turned and shouted, "Frag Out!"

The explosion lifted the SUV as though it had hit an IED. It was engulfed in flames immediately, and burning figures —those that could—tumbled out onto the street.

More bullets cut through the icy air as I ducked down behind the van. Around the burning SUV, the snow on the ground was quickly melting. Shooters from the vehicle Morozov was in were trying to flank us.

Helen and Norris kept up a steady rate of fire as we backed away to take cover across the street. Once there, we opened fire to cover their retreat. I heard Groves say into his comms, "Slick, how far away from the facility are we?"

"About a block."

"Okay. Holly, we can proceed on foot."

I nodded. "Roger that."

Groves dispatched Norris to take point while Cross and Helen covered our rear. No time for dilly-dallying, we sprinted, creating a chasm between us and the pursuers. Morozov, relentless as a tick, burrowed deep under our skin —a tenacious adversary who refused to release his grip.

"We're obviously on the right track," I shouted at Groves.

"I would concur, ma'am."

As we turned the corner of a massive building, a breathtaking vista unfolded before our eyes. Atop what appeared to be expansive parklands, intricate structures stood sentinel. The ground lay cloaked in a pristine blanket of snow, and there, etched into the frozen canvas, were the unmistakable footprints of Norris, marking his swift passage across this wintry expanse.

"Boss, I'm in the mouth of the garage. Come ahead fifty meters."

"Roger, Chuck, on our way."

We caught up with him and jumped down onto a concrete driveway. Helen, Rose, and Cross ran in behind us, then Helen and Cross took up a defensive position. I said into my comms, "Slick, talk to me."

"Ma'am, the SUV from the ambush site has been joined by two more. I've managed to intercept radio transmissions. Morozov is calling in reinforcements from across the city."

"Just for a woman and child?"

"From what I can gather, there is something else at that facility they don't want found."

"Let's find it then," I said. "Ian, let's go in."

"Chuck, lead out. Let's find what they're determined to keep secret."

We went down the ramp into the underground garage. It was empty except for three black SUVs. I deduced that since there was no one in them, they belonged to the Lehner Corporation.

"Slick, copy?"

"Yes, ma'am."

"What exactly do they do here?"

"Wait one. It's not exactly stated. Umm, electronics... microchips for...missile systems."

I glanced at Groves. He said, "R-12?"

"Slick, does the R-12 take the chips they manufacture?"

"Not unless the rocket systems are updated," he replied.

A myriad of thoughts ran through my head all at once, causing a bottleneck in my brain. Then it popped like the cork had been forced. "They're after chips for the R-12. Lehner is making them. They kidnapped a rocket scientist, and now we've stumbled onto why. They need someone to fit the chips."

"But what do they want with R-12 ballistic missiles?" Groves asked. "I thought they were all out of date."

"Obviously someone still has some. This is a lot worse than first suspected."

"Did you have any idea at that time what they were up to, Miss Smith?" Christine Ryan asked.

"No, ma'am. As I just said, whatever they were up to was a lot worse than we figured."

"So, while going there to find a woman and child, you stumbled onto something else entirely."

"Yes, ma'am. Something else entirely."

"Continue, Miss Smith."

We went underground looking for an entrance into the facility. "Maybe this had something to do with @Dolos," I said to Groves.

"Possibly."

"Shall we go?"

"Yes."

A bank of elevators sat at the far end of the underground garage. The power was still on. My guess is it was on a timer. We got into the elevator and paused. My hand shot out to stop the door closing. "Ian, what do you think?"

He turned to face me and looked at the numbers. It went from garage, up through basement, to ground level. However, it was the other numbers that held our focus. The ones that went down five levels. "Which one?" I asked.

"Start at the bottom and work up."

"Let's do it."

I hit the button and felt the elevator drop. We watched the numbers anxiously until it got to five and the doors slid open.

"Where do we start, boss?" Norris asked.

"Clear each floor as we go."

The fifth level was offices and research labs. As we went through each methodically, we found nothing important. The fourth level was much the same. The third, however, was where we hit gold. And blood. This was the on-site hub for the manufacture of microchips.

In a dimly lit room, two guards stood watch, their automatic weapons at the ready. Initially unaware of our presence, we seized the opportunity to gain the upper hand. However, even when confronted, they refused to yield. Desperation drove them to reach for their weapons, and we were left with no alternative but to defend ourselves.

Blocking it out of my mind, I said, "Spread out and start searching."

"What are we looking for?" Rose asked.

"There can't be many of the R-12 missiles around anymore so maybe a small box, carry case, something like that."

"Ma'am, copy?"

It was Slick. The line was rough, but at least it was secure. "Go ahead."

"Thank God, I've been trying to raise you. Four vehicles

have arrived topside. I've been able to identify Gennady Morozov. They're..."

"Say again, Slick, I missed your last."

"They're inside."

DING.

The elevator door slid open. "Oh shit. Get Down!"

A sudden onslaught of armed assailants spilled out of the elevator, their weapons blazing. Bullets sliced through the air, forcing us all to seek refuge. Among them, a burly Russian stepped forward, wielding a light machine gun. As he depressed the trigger, the weapon roared to life, escalating an already dire situation.

Bullets smashed into walls and furniture. Equipment seemed to disintegrate before our eyes. Amid it all, I glimpsed Morozov strolling nonchalantly through the facility, seemingly unburdened by the cares of the world. His approach to a nearby desk was deliberate, and he deftly retrieved a diminutive container.

"Morozov has the chips."

"Stop Morozov," Groves shouted.

Our guns blazed, but the moment had slipped through our fingers. The elusive Russian vanished, leaving his retreating comrades in his wake. They scrambled into the waiting elevator, and just before the doors sealed shut, one of his henchmen hurled a fragmentation grenade into the room.

The explosion created utter chaos. Shards of debris flew, and the shockwave slammed us against the walls, disorienting and bruising us. Yet, somehow we managed to claw our way back to our feet, adrenaline surging, and staggered toward the stairwell. The mission wasn't over. It had just begun.

I looked at Groves. "We need to stop him."

Trying to sprint up the stairs to the garage felt like an uphill battle. With our energy depleted by the concussive force, I wouldn't have been surprised if a tortoise could pass us. "Motherfucker," I growled savagely.

"We have no hope of stopping them."

I made two calls immediately. One was to John informing him of our situation.

"Who was the second call to?" German asked.

"I'm not at liberty to say at this point, sir."

His eyes flared. "Miss Smith, this is an inquiry to ascertain the truth about an operation you were in command of. The ramifications of which could see you in prison for a very long time. It is imperative that we get all the facts."

There was a period of silence, then, "No comment."

"Miss Smith, I must—"

"Shall we continue, Mr. German?" Christine Ryan asked.

German sighed. "Very well. Let's move onto what you did next, Miss Smith."

"John, I have to be quick. Everything hinges on finding that scientist. Morozov just acquired chips that I believe will be used in R-12 ballistic missiles. We need to find out anything we can."

"What about the woman and child?"

"No joy."

I disconnected the call and looked across at Groves. "I'm all open to suggestions."

What he verbalized was what I had been thinking, but I was too scared to voice my opinion on the matter. But still, it shook me to the core. "You have a rat in your ranks."

"I agree."

"Rose, work your magic and get one of those SUVs unlocked and working."

"Yes, sir."

Groves turned his attention back to me. "Holly, you need to figure this out fast."

"There are only four of us. John, Raymond, myself, and Slick."

"Has this been happening all the time?"

I told him about Brian Short. "We figured that with him gone, there would be no more problems. But if anything, they've gotten worse."

We heard the SUV start and hurried across to it. Once we were aboard, Groves drove out of the garage. "We'll head back to the safehouse. We need to find this mole before it goes any further."

I thought about the woman and child. That was how I started to refer to them as, because the further the day wore on, the more likely it was we wouldn't be able to save them.

———

Meanwhile, Morozov made a call to Shatov. "What is happening?"

"We have the chips. The scientist?"

Shatov said, "We have him. All we need is for the weather to let up and we can fly out of here."

"They almost got the chips," Morozov said.

"But they didn't."

"Things are getting out of hand, Mikhail. We should have killed them before now."

"You know why."

"Yes, but killing them would have served the same purpose."

"Damn it, Gennady. If we had killed them, there would have been the risk of it being taken away from MI6. That would have taken it out of Melinoe's hands. We need Melinoe in place until this operation is over. Stick with the plan."

"What if they discover Melinoe?"

"Then we deal with it."

"So, we keep sacrificing men while we keep them busy."

"It is called controlling the situation," Shatov said.

"Then why the price on their heads? I don't understand."

"What price?" Shatov was confused.

"The fifty million. Why do you think the city is flooded with teams of gunmen?"

"Aren't they your teams? I thought you had it under control?"

Morozov said, "They are not my teams. My teams have been busy."

"Then whose teams are they?"

"I will look into it."

"Do that. Put a stop to it before they ruin everything. Once we have accomplished what we need to in Berlin, then you can kill them all. And not a minute before."

The call disconnected and Morozov made another call. "Keep going. Make sure you kill them. I will give you the information when it comes to hand."

———

So that was where we were at for then. We didn't know until later that Morozov was working against orders. Dolos was just a name, and soon we were to get another.

When we arrived back at the safehouse, Slick was waiting for us. "Holly, I have another name. I picked it up in chatter."

"What is it?"

"Melinoe."

"Is it significant?"

"Melinoe was the Greek Goddess of ghosts."

"What do you make of it?" I asked him.

"Dolos is the spirit of trickery, and the other is the Goddess of ghosts. They have to be codenames for something or someone."

Suddenly Groves appeared. He was flanked by Rose and Helen. Everything I saw in their eyes told me to run. Instead, I stood fast. "What is it?"

"We've been ordered to detain you and Slick until MI6 gets here."

"You what?" I was stunned.

"Sorry, ma'am. They will have a team here within thirty minutes."

"What is this about, Ian?" I asked, pretty much knowing what the answer would be.

"The murder of Arthur Michaelson."

"But I already explained what happened."

"Yes, ma'am, you did, but they want to hear it from you."

Slick entered the room with Norris and Cross. "What the hell is going on, ma'am? I've been told to stand down."

I looked at Groves. "Stand down?"

"Yes, ma'am."

"But we have people in the field and computer chips possibly on their way to be inserted in missiles."

"You also have a mole in your system."

"A mole?" Slick was surprised. "What fucking mole?"

"The one that is feeding information to the Russians."

Slick straightened up. "And who the fuck might that be? Not me, not Holly. I can't see Reaper or Knocker fucking doing it."

"Take it easy, Sam."

"Be fucked," he snarled and turned to leave.

"Where are you going?" Groves asked.

"Back to work, we've still got a team in the field. If you don't like it, fucking shoot me."

Then he walked out.

"Slick."

"Yes, ma'am?"

"Find the woman and the girl."

"What about Reaper?"

"They are off comms. Keep it that way. The less MI6 knows about them, the better. They'll improvise."

"Yes, ma'am."

I focused on Groves. He shrugged. "This isn't my doing."

"I know."

The MI6 team appeared thirty minutes later. They materialized out of the blizzard that had just encompassed Berlin. Once inside, Ian Groves and his people were dismissed.

"Good luck, ma'am."

"Thanks for your help, Ian."

Two colleagues confronted me: Sabrina Harrison and Ethan Wilson. Sabrina exuded an air of ambition reminiscent of someone who would trample on anyone to ascend the promotional ladder. Her blonde hair was pulled back severely, framing a face that perpetually wore an expression as if she had just bitten into a lemon. The man beside her, Ethan, seemed to hang on her every word, a willing servant. I couldn't help but feel sorry for whoever had married this domineering woman.

The other two appeared with Slick in tow. Jason Carpenter and Carol Lester. Carpenter was a large man, radiating the aura of being the team's muscle. Which left Lester, most likely the brains. Slick dabbed at a small cut above his eye as he sat beside me.

I stared at them. "What happened?"

"He failed to comply."

"Fucking asshole. We have an ongoing mission that needs to be continuously monitored."

"Not anymore," Sabrina said smoothly. "That mission is over. This debriefing is to find out about the cold-blooded murder of Arthur Michaelson."

I remained mute.

Sabrina took out a recording device and said, "Shall we begin?"

"You're wasting our time," Slick snapped. "A woman and a child's lives hang in the balance, and we are responsible for finding and saving them."

"Both Russian nationals which makes them not our concern."

"Not according to Christine Ryan," I snapped.

"It was Miss Ryan who authorized this inquiry."

"How about missile computer chips that go into R-12 ballistic missiles?" I asked.

"Again, not our problem."

My frustration was palpable, anger a boiling pit of lava threatening to spill over. They were here screwing everything up. Interfering with our mission.

"I'll start with this question. Where are Mr. Kane and Mr. Jensen?"

"Somewhere in Berlin trying to find a rocket scientist," I replied.

Her eyes narrowed as she tried to decipher whether my response was a lie. "Where are Mr. Kane and Mr. Jensen?"

"We are out of contact with them. They ditched their comms because someone was tracking them."

"By someone, you mean…"

"General Gennady Morozov and several teams of assassins."

"Assassins?"

I nodded. "Yes, they were after the bounty on their heads."

"What bounty?"

"General Mikhail Shatov put a fifty-million-dollar price on Kane and Jensen's heads."

"Why?"

"Because we're getting too close."

"Too close to what?" Sabrina asked.

"We don't know."

"Surely you must know something," she said, raising a skeptical eyebrow.

"I know this is a waste of time."

Sabrina stared at me. "You said someone was tracking you via comms. How do you know this?"

"I didn't. It was who figured that out with the help of Hunt."

"Convenient that the murderer of an MI6 officer claims that they are being tracked by their comms and then go dark. Now no one knows where they are."

I had purposefully omitted the detail that there was a cell we could call. "If you say so. It made sense at the time however, because when they went anywhere, they were attacked."

"At the time?" she asked questioningly.

"Yes, ma'am."

"Care to elaborate?"

"No, ma'am."

Sabrina said, "Withholding pertinent information could well lead to you being charged with an offense, Miss Smith. Remember that."

"Yes, ma'am."

"Now, please elaborate on the last statement."

"When we were with Ian Groves's team, we were in a van, and Morozov and his people pulled up beside us at a set of traffic lights."

"Could they have tracked your comms?"

I shook my head. "We were using the Global team's comms."

"The Global team's comms." She said it slowly, annunciating every word. It was annoying and I wanted to punch her in the face.

"Yes, ma'am."

"Hmm, we'll come back to that. Let's go back to the murder of Michaelson by your man."

She made *your man* sound repugnant. "It was an unfortunate incident, not murder."

"Unfortunate incident, Miss Smith?" she replied. "Hmm."

From the table beside her, she dragged a laptop across the surface, opening it once it was in front of her. Sabrina clicked the touchpad and then turned it for Slick and I to see. "I'm just curious how this can be an unfortunate incident."

I looked at the screen and immediately saw a problem. "That isn't the whole screen. There was more to it."

"It is what we have. From what I see, we don't need any more."

I glared at Sabrina. "There is a kill order on one of my people. He deserves to have this investigated thoroughly."

"What is there to investigate, Miss Smith?" she asked. "The tape says it all."

"It does not."

"Moving on."

"Wait," Slick growled. "What kind of railroad fucked up

interview is this? You either want to hear what we have to say, or you don't. Which is it?"

"Moving on. You mentioned something about chips?"

"You said they weren't your problem," I reminded her.

"Tell me about them."

I felt dry in the throat. "I would like a drink."

Sabrina looked at Carpenter. She nodded and he disappeared. Sabrina said, "The microchips."

"We deduced that the kidnapping of a scientist and the microchips were linked. Which was why—part of the reason —we were at the facility owned by Willi Lehner."

"How did you come to that conclusion?"

"By listening into a phone conversation between Lehner and Morozov."

Sabrina's gaze was steady. Carpenter came back with a drink. He put it in front of me, and as he did, his shirtsleeve moved slightly up his arm, exposing a tattoo. I thanked him for the water and took a sip then a couple of mouthfuls.

"Where is Mr. Kane going?"

"I don't know. To look for the scientist."

"Why did you come back here?"

"To regroup," I replied. "We had a couple of things to look into."

"What things?" Sabrina asked.

"Dolos and Melinoe."

For the first time, I saw her eyes flicker and she glanced up at Carol Lester. It was almost imperceptible, but I saw Carol's head move. A nod. Not much of one but it was there.

I said, "That water must have gone straight through me. I need to use the bathroom."

Sabrina nodded. "That is fine. We will question your companion while you are indisposed."

Leaving the room where we were being interrogated, I headed for the bathroom. While going through the motions and making all the right noises, I accessed a hidden panel in the wall. Concealed inside was a Glock handgun. I tucked it into my pants and made sure it was not visible. Then I went back out to where they were interrogating Slick.

Sitting down, I made myself comfortable, also making sure I could access the weapon when required. Beside me, Slick was explaining—or trying to—that there was more to the video than what they were seeing.

"If you just let me show you, we can clear this all up and you can have the kill order rescinded."

"I'm not sure that anything will excuse that," Sabrina said.

Slick gave me an exasperated look. "Is it me, or do these people just not give a shit about anything?"

"I know, love, it's like talking to a fucking gate post."

I stared across the table at Sabrina, her face devoid of emotion. I pictured myself raising the weapon and putting a bullet in her forehead. Her blue eyes looked at me suspiciously and she opened her mouth to speak. But someone else beat her to it.

"Would someone like to tell me what is going on?"

CHAPTER 9

THE GLOCK IN MY FIST ROSE ABOVE THE EDGE OF THE TABLE AND fired. The bullet went where I pictured it and punched into Sabrina's forehead, blowing her brains over Carpenter, who stood against the wall behind her.

Throwing myself from my chair, I hit the floor hard. The Glock I held shifted aim and I fired up under the table into Wilson's middle. Three times the Glock roared, and each time, Wilson jerked. The last time was when the bullet shattered his spine.

There were still two threats in the room.

I kept rolling, cleared the table, and came up firing. This time Carpenter was my target. Four more rounds and he was sliding down the wall, leaving a bloody streak, a gun half drawn. The threat from him was done with.

I spun and brought the Glock around, my sights set on Carol Lester. Her weapon was drawn but pointed downward. The shock and severity of the violent outburst and the demise of her colleagues had delayed her reactions. My stare was steady, my voice like granite. "Don't do it, bitch."

She failed to listen, and I shot her.

Only to wound, mind you. The bullet punched into her shoulder, spinning her around and causing her to drop the gun she'd been holding.

Finished, I raised my hands to show I was no threat. Lisa Goodall stood with her service weapon pointed at me. Two of her people were doing the same. "Put the gun down!" Goodall snarled at me. "Now."

"Okay, okay, I'm putting it down." I crouched slowly. The Glock was placed on the floor and I rose to my feet. "There, I put it down."

"Restrain her."

While this was happening, Slick sat stunned, his mouth agape. Then, "What the fuck was that?"

"Check Carpenter's arms for tattoos," I said quickly. "Do it, Slick."

"Stay where you are."

Slick hesitated. I said, "Do it, Slick."

He ignored another barked order and did as I asked. He crouched down and pulled back Carpenter's sleeve. The tattoos were revealed. "Russian military," Slick said. "I'd know them anywhere."

Although I was cuffed with cable ties, I turned to glare at the woman I had wounded. She was on her feet but suffering great pain. I spoke to her in Russian. "Who are you?"

She said nothing.

"Who the fuck are you, huh?"

"Holly, sit down," Goodall ordered me.

"You were in command," I said to her. I stepped closer. "I know you were. I saw how she looked at you."

She said nothing.

"Answer me!" I shouted and used my bound hands to hit her wound.

Groaning in agony, the woman known as Carol Lester buckled at the knees. One of Goodall's minders lurched forward and dragged me back. He forced me into a chair at the desk. Goodall looked at her minders. "Get a team in here to clean up this mess. Holly, you are with me. If you try anything, do anything that I don't like, I will shoot you."

"Ma'am."

She then looked at Slick. "I suppose you'd better come too. Then you can explain what the bloody hell is going on."

––––––––

An hour later, Goodall stared at us and said, "Let me get this straight. Those people you killed and wounded are Russian?"

"Yes, I think we've already explained that."

"And why they were here is yet to be established?"

"I would say they were gathering intel before they killed us."

"Then there is the intelligence about computer chips for R-12 missiles, two names that we are yet to uncover the meaning of, a kidnapped scientist, a fifty-million price on your operators' heads, and a woman and child who have been kidnapped and whose lives are on a time limit."

"Don't forget the MI6 kill order."

"That has been rescinded. I don't even know where it bloody came from. Tell me about the woman and child."

I nodded. "The woman and child are a distraction."

"What for?"

"For what is really happening in Berlin."

"What would that be? From where I am, Berlin is a war zone, not to mention the weather."

"How did you get in, ma'am?" I asked.

"A couple of bloody brave pilots and some bloody brilliant flying. Again, why are they distracting you?"

"It has to be something to do with the missiles," I replied. "That and the fact there are two generals in the city."

"Two?" There was concern on her face.

"Yes, ma'am. Shatov and Morozov."

"Do you know where they are?"

"No."

"Kane?"

I stared at her for a moment. Inside my mind, I was debating what to say.

"Well?" Goodall asked.

"He's looking into the missing scientist."

"Call him in."

"What?"

"Call him in," she said again.

"I can't do that," I replied.

"Why not?"

"Because I can't."

"Can't or won't?"

I remained silent.

"Ma'am, if I may?" Slick said.

It was Goodall's turn to stare. "If you must."

Slick grabbed her computer and linked it to our network. He then brought up the file with Michaelson's death and hit play. "Watch and make your own conclusions."

She watched it. All the way through. Goodall never blinked. Once it was done, her head came up. "I see."

"You'll note that—"

"I saw it," she replied, cutting Slick off. "All right, I'll relay it back to HQ. The question is, what do we do next?"

"Question the woman we have in our custody."

Goodall nodded. "Yes, I do believe we should."

———

The impostor had been moved to another room. Goodall and I sat down opposite her. Her face was pale, and she was in pain. Goodall said, "We have a few questions for you and then we'll see what we can do about that wound."

The woman stared at the wall over our shoulders.

"What is your name?" Goodall asked.

She said nothing.

"Who sent you?"

Again, nothing.

Slick entered and placed a sheet of paper in front of me. He'd downloaded information from the woman's phone.

She was definitely the one in charge of the group. I looked up. "Your name is Olga."

Her eyes flickered.

Goodall looked at me curiously. I pushed the paper to my right. She looked down and then back at the woman named Olga. "It seems you made and received a lot of calls to the same number. Who is the person on the other end?"

Olga remained silent.

"Is that the person pulling the strings?"

Nothing.

I said, "Whoever it is, they're the ones giving the orders, aren't they? Too many calls not to be, Olga. Give us a name."

She continued staring at the wall, her face stony.

"We are getting nowhere here," Goodall said.

I said, "The sooner you answer the questions, Olga, the quicker you get attention for the wound."

"No comment."

"Well now, you're talking at least. Who is Melinoe?"

Nothing.

"Is Melinoe the one giving the orders?"

Once more, Olga focused on the wall. I was beginning to see a pattern.

"Is Morozov Melinoe? Is that it?"

"Who is Morozov?" she asked.

I stared at her, trying to gauge what she knew.

Goodall said, "We're wasting our time, Holly."

Olga was in pain. That pain was increasing. I had another idea. I got up from the table and said, "Be right back."

When I returned, it was with a syringe loaded with a certain type of pain killer. Plus a little extra. I won't reveal what it was.

"I have pain medication for you." I walked over to Olga and stabbed the needle through her clothing and into her arm. What can I say, I'm not a physician.

Then I waited. It took a few minutes, but before too long, she was flying higher than a kite. Goodall looked at me. "What did you do?"

"I gave her pain meds."

"How much?"

"Enough."

"Christ, you gave her too much."

"Did I?" I looked at Olga. "Olga, can you hear me?"

She looked at me, trying to focus. "Yes."

Her voice sounded tired.

"Melinoe. Do you know who he is?"

She nodded.

"Now we're getting somewhere. Is that where you get your orders?"

"Yes."

"What were your orders?"

"To find out what you—you knew."

"Then what?"

"Kill you."

"Who is Melinoe?"

"I don't know. We only talked by phone."

"Are they Russian?"

She shook her head and leaned to the side. "No."

"Who?"

"No."

Her head got lower until she was half-asleep.

"Great," Goodall huffed. She glared at me.

I shrugged. "We got more out of her than what we were achieving before."

"Let's take a break."

"We can still push her some more."

"No, take a break."

I found Slick at his computer. "Find out where that number goes?"

"I'm working on it. It pinged in Berlin. Right now, it is turned off. If it ever goes back on, I'll jump on it."

"Do your best. At the other end is Melinoe."

"Yes, ma'am."

———

"Miss Smith, what became of your prisoner?" German asked.

"She died."

"From what, may I ask?"

"It was assumed an overdose of pain medication."

"Medication that you gave her."

"That was the theory."

"I'm not interested in theories, Miss Smith. Only facts."

"Yes, sir."

"So, the fact was, your prisoner died from an overdose that you administered."

"No, sir."

His eyebrows shot up. "No?"

"No."

"But in the report submitted by you, it is stated that this Olga, whoever she was, died of an overdose."

"Yes, sir, that's correct."

"I'm confused. Please explain."

"She died of an overdose, sir. But I didn't give it to her. She was murdered."

"Good Lord, please carry on."

Slick came to me half an hour later. "I have a problem. A big problem. No, actually, I would go as far as to say *we* have a problem."

"Don't keep me hanging."

"Lisa Goodall has been in Berlin since the night before we arrived."

"Okay, no, that can't be right."

"The cell that the number belongs to went live ten minutes ago for one minute. The trace puts it here inside this building."

I felt the walls closing in on me. "Fuck. Is she—she has to be Melinoe."

"It would seem so, ma'am."

"That means we can't trust her two friends, either."

"No, ma'am."

"Get the others back here now. This is important."

"Yes, ma'am."

Slick had just disappeared when Goodall reappeared. "There you are. We have a problem."

"What?"

"The prisoner is dead. Whatever you gave her killed her."

"Shit."

We went into the room where the woman had been sleeping. One of the others had patched her wound as best they could. "Are you sure she's dead?"

"Yes."

"Who found her?" I asked.

"Lionel," Goodall replied. "I hope you understand the gravity of this, Holly. You knowingly gave a prisoner too much pain medication, the result of which caused her death. Not only will it end your career, but it will send you to prison for a very long time. I have no option but to place you under arrest until such a time when you can be transported to the proper facility or back to London."

Right now, I was screwed.

KANE AND JENSEN

CHAPTER 10

GERMAN SAID, "AT THIS POINT, I THINK WE'LL COME BACK TO *Mr. Kane. His story is relevant, and as we know, it will converge with Miss Smith's."*

I stared at him and nodded. "All right."

While things were happening with Holly, we continued our mission to source intel about the scientist. Our first requirement was transport, so we took one of the trucks graciously provided by our attackers. I grabbed Hunt's cell and called Slick. "I need a name and location for where the scientist was taken from."

"I'll do you one better. I'll send you the address of his residence."

"Send it to this number. I'm compromised."

"Roger that."

Once the address came through, we headed into central Berlin. The scientist's name was Sepp Kahn. He was a widower in his late sixties who lived alone since a massive stroke had taken his wife two years earlier.

We parked on the street outside the apartment block he lived in. Knocker and I climbed out and took our Glocks. I half expected a team of shooters to appear from out of the bleak morning to continue the attempts to collect the bounty on our heads.

However, the street was clear except for a couple of cars parked further along, both still covered with snow, so they hadn't been recently driven.

The entry to the apartment block was clear so we rehomed our weapons. We used the stairs to get to the level we required and walked along the open landing until we found the right door.

It was locked, of course, and no one appeared to be home, but Knocker had a way of unlocking these things. While I stood directly behind him, he got the door open, and we entered the apartment.

"What are we looking for, Reaper?"

"Anything that will help."

Starting a systematic search of the premises, we were ten minutes in when Knocker found the first item of interest. A photograph of a group of people wearing suits. It was old, having been taken in the late eighties. "Reaper, look at this."

I walked over and glanced at the photo, picking out Shatov's face immediately. When I looked harder, I saw the other generals as well. The ones we knew, anyway.

With the picture in my hand, I walked over to a photo of Kahn. "I'm guessing one of the others is our man."

Placing them side by side, I soon picked him out. "They all know each other."

Knocker said, "We need to identify the others."

"I agree." Placing it in my pocket, we continued the search for at least twenty more minutes. But if there was something else to find, we missed it.

"Let's go, Knocker."

"Where?"

"To see where he was taken from."

When we emerged back outside to the biting cold, the others met us and climbed back into the truck. With a low buzz, Hunt's phone rang and he answered it, quickly passing it to me. It was Holly.

"John, where are you?"

I told her.

The call disconnected, so I went to return the cell.

Hunt said, "Keep it."

While Knocker drove, I produced the photo and showed Hunt and Hawk. The street we were driving on had been recently plowed, so we were able to travel at speed toward the facility where the kidnapping had occurred.

There was security everywhere. Plus police. We stopped along the street from the group of buildings. "How are we going to do this?" Hunt asked.

"Anyone fluent in German?" I asked.

"That would be me," Hawk replied. "Comes from having a German boss."

"That's good," said Knocker. "I only know how to say fuck."

It wasn't true, but it was his way of saying that his abilities wouldn't pass muster.

I said to Hawk, "You're with me then."

Approaching a guard stationed by the security gate, Hawk asked, "What's the plan?"

"Let's wing it."

"Great, I feel like a fucking bird."

Stepping in front of us to block our way, the guard asked, "What do you want?"

"We have to see Professor Kahn," Hawk said.

"You can't."

"Why not?"

"Because he isn't here."

"Then where is he?" Hawk asked. "We had an appointment."

"What about?"

"A component he's been working on. We're from Bremen Aerospace Technologies. He was looking at something for us."

"Like I said, he isn't here."

"Then where is he?" Hawk tried again.

"I cannot tell you."

"Who can?" Hawk asked, feigning agitation.

"I will—wait here."

He went back into his little hut and looked to be making a call. A couple of minutes later, he reappeared and said, "Come with me."

Following him to the main building, we went inside through the entrance foyer past a gaggle of police questioning a group of people.

Hawk asked our escort, "Why so many people with the weather the way it is?"

"We have a rail line beneath the building."

Hawk glanced at me. I'd caught what the guard had said, and I was curious as to why they would have such a thing.

"A rail line? Really?" Hawk prompted.

"Yes, we use it to transport the goods we manufacture. It saves using lorries."

He took us upstairs and into an office area where we found a receptionist. She smiled at us and said, "Mr. Fischer will be with you shortly."

The guard nodded at us, satisfied that he'd performed his duty, and disappeared. Hawk turned to me and said, "Interesting fact about the rail line."

"What I find even more interesting is that all these police have turned out for a simple kidnapping."

In the doorway to an office, a man in his late sixties appeared. He was of average height, gray-haired, and dressed in a suit.

"Gentlemen, please come in."

He disappeared into the office, and Hawk said, "Bingo."

I nodded, recalling a face very like one of the men in the photo in my pocket. Hawk and I went inside, closing the door behind us. Fischer turned and addressed us from behind his desk. "I don't have much time, gentlemen. State what you want."

"Do you speak English?" Hawk asked.

Fischer frowned. "Yes, I do."

I nodded. "We'd like to ask you a few questions about Sepp Kahn."

He flinched straight away. "I do not have time for this."

"Did Sepp know a man name Morozov?"

"What? I don't know."

"What about Mikhail Shatov?"

"You will have to ask him, if he is ever found."

I stared at him, waiting.

Fischer said, "If you'll excuse me, I have to get back to work."

My left hand went into my pocket and came out with the picture. I tossed it onto the man's glass-topped modern desk. "Pick the picture up, Mr. Fischer."

The man hesitated until he noticed Hawk's hand was filled with a P226. The German's eyes went wide.

"Look at the photo, chum."

A trembling hand reached out and picked up the photo. I said, "You'll see some old friends in there, Fischer. I recognized you, but also there are Shatov, Morozov, Noskov, and Misha Durov, who is dead by the way. Also in there is Sepp Kahn. The others we don't know. However, we want to know your relationship with them."

"I've never seen—"

Hawk strode forward and clipped him with the P226. The man was stunned while Hawk rifled through his desk drawers. He found a roll of tape and fixed his arms to the chair.

"What—what are you doing?"

"Shut the fuck up or I'll hit you harder," Hawk growled. "Next time, I'll scramble your brain."

"What are—"

"Mr. Fischer, look at me," I said in a calm voice. When he was focused on me, I continued. "We're going to ask you some questions, and you will answer them. If you don't, your day will become considerably worse. Do you understand?"

The man gave a terrified nod. "Yes."

Hunt's cell buzzed. I answered it.

"John, I have to be quick. Everything hinges on finding

that scientist. Morozov just acquired chips that I believe will be used in R-12 ballistic missiles. We need to find out anything we can."

"What about the woman and the child?"

"No joy."

The call done, I put the phone away and stared at Fischer. "That changes things."

Fischer looked nervous. Sweat beaded on his brow.

"What is your relationship to Morozov?"

He hesitated.

"Jake."

"No, wait. We were all friends. We did work on a special program together before we went our separate ways."

"What program?"

"Missile research. You have to remember, it was the Cold War. We did it, the Americans did it."

"Was Willi Lehner part of the group too?"

He nodded.

"Why isn't he in the picture?"

"He wasn't there that day."

I nodded. "Okay, let's get this straight, because there seems to be a lot of moving pieces. Kahn works on rocket engines for ballistic missiles?"

"Yes."

"R-12?"

Fischer nodded. "He once did."

"Lehner manufactures chips for the motors?"

"Yes."

"For the R-12?"

"Yes, the motors won't work without them."

"What did you do?" I asked.

He stared at me.

"It's a simple question, Fischer. Kahn worked on the rocket engines, Lehner made chips for them so they would function correctly. What was your part in all this?"

"I—we built the rocket engines."

My gaze hardened. "You made rocket engines to be fitted to R-12 ballistic missiles?"

"Yes."

"And they won't work without the chips?"

"No."

"How many rocket motors?"

"Ten,"

"For ten R-12 missiles?"

"Yes."

"Holy shit," I muttered. "Where did they go?"

Fischer shook his head. "I—I don't know. They left here in a couple of boxcars last night. They couldn't have gone far because of the weather."

The Generals now had in their possession chips, motors, a scientist to fit them, and I could only assume they had missiles to go with them. No wonder they wanted us to look the other way. Another question: was this Stalin's Spear?

"Ever heard the name Stalin's Spear?"

"No," he lied.

"Who else is in the photo?" I asked him. I stabbed at another figure. "Who is that?"

"Valeri Lash," he replied.

"Valeri Lash?"

"Yes."

"As in Sergey Lash, the president of Russia?" I asked.

"Yes."

"Who is this?"

"Denis Sobolev."

"What does he do?"

"He is dead. Cancer, early two thousand."

"And this one?"

"Philipp Lahm," Fischer said. "He is a nuclear scientist."

While we contemplated what we had heard, Hunt's phone began buzzing wildly in my pocket. I answered it and heard Knocker's voice. "Get out, Reaper, you've got incoming. Five black SUVs and a technical just blew through the main gate."

"Shit. Hold position. We'll come to you."

I looked at Hawk. "Turn him loose. His friends are here to clean up. We'll take him with us."

"No, you can't, they will kill me."

"You should have thought of that before you got involved with them."

Within moments gunfire could be heard in the lower levels of the building. In time, the Berlin news stations and papers would call it the worst twenty-four hours for street fighting since Russia had invaded the city in World War Two. Well, guess what, they were back, and hell had come with them.

The cell I held rang again. This time, it was Slick. "Reaper, you have to come in. Shit has really hit the fan."

"Yeah, no problem," I replied, sarcasm thick in my voice. "If I'm damn well alive."

Then I disconnected the call and prepared for war once more.

While I took point, Hawk brought Fischer with him. Leaving the office, we found a floor in chaos as workers tried to either hide or escape the violence slowly encroaching on their workplace. One look at the weapons we held only served to heighten their panic, and several women screamed and scattered.

At the stairwell, we started moving down. Ahead of us were two men in suits. They stopped suddenly, turning in panic.

Before they could start back up, gunfire erupted, and the pair fell into bloody heaps on the stairs.

Coming up the stairs behind the fallen bodies, an assailant holding an AK-12 appeared. These guys were Russian.

The Glock in my grip hammered three times, each round punching into the shooter. He fell back and slid out of sight.

Our boots on the stairs squeaked softly as we made our way down to the landing then turned to face the next flight.

The man I had shot lay in a tangle at the base of the stairs, blood beginning to pool around him.

Through the door beside the dead shooter, two more assailants appeared, looking up at us before spraying a fusillade in our direction.

"Back," I snapped. "Back the fuck up."

We retraced our steps up the stairs, stepping over the bodies of the two dead workers. Once at the top, Hawk stopped and waited. "I'll catch up, Reaper."

As we stepped back out into the hallway on the top floor, I shoved Fischer along in front of me. Behind us, the sharp cracks of Hawk's handgun were audible. Quick footsteps on the tiled floor made me turn, and I saw Hawk running toward us. "That'll get them thinking for a few seconds—shit!"

Gunfire!

The bullets were emanating from ahead of us. The assailants must have utilized another stairwell we weren't aware of. Hawk and I acted instinctively, diving to the floor to take cover. Fischer, on the other hand, was too slow and received two stray rounds to his chest. We needed to consider that he might have been the primary target.

From our positions on the floor, our weapons came to bear. Hawk and I opened fire and the two shooters dropped onto the cold floor.

Jumping to our feet, I moved to assess Fischer while Hawk checked the shooters. Fischer was dead, his eyes wide, blood running freely from the holes in his torso. Emptying the pockets of one of the shooters, Hawk pulled out a phone. Then he picked up their two AKs and tossed one to me.

"Don't waste ammo."

I checked the weapon, and we kept moving, locating the door to the stairwell they had used. Opening the door cautiously, I peered down the stairs, making sure it was clear before moving on. At the base of the first flight, we found the crumpled body of a woman. She'd been shot in the back, obviously running for her life. These monsters had no compunction about killing anyone in front of them.

Throughout the building, continuous gunfire echoed. It was obvious that the shooters were cleaning house.

Making for the foyer, Hawk and I had to traverse the ground-floor walkway, enclosed by floor-to-ceiling plate-glass windows that gave a clear view of the large driveway turnaround and out to the front gates. It was then we noticed the technical. A flatbed truck with a heavy caliber machine gun attached to it.

And the gunner saw us.

Then things got hairy.

The heavy machine gun swiveled in our direction and the man behind it began firing. The chug-chug-chug seemed to echo off the building. The plate-glass windows shattered under the assault, and rounds punched into the wall behind us as we sprinted into the foyer, dodging falling plaster and debris.

Ahead of us, another assailant turned and stepped toward us. I brought the AK up, pointed it in his general direction, and fired.

By the time the magazine was empty, there'd been more misses than hits, but several had found flesh, and the floor rushed up to meet the dead shooter. Discarding the weapon as we dived behind the front desk, we weren't the only ones to take refuge there. The receptionist was there, blue eyes open in death, her body lying in a pool of viscous blood.

Heavy caliber bullets continued to destroy everything they touched. One resembled a missile as it blew through the counter near my head. I glanced at Hawk. "We need to stop that prick."

"Just as soon as you tell me how," he fired back at me. Another close round. "Fuck."

I reached for the cell and made a call. "Knocker, we're pinned down. That Technical needs to go."

"On our way."

While we waited, more rounds were incoming, causing

further damage. A screech of tires. The crunch of grinding metal. The firing stopped.

Peering cautiously around the counter, I noticed our transport had smashed into the technical. The front was pushed in, and from the damage I saw, it was going nowhere. "Shit," I groaned.

Hawk said, "That's fucked."

"Yeah."

A flurry of Russians began to gather, their attention drawn by the bingle out the front. Hawk swung his AK around while I lifted my Glock. Opening fire at the gathered Russians, our bullets slammed into flesh. Three shooters met their demise because they had failed to show caution.

We rushed outside and found our friends examining the truck. Knocker looked at me and shook his head. "Going nowhere, Reaper."

"Well then, we'll grab one of their SUVs."

The nearest vehicle met our requirements, and we clambered inside. Hawk assumed the driver's seat. In retrospect, that decision proved to be an error. Both Hawk and Knocker exhibited unexpected similarities in their driving capabilities. Interestingly, rumors circulated that Hawk had a penchant for boosting high-performance automobiles.

The surface of the streets was icy, and the weather had deteriorated once more. Peering in the side mirror, I caught a glimpse of two SUVs giving chase. As we took a corner at speed, the rear of the SUV came around to meet us.

Three times.

"Christ on a bloody crutch, Jake," Knocker growled. "What the bloody hell do you call that?"

"Ballet, old cock, ballet."

He straightened it up and floored the pedal again. I said, "Just try not to kill us, Hawk."

I dialed Slick. "I need to talk to Holly."

"You can't."

"Just put her on, Slick, damn it."

"She's under arrest, Reaper."

"What?"

"Long story."

"Okay, listen carefully. Last night, Morozov's people took ten rocket motors for R-12 missiles from Fischer's facility. As you know, they also managed to acquire the chips to make them operational. Sepp Kahn, the kidnapped scientist, is the man who can do just that. What you need to do is find out where the motors are going. Or, where they are holding the missiles."

"I'll do what I can, Reaper, but you need to come in to sort this mess out."

"We're on our way now."

I looked in the mirror again but saw nothing. "Seems as though they're gone."

Hawk nodded. "Looks like."

"Did I just hear you right?" Hunt asked.

"Yeah. The purpose of keeping us preoccupied was to further their other agenda."

"R-12 missiles, motors, chips—we're headed for war, Reaper," Knocker said. "Mark my words. These bastards are cooking up something big, and I bet it goes fucking bang."

And it did. Ten seconds later, when the black SUV rammed us from the side.

The vehicle we were traveling in flipped up onto two wheels and then lobbed onto its side, skidding and spinning at the same time. Glass was sprayed all over us and we were thrown around like vegetables in a stir fry. I hit my head and stars flashed before my eyes.

When our SUV stopped spinning, we were disoriented, unsure of which way was up. As cognition dawned, I released my belt and moved to climb out.

In the back seat, Knocker was clambering up through the smashed window, grabbing the door handle as he dropped to the ground, staggering until he gained his balance. He emitted a curse and then began to struggle with two other figures. I heard words but couldn't make them out. By the time I was halfway free of the wreck, hands grabbed me roughly and dragged me clear.

A hood was pulled over my head and I was thrown into a van. I heard Knocker cursing and then the door was slammed shut. Moments later, the motor was turned over, and two other doors closed before the van started moving. More voices, and at first, I couldn't make them out. Then I realized they were Georgian.

"Knocker?"

"Reaper?"

"Hunt?"

Nothing.

"Hawk?"

Nothing.

Gunshots were conspicuously absent, which indicated that our friends were both still alive, even if they weren't with us. Small mercies.

As the van bumped along, I could feel it turning left and right, losing track of our route after ten minutes. About twenty minutes into the journey, the vehicle stopped. When the van doors were flung open, we were dragged out and dumped abruptly onto a concrete floor.

Two of the Georgians grabbed our arms, dragging us roughly to some chairs, binding our hands and feet to the metal arms and legs. When our hoods were removed, I blinked rapidly, trying to clear my vision. At first, I only saw the silhouette of a man standing in front of me. Then his face took on some clarity.

"Fuck me."

"Hello, gentlemen, welcome to Berlin."

It was Igor Ionov.

"Damn it, Reaper, I thought we were done with him," Knocker growled.

I glanced at my friend. "Are you okay?"

"Fucking head hurts."

"Mine too." My gaze turned back to Igor. "What do you want this time?"

"My friend, you are worth fifty million dollars." He shrugged. "You and the ass turd."

"Who are you calling a fucking ass turd, dog nuts?"

"Do you know what you're mixed up in, Igor?" I asked him.

"It does not matter. Being a capitalist, I work for myself, and money is all that I care about."

"So, you've teamed up with the Georgians."

Igor had beefed up somewhat since our last interaction in Turkey. His hair looked a little thinner, but otherwise, he appeared to be taking good care of himself. "What do you know about R-12 ballistic missiles?"

"Nothing, and I don't care. I have a call to make, informing the people who are looking for you that you are here with me."

Knocker shook his head. "Yeah, bad idea."

Igor stared at him. "Rubbish."

"Everyone they come into contact with dies."

"Dies?" He looked at me.

I nodded. "Yes. They haven't left any loose ends so far. You make that call, they'll pay you, all right. Only it won't be in cash. Just bullets."

"You lie?"

"How long have you been in Berlin?"

"Long enough."

"Do you know why there is a bounty on our heads?" I asked.

"I'm guessing it is because you are assholes."

I let the words slide. "It's because they're up to something big. Have you ever heard of The Gods of War?"

"Ha. Tales told by old men," he sneered.

"Mikhail Shatov," I said. "Misha Durov, Lazar Noskov, and Gennady Morozov. And one more."

"Should those names mean something to me?" Igor asked.

I looked around the warehouse. "Four of them are dead.

One of them, Durov, is dead for real. Reach into my pocket and you'll find a picture."

He gave me a puzzled look and then did as requested. He peered down at the picture.

I said, "They are all in the photo. Plus, there are others. One is a rocket scientist who specializes in R-12 rockets, and the other makes jet engines that propel ballistic missiles. Another guy in there is Valeri Lash."

Igor's head snapped up. "Lash?"

"That's right, even your illustrious new president is involved somehow."

Fleetingly, uncertainty washed across his face. "He is not my president. He is a psychopath."

"That instills me with so much confidence," Knocker said.

"How long have you worked with the SVR?"

"I do not work with them anymore. Lash reverted all the intelligence agencies back to the KGB. Returned us to the Stone Age."

"Have you ever heard of anything called Stalin's Spear?"

He had. "It was a plan formed by the old generals to fight back against the west just in case Mother Russia was threatened. It first came to light in nineteen sixty-two when America deployed missiles into Italy and Turkey. The Soviet Union responded by doing the same in Cuba."

The Cuban Missile Crisis. Shit. "What happened to the missiles that were there?"

"Taken away under an agreement formed by the presidents of the time. Why?"

"Haven't you heard a thing I have just told you?"

He thought for a moment. Then it dawned on him. "You are saying that these men—these generals—are preparing R-12 ballistic missiles for something called Stalin's Spear?"

"It would appear that way," I replied.

Igor stood still, his mind ticking over. He signaled to one of his men. "Cut them loose."

Giving his boss a curious look, the man carried out his

order. We stood up and I rubbed the circulation back into my wrists. "Thank you, Igor."

"Do not thank me yet. If I find out you have deceived me, I will have my men kill you."

"We're not lying, mate. I only wish we were," Knocker said.

"I will see what I can find out."

With a nod, I said, "Memorize this number."

When he had the number, he said, "I will call when I know something. If not, I will find you."

"Just be careful."

He grinned. "As you Americans say, this is not my first rodeo."

"We need a ride."

"It can be arranged."

I took Hunt's phone and made a call. "Where are you?"

"Looking for you. Are you both all right?"

"Yeah, get back to the safehouse, we'll meet you there."

"He was going to let you go, just like that?" Christine Ryan asked.

"Yes, he realized the same threat we did."

"You shared top-secret intelligence with a foreign operative," Holland accused me.

"No, I didn't," I replied. "I shared information in the hope of saving our lives and getting something back in return. Which we did. Besides, he wasn't a foreign operative at that time."

I stared at the CIA director. He remained silent, but I could tell there were a lot of questions tied up inside that he wanted to get out.

"What did he find out?" German asked.

"I'll get to that, but first, we had another issue. There was a spy in our ranks."

CHAPTER 11

WHEN WE ARRIVED BACK AT THE SAFEHOUSE, HUNT AND HAWK were already there. But the surprising part was that Goodall was there too. She explained to me what had happened and then told me that Holly was under arrest.

"I want to see her."

"No, I don't think that is a good idea. Once the weather lifts, she will be sent back to London for interrogation."

"Interrogation? You make it sound like there is more to it."

"We need to investigate the leaks," Goodall informed me.

"You're wasting your time. It's not her."

"The higher-ups can decide that. Get your cuts patched. Then you can debrief with me on what you discovered."

"Yes, ma'am."

While I was seeing to my injuries, Slick came looking for me. "Boy am I glad you're back. There is shit going down here you'll never believe."

He explained their mission and the chips. He then told me about the impostors and how Goodall and her people had turned up and saved the day, or rather Holly did by shooting the shit out of the Russians. But then he informed me of the coincidence of Goodall already being in Berlin.

"Okay, so?"

He looked at me, waiting for me to join the dots. "The Russians were getting their orders from someone named Melinoe. It means ghost. There was a number in the commander's cell. I rang it and it pinged in Berlin. It came a while ago for one minute and then went off. It pinged from in this safehouse."

"Shit. You're telling me Goodall is an impostor too?"

"I can't be sure. But it fits."

"Tell me what happened with the woman who died," I said to Slick.

"Holly gave her a little extra pain medication to relax her for questioning. Not the first time it's been done. I've seen Brick do it before."

I nodded. We'd used the same interrogation technique on wounded prisoners in the past. "Keep going."

"Anyway, they got some intel but then Goodall called time on the interrogation."

"Why?"

"Well, looking back, maybe they were getting too much, and Goodall was worried that things might come out."

"Okay. Did anything pop on the missiles or motors?"

"Still working on it," he replied.

"Fine, make it quick. Where is the body?"

"Down in the basement."

I looked at my watch. It was two p.m. The woman and child had nine hours to live.

Leaving Slick to his search, I went and found the others. Staring at Hunt, I said, "You still up to date with your medical training?"

"Sure."

"Come with me."

We headed downstairs into the basement of the safe house, finding a single body bag. The others had been disposed of, but this one would go back to the UK for examination in the case against Holly.

"What are we doing, Reaper?"

"Looking for anything that's not right."

"Such as?"

I gave him the short version of what Slick had told me. Hunt frowned and said, "You think that someone else might have gotten to her?"

"Yes."

"Then let's check her out."

For ten minutes we looked over the dead body. The cold in the basement acted like a cooler and slowed down natural processes. It took a little time, but Hunt was the one who found it.

"Look at this, Reaper."

I walked around to stand beside him, noticing what he wanted to show me. Up under the hairline at the back of the woman's head was a puncture mark where something long and thin had been thrust in deep and killed her.

"Someone didn't want her to share," Hunt said.

"Yeah. But who?"

"Everything points at Goodall."

"Let's find out."

Heading back upstairs, I gathered everyone together. Goodall threw me a quizzical look, especially when Knocker appeared with Holly in tow. "What is she doing here?"

"She needs to be here," I replied.

Goodall said nothing.

Hunt and Hawk took up positions on the perimeter of the room where they could observe everything.

"Right, let's get started."

"Started on what?" Goodall asked.

"Somewhere in this room is a traitor, a plant known as Melinoe, and I mean to find out who it is."

"Rubbish," Goodall snorted.

"Somehow, the generals have known our every move. The only way they could achieve that was to have someone on the inside. At first, I thought it was Michaelson because he was responsible for setting us up with comms and the generals were linked into them. But still, after that they knew where we were. Going back before that, before we came to Berlin, they were working out our moves to a point. That means there is more than one working inside MI6."

"You are clutching at straws, Mr. Kane," Goodall said to me, a defiant look on her face.

Turning to Slick, I said, "Your turn."

"I went through the dead woman's cell and tagged some numbers she'd called. All went to burner phones which haven't come back online at all. But there was one. It came online for one minute not that long ago. In this safe house."

He paused and let his statement hang in the air.

Goodall said, "You're saying it is one of us?"

"Yes, ma'am. That person had contact with the Russian woman we knew as Sabrina."

"They were giving her orders or passing them on," I added. "From whom we don't know. Slick."

"The good part is that now I know the number, I can call it and find out."

Goodall looked puzzled. "How, if it is turned off?"

"I can turn it on." He hit some keys on his laptop, and before we knew what was happening, a buzzing sound filled the small room.

All eyes became focused on the person the sound was emanating from. Goodall's eyes went wide. "No!"

I walked over to her and removed the cell from her pocket. The screen was still lit, and it was buzzing. "Slick, kill it."

"I—I've never seen that before in my life, look."

She dug into her other pocket and took out a second cell. "This is mine. I don't know how that got there."

It was a familiar tune played on an old guitar. Feign shock and deny, deny, deny. Holly stared at her. "You fucking bitch."

"I'm not done yet."

"What do you mean?"

"The woman didn't die from an overdose. She died from something long and thin being pushed from the base of her skull into her brain. Which means Goodall is in the frame for murder too."

"I didn't do this, I tell you," Goodall reiterated. "Once I prove it, you'll all be put in some dark hole in the bloody desert."

I looked at her two companions. "What do I do with you two? The question remains, can you be trusted?"

"You can trust us," said the bigger of the two men.

"Fine, she's your responsibility until we get out of here."

"Yes, sir."

They escorted the protesting woman from the room and out of our sight. I looked at Holly. "You okay?"

"I knew you would save my ass."

"Yeah, well, I'm not sure about that. The Generals know where we are, so that means it's time to vacate before they move on us here."

"What did you find out?"

"You are going to love this."

I filled her in, and when I was done, she stared thoughtfully at the floor. "This is a big fucking mess, John."

"Yes, ma'am. We need to find the chips or the motors. And the missiles."

My cell rang.

It was Igor.

"I have news for you."

"Great, tell me."

"Not over the phone. Meet me in Viktoria Park by the Nationaldenkmal Für Die Befreiungskriege."

"When?"

"Thirty minutes," Igor replied.

The call disconnected and I looked over at Knocker, "We have to go."

Hunt said, "We'll come with you?"

I shook my head. "You two have done enough already, Bord. We appreciate everything you've done, but we'll take it from here."

"What about the price on your heads?"

I grinned. "Can't be many people left to try and collect it."

"We can still help," Hawk pointed out.

"Reaper, got a minute?" Knocker asked.

Knocker and I moved to one side. He said, "Holly and Slick need to find a new base of operations. Might be best if they were mobile."

"They can take Goodall's ride. We'll take the one that the Russians came in," I pointed out. "But you are right."

"Bord and Jake can go with them to keep them safe. Saves us worrying about them."

"What about the others?"

"They can take them to the embassy, leave them there. It becomes their problem."

"All right, we'll do it that way."

I turned back. "Bord, I have a job for you and Jake."

Amid the falling snow, we arrived at the park to discover a tense and apprehensive Igor waiting for us. His words carried weight: "This situation is bigger than you realize."

The gloomy, overcast sky loomed above, casting a heavy veil over our surroundings.

"How so?"

"I reached out to a friend. He hears things. When the October Affair ended, not all the missiles were removed from Cuba. You must understand that the trust was no thicker than a filament, so they retained some, securing them in a clandestine facility, just in case the filament snapped. It was against the agreement made by the United States and Soviet Russia at the time."

"What a load of horseshit," Ken Newman burst out.

I stared at him.

German said, "Do you have something to say, Mr. Newman?"

"I do. That smacks of Russian propaganda."

"If you will shut up and listen to the rest of the hearing, you might learn something," I snapped at him.

"Continue, Mr. Kane," Christine Ryan said.

The intel on the presence of missiles still in Cuba had provided an answer to a specific question yet left our main inquiry unanswered: What exactly were these missiles intended for? What were the generals up to?

"You think they're getting ready to launch on the US?"

"If they did, there would be hell to pay. The problem is, I think Sergey Lash might be crazy enough to do it."

"But why? You said yourself that Stalin's Spear was designed to be enacted if Russia was threatened."

"What if it was for something else?" Igor asked.

"What do you mean?"

"Lash has always said that Russia should reunite again. He has already changed its name back to the Union of Soviet Socialist Republics. But he still needs to put it all together."

"He couldn't. NATO would stop him."

"What if the Cuban missiles are designed to be a knife at the American throat to stop them from intervening to prevent it?"

"Is he crazy enough to believe that?" I asked.

"Yes."

"There is still England," I pointed out.

"I did not say I had all the answers." There was frustration in his voice. "Just theories."

"Did you hear anything about the motors?"

"Yes, they—"

WHAP!

"Fuck, sniper!" Knocker exclaimed.

One look at Igor was enough to know he was dead. "Move! Move!"

"He's in the trees to our left," Knocker shouted.

"Flank him," I called back as I grabbed my Glock. I became painfully aware of the presence of people playing in the snow. "Damn it."

Splitting up, we tried to work our way around the position where the shot had emanated from. By the time we got there, he was gone. He had, however, left wide-spaced prints in the snow, evidence of his hasty exit. They ended at the street where he'd obviously had a vehicle waiting.

"Damn it," Knocker snarled. "Why is it when we get to go forward one step, we get shuffled back two?"

"Because we're good guys in a shit movie," I replied. "This is what always happens in shit movies."

"Well, I'm sick of this shit movie."

———

While we were busy chasing our tails once again, Shatov was contacting Morozov, and he wasn't happy. "What have you done, Gennady?"

"Sir?"

"It was you who put the price on their heads," he snarled. "You, not me. Are you trying to subvert everything we have worked for all these years?"

Morozov had been found out and needed to smooth it over. "Sir, they are ruining everything. They know about the rocket engines, the chips, the scientist, everything. And now Melinoe has gone quiet. What I did was for the betterment of our great country."

"I told you they could be taken out once we achieved our goals. Instead, you have set Berlin ablaze while everything vital to the plan succeeding is stuck in the damn city. It was under control. At least Dolos is out of reach, or I am certain you would have that plan in ruins as well."

"I did what I thought was best."

"No, you did what you wanted to do, now we have to clean the mess up."

"Tell me what to do, Mikhail."

"Get the train to Kiel. I don't care how, just do it. I want the engines on the ship."

"What about the chips?"

"I have someone coming to you. They will transport

them once the storm has gone. Codenamed Archangel. And get rid of that damn bounty."

"And Sepp?"

"Get him to Prague."

"It will be done."

"Do not defy me ever again, Gennady. I will not stand for it."

"Yes, Comrade."

"One more thing. You will escort Sepp. Whatever happens, he must get to Prague. It is vital."

"It will be done. And the woman and child?"

"Detail a team. End it now."

"Yes, Comrade."

———

"This is all so confusing," German said. "So much going on that I can't even keep it straight in my head."

"You should have been trying to unravel it in real-time," I replied. "I will try to explain."

"Please do."

"The generals opened a new oil field because they needed that resource. Diamonds from the Congo mines gave them the money needed to carry out their plan."

"Stalin's Spear?"

"Yes. While that was happening, they managed to get Sergey Lash into power as president. He, however, had his own agenda. But they all had one thing in common."

"They wanted to reunite the old USSR?" Holland asked.

I nodded. "Yes."

German mused, "That part is relatively straightforward. Explain Berlin."

"Berlin was where we first came across Dolos and Melinoe," I told them.

"Melinoe the traitor."

"Correct."

"And Dolos?"

"At that time, we didn't know."

"Fine, continue."

"Morozov and Shatov set Berlin up to get us looking the wrong way. We were to chase the kidnapped woman and child while they did their thing with the missiles."

"Instead of just killing you?"

"Yes, I still haven't figured that one out. Maybe if they had, then things might have been different."

"Go on."

"What Shatov didn't count on was Morozov going against his orders, and us figuring out that it was a distraction. We stumbled across it quite by accident but soon discovered intel on the chips, the engines, the scientist, and most problematic, the missiles. We had an inkling of what their overall plan might be, but we couldn't be sure. If we cried wolf too early…you know."

"So instead, you waited."

"And just as well, or we wouldn't have found out what we eventually did."

"You mean Dolos?"

"Yes."

"And Archangel?"

"Archangel was a professional trafficker or smuggler if you like."

"Okay, I think I have my head around it so far. Now, according to the notes I have, things went a little pear-shaped after that."

Holland snorted. "Pear-shaped? They had already turned the city into a war zone. They were about to take it to the rest of the damned country."

"That would be a fair assessment, sir."

"Okay, let's hear the rest of it so we can get out of here. Unless you would like a break?"

I looked at Knocker and Holly. They shook their heads. "No, we're fine, sir."

CHAPTER 12

AMID THE CHAOS, WE REGROUPED WHILE EVADING PURSUIT. After meeting up, our search led us to a forgotten factory, its walls echoing with the ghosts of past industry. The air hung heavy with the scent of aged wood and long-abandoned polish. Within those weathered walls, we huddled together, our breaths visible in the dim light. Our conversation was tense, our options limited. One objective remained: locate Morozov. The enigmatic and elusive figure lingered somewhere in the maze of Berlin streets. Our task was clear: unravel the city's secrets, trace the threads that would lead us to him. Time pressed upon us, urging us forward, and we set forth, determined to find the man who held the answers we needed.

"Slick, run down anything you can, pull any string available," I told him.

"Trains," said Knocker.

I stared at him. "What do you mean?"

"The rocket engines were dispatched on a train. There can't be that many moving at this point. I'm guessing that they need to get them out of Berlin in a hurry. If we can find the right one, we might get somewhere."

"Agreed," I said. "I don't know why I didn't think of it."

"I might have something," Slick said, looking up at us from his screen.

"That was fast," Knocker said cautiously.

"No, another name. I was monitoring the dark web for chatter, and something popped. Archangel."

"You'll have to tell me who that is," I replied.

Holly said, "Are you sure that was the name?"

"Yes, ma'am."

Glancing at Knocker, I said, "I assume someone will tell us who Archangel is."

"In Berlin, Slick?" Holly asked.

"Yes, ma'am."

She turned to Knocker and I. "Archangel is the name used by a European smuggler. Nothing big, just small stuff. But valuable."

"Like chips?" I asked.

"Yes," Holly nodded. "We've come across her before. The experience cost us two agents."

"Her?"

"Yes. Natalia Semenova. She used to be one of Russia's top agents. Now she's freelance. She's very capable."

Slick turned his laptop around and showed us a picture. Tall, dark hair, and petite facial features. Almost childlike but very attractive.

Holly said, "Don't let her looks fool you, she is very dangerous. She may look like she works alone, but her man is never far away."

"What man?"

"Nigerian. Reuben Garba. Big man, former soldier with the Nigerian Army. Natalia recruited him while in the country on another job. Extremely loyal to a fault, he will sacrifice his life for her, so don't ever doubt that he won't."

I looked at Slick. "So what do you have?"

"Nothing yet. Like I said, it is just a name."

"Dig faster."

He was about to say something when his brow furrowed. "What the hell?"

"What is it?"

"I had a facial recognition program running in the background, searching for the woman and child as well as Morozov and…well, you know."

"What popped?"

"The woman and kid."

"Where?"

"Berlin Museum."

"What are they doing?"

"I don't know, but according to this, the museum is closed due to inclement weather."

I looked at Knocker. He nodded. "Smells like my Aunt Martha's week-old socks."

"I agree, but it might be the only chance we get to rescue them." I looked at my watch. We had six hours left. In the eighteen hours that had sped by, we'd only seen them when the Russians had wanted us to. Such as now. "Fuck it, we go."

Acquiring suitable weapons was a priority. All we had were our Glocks. "Got any idea where to get some firepower?"

"Fritz Hammel."

"I'm almost loath to ask. Who is Fritz Hammel?"

"Arms dealer based here in Berlin. Has a warehouse about three miles from here he operates out of."

I tossed him the keys. "Fine, you drive."

"Wait," Holly said. "Take Hunt and Hawk with you."

"I'd feel better if they were with you. We'll be fine."

"But you're walking into a trap," she pointed out.

With a nod, I said, "Yes, but we'll be ready. They won't. Besides, by the time we get there, it'll be dark. Just keep Slick busy finding whatever he can to point us in the direction of the chips. Once we acquire them, they can't carry out their plan."

Knocker and I left the factory and went to see his acquaintance. The warehouse was clean and new-looking. We pulled up outside on the concrete apron just as full dark was almost complete. The snow had stopped, but the air outside was still frigid, even though the wind had dropped.

"How do you know this guy?" I asked Knocker, torn between placing my hands in my pockets to keep them warm or keeping them free for any eventuality.

"Old friends," he replied.

"Anything I should know?"

Knocker shrugged. "Not really."

"Okay, you go in first. Just in case I get lucky and walk into a bullet."

We stepped out of the vehicle, leaving behind the warmth of its interior. The massive sliding doors stood shut and secured, but a standard pedestrian door nestled within the right side panel caught our attention. Knocker, ever curious, gave the handle a gentle tug. To our surprise, it yielded, swinging open with a soft creak.

As we crossed the threshold, the interior revealed itself—a cavernous space illuminated by industrial-sized lights suspended from the ceiling. Their glow was stark, reminiscent of the slow warmth that creeps in when these powerful globes first flicker to life.

The air smelled faintly of oil and metal, and the echo of our footsteps reverberated against the walls. In this unexpected sanctuary, we exchanged glances, anticipation hanging in the air like the lingering buzz of those overhead lights.

"Knock-knock," Knocker whispered, breaking the silence.

Of the four men who were inside, three of them were armed. The fourth man had a neatly trimmed beard and wore a black suit and a tie to match.

Knocker smiled. "Hello, Fritz, it's been a while."

It took one glance at the grinning Brit for the bearded man to indicate with his hand to two of his men. "You and you. Kill him."

Knocker's arms shot out in front of him. "Whoa, whoa. Hold on, Fritz. I came here as a friend."

"Kill his friend too."

"I'm guessing that your last meeting didn't go so well?" I said to Knocker.

"I'll admit it could have gone better," he said to me.

"You destroyed a shipment of weapons that I was sending to Latvia," Fritz snarled.

"Failed to mention that, Knocker?" I said to him. "You'd think that might have been pertinent information when you first proposed the idea."

"Might have forgotten, totally slipped my mind."

"Shit." I looked at Fritz. "Yeah, shoot him."

"Hold on, you can't shoot me," Knocker snapped.

"Why not?" Fritz asked.

"Yeah, why not?" I asked as well.

"Because."

"Because what?"

"I'll think of something in a moment."

Fritz looked at me. "Why are you here?"

"We need weapons," I told him.

"You have come to the wrong place."

Looking around I pointed out the crates stacked throughout the warehouse. "Somehow, I don't think so."

"They are legitimate business dealings," Fritz informed me.

"How legitimate?"

"Tinned food."

"Bullshit," Knocker growled. "I bet I could open any number of crates and find a shitload of FN SCARs."

"Shut up, you are dead. I just haven't shot you yet." Fritz looked at me. "What guns do you want?"

"If you have SCARs, I'll take a couple. Spare ammo, body armor. Spare ammo for Glocks as well. Grenade launcher, ammo for it. Fragmentation grenades as well."

"Huh, you going to war, American?"

"Already have been since last night," I said casually.

Fritz stared at me as his mind contemplated my response. "You?"

"Me what?"

"The old amusement park? Train station?"

"Among other places."

"The market?"

"Yes. Look, we don't have time for this. We need the weapons."

"How will you pay for them?" Fritz asked.

"I don't know."

The arms dealer made a guttural sound. "What do you think this is? A fucking charity store?"

"No, but if we can't get the weapons, we can't stop the Russians from starting a nuclear war."

"A nuclear war?"

"Could be," I replied, dialing back the tone. After all, we couldn't be sure what their intentions were. "We need to stop them."

"All right, I will help you. Only because I do not like Russians. They try to rip me off."

We picked out what we needed, and he threw in a Dragunov sniper rifle. "Present from me."

"Thanks, Fritz."

Loading our material into the vehicle, we farewelled Fritz and his men, then set off for the museum to liberate Kira and Polina.

"Talk to me, oh great one." The comms were hooked up through my cell.

"I've hacked into their security camera system, Reaper. The alarms are off-line and I'm guessing that they're lying in waiting for you. The targets are on the second floor among the paleontology display. Both are seated on chairs, and the shooters have formed a collapsing perimeter. It's going to be tough. More shooters are spread strategically throughout the museum. I'll do my best to guide you through."

"Copy."

We loaded our weapons and I looked across at Knocker. "You ready?"

"Like the bloody battery," he responded.

"What?"

"Eveready Battery?"

"Idiot."

"I thought it was good."

"Shit."

We started toward the museum along the snow-covered walkway. The icy stairs leading to the main doors were treacherous.

I said, "Talk to me, Slick."

"To your right on entry, there's a shooter near a large statue and another to the immediate left of the doorway."

"Copy." Looking at Knocker, I said, "You go right."

"Roger that."

I let the SCAR hang from its sling and took out my suppressed Glock. Shoving the heavy wooden door open, we entered.

Immediately, I took the close target on the left. Two shots to the chest, one to the head. I didn't spare a thought for the target on the right because I knew Knocker had that one covered. Instead, I swept my area to make sure there were no additional threats.

Behind me, I heard the shots from the SCAR. Just two and then, "X-ray down."

"Clear left."

"Clear ri—contact up!"

I spun. Bringing the Glock up. I needn't have worried because Knocker had the situation under control. The SCAR cleared its throat again, the bullets taking out the target and a priceless Ming vase beside him.

"Oops."

"You know that was probably worth a hundred grand, right?"

"You think they have insurance, Reaper?"

"Wait," German said. "You were rescuing hostages, did you not think that it might be better to be more covert?"

I looked at him. "We made the conscious decision that the awaiting forces were using the hostages to draw us in. Ergo, they would keep them alive."

"That is a big assumption."

"Yes, but not unlikely."

"All right, continue."

"Slick, talk to me."

"Head up the stairs, Reaper. They are toward the back."

"Copy."

Taking point, I put the Glock away and once more had a firm grip on the SCAR. When I reached the landing, I made sure that the shooter Knocker had put down was actually dead. That done, I kept moving.

This section of the museum was part of an African diorama. Lions in long grass, zebras, a giraffe, wildebeest, baboons on rocks, leopards in a tree, and, of course, an elephant. It brought back memories of operations we'd performed on what was called the dark continent.

"Reaper, you have two more assailants coming in from your two o'clock," Slick told us.

I looked around. "Where?"

"Two o'clock. They should be in your field of vision."

"I can't see anything because of this fucking grass."

Automatic weapons fire ripped through the display, hammering into animals and cutting down clumps of African grass. A baboon toppled sideways from its perch atop a rock.

I threw myself to the floor. "Contact front."

Knocker followed suit as the bullets sliced the air above us. I heard Slick say, "Do you see them now?"

I ground my teeth. "Fuck off."

"Thought so."

Crawling along the floor, I took up position behind the largest thing in the room. The elephant. Obviously, they still couldn't see us because they were spraying bullets wildly around the room.

"Slick, can you see me?"

"Roger."

"Can you see them?"

"Roger, they're at your two o'clock."

I aimed the SCAR, adjusted my fire selector, and opened fire. The weapon rattled to life, sending spent cartridge casings bouncing across the floor. Slick said, "Great shot, Reaper. You just killed a wildebeest."

"Christ."

A sudden fusillade came toward me punching into the elephant. I sought shelter behind a thick leg and felt the animal shudder under multiple impacting rounds. Poor bastard wasn't even safe in death. "Sorry, buddy."

Knocker's voice came over comms. "Fuck this, Reaper, I'm going high."

"Don't do anything stupid, Knocker," I cautioned him.

"You know me."

"Yeah, I do. Hence the warning. Shit."

I burned through another magazine of 5.56 rounds to draw fire so Knocker could get into position. While reloading, I caught a glimpse of him climbing Baboon Rock. This could not end well.

A shout from our adversaries echoed around the room, indicating that he'd been seen. The shooters changed their target to Knocker on the rock. He began to open fire and I saw him fall back. "Damn it."

Moving quickly in a flanking move to get around the shooters, I had no knowledge of the fate of my friend: dead or alive? The first shooter came into view, and I shot him with the SCAR. Pressing forward, I found the second shooter not far from the first. He swung his weapon around to fire at me, but I was already firing as he started.

My bullets punched into flesh, knocking him back. I moved forward and fired again, making sure he would stay down.

Turning to face the rock, I called out, "Knocker, you there?"

At first there was nothing, then, "Shit, that was acrobatic."

"Come on, these guys are down. Slick, where to?"

"Keep going. Next stop is the underwater display."

Moments later, I heard Knocker say, "What the fuck?"

He was looking up. The room was massive with what resembled a catwalk, a rail along one side instead of a wall, overlooking the center of the museum. From there, people could see down onto the ground level. It had to be big to fit the life-sized blue whale hanging from the ceiling. "Big," I agreed.

"Bloody huge. On a normal day, I would stop and stare at it, but—bloody hell that's big."

Hanging not far away from it was a great white shark, a manta ray, and a sunfish. "Slick, what do you see?"

Waiting for his response, I swept my SCAR back and forth, left to right, looking for targets, hidden or otherwise.

He said, "Reaper, you have three shooters moving along the gantry above you, trying to get to a better vantage point."

My weapon swept up toward the next level catwalk. At first, I couldn't make anyone out, but then they stepped into view from behind the whale.

"Contact up!" I called out and opened fire.

Knocker dropped to his knee and opened fire with his SCAR. Bullets hammered into the gantry and ceiling. Even the whale managed to stop a few. A shooter fell over the rail, tumbling like a crash test dummy to the floor. Meanwhile, his friends kept up their rate of fire and bullets ricocheted all around me.

"Frag out!" Knocker shouted.

"No!"

"Too late."

I dived to the side, using the whale's form as cover, as the grenade arced through the air. He'd cooked it, and as it

neared the two shooters on the gantry, the grenade detonated. I lay on the floor, looking up. Most of the orange blast
was blocked by the whale's form. The two shooters were
blown off the gantry and fell to the hard floor below. Meanwhile, the whale became its own swinging killer.

With the parting of a couple of the heavy-duty wire
cables that held it aloft, it began to plummet downward, but
the final remaining cable snapped taut, making the cetacean
swing like a wrecking ball.

"Shit, Knocker," I growled as I rolled desperately out of
the way. I felt the breeze of its passing barely inches away.

It hit the floor, its momentum sending it skidding across
the surface. The last cable snapped, giving way, turning the
whale into a sliding missile, intent on demolishing the
second-floor rail. Smashing through, it disappeared with an
almighty crash.

I shook my head. "Shit, Knocker."

"That was wild, huh?" he said with a grin as he came and
stood over me.

"We're here to rescue people, not trash the joint," I
growled, getting to my feet.

He slapped me on the shoulder. "Follow me. Slick, next?"

"Keep going until you reach the stairs on the far side.
Follow them down until you reach another large room.
You'll find them in there."

"What's it look like?"

"There are two guards with them, but I'm still showing at
least another five throughout the museum."

"What are they doing?" I asked.

"Waiting."

"For what?"

"No idea. But they're not moving." There was a pause.
"Something isn't right."

"You don't say."

Knocker reached the landing first and stopped. I came up
behind him and touched his shoulder, sending him ahead
down the stairs. Noticing the two guards immediately, he

fired four shots, two into each. They dropped to the floor like stones.

We hurried across to the woman and child. Both had gags and were crying. I said, "It's okay, we've come to get you out."

I pulled the gag down from Kira's mouth. "You have to leave. It is a trap. Leave us."

"We're not leaving without you," I told her.

Knocker freed Polina. "Hey, kiddo, you ready to get out of here?"

"Y-yes, please."

"Reaper, whatever you did, it triggered a response. I'm now picking up more movement throughout the museum."

"Weren't they there before?"

"Not these ones."

"And you're only just seeing them now?"

"It's the weather."

"The weather," Knocker growled. "It seems the weather is responsible for a multitude of sins."

I looked around the room. It was cluttered with dinosaurs and fossil displays. I grabbed Kira and guided her to a large herbivorous creature. "Stay here. Keep down and we'll come back for you when we're done."

"Don't leave us," Kira pleaded.

"We'll be back. I promise."

I checked my loads, looked at Knocker, and we nodded. Then we went to war once more.

Instead of planets with craters, these ones had holes. From our position, the planetarium resembled a war zone. Some of the planets had fallen from their suspension cables, the night sky overhead had numerous black holes, and a lunar lander previously standing on four legs now had toppled over on three.

There were three bodies on the floor and numerous

others throughout the building. A fire in the rainforest room and alarms going off everywhere. I reloaded my weapon and looked across at Knocker. The battle had been fierce, and we were both feeling the effects. "You okay?"

"That was intense. These Russian pricks put up a good fight."

"Yeah. Let's get out of here before more trouble comes our way. Slick, are we clear?"

"Yes, but you have emergency responders a few minutes out trying to get there on icy streets as quickly as they can."

"Copy."

We gathered Kira and Polina and got out of there before the responders arrived. Knocker and I dropped them outside the embassy. "Holly called ahead. You should be fine here," I told Kira.

"I don't know how to thank you. Andrey said you would help."

"He was a friend. I wasn't about to let him down," I lied. The truth was, I was about to give up on them when the other thing popped up. I couldn't tell her that though.

I called Holly. "The packages have been dropped at the embassy. What now?"

"We have a problem."

"What?"

At this point in time, she delivered the worst possible news. The weather was clearing.

CHAPTER 13

WE MET UP AT A DESERTED BAR UTILIZED BY COLD WAR AGENTS from both sides back in the day as a meeting place to pass information back and forth. All the furniture was covered in a thick layer of dust, but other than that it looked as though it had not been disturbed since the day the doors had closed.

Knocker stood behind the bar counter holding up a bottle of whiskey. "Drink, Reaper? Sure to have aged well."

"Sure to have aged," I said, screwing up my nose.

He found a glass, wiped the dust out of it, and poured some of the contents of the bottle into it. He held it up against the light. For some reason, the electricity was still connected. However, we weren't about to complain.

Knocker grinned. "Looks okay."

He swallowed it in one gulp. I stared at him and waited for the explosion. Instead, he grinned. "That was good."

"Alright, pour me one."

Knocker repeated the process and handed me the glass. He was right, it wasn't bad at all.

The door to the bar opened, and instantly, our weapons leaped into our hands and pointed at the figures in the doorway.

"Whoa," Hunt said, holding his hands out in front, showing us they were empty. "You guys are a mite jumpy."

"Been shot at a lot recently," Knocker said, picking up another full shot glass of amber liquid.

They came in and Knocker cleaned more glasses and poured everyone a drink. We gathered around a table and Holly said, "Anything to report?"

"We took Kira and Polina to the embassy. What's news on your front?"

"Nothing on the train or the scientist. But we may have something on Archangel."

"What?"

"I got a couple of pictures off the feed from the Berlin Ramada," Slick said. He turned his laptop around for us to see. "This is Natalia Semenova and her bodyguard. They were seen going into this hotel and coming back out thirty minutes later."

The picture changed and they were shown leaving with a small briefcase.

Slick continued, "Ten minutes later, we got this."

This time, the screen showed Morozov and two bodyguards.

"Our friendly neighborhood Russian," Knocker said.

"Yes."

"Do we know where he went?"

"No, but Natalia Semenova is currently at an airfield outside of Berlin waiting to get clearance for her plane to leave."

"How did you manage to find her?" I asked.

"It wasn't easy. But she is definitely there."

"People?"

"Don't know. One for sure: her bodyguard."

"Pilots," Knocker said. "Plane isn't going anywhere without them. And you can count on at least an additional two guys for security."

"Anything on the name Dolos?" I asked.

Slick said with a shake of his head, "I've tried to find something, but it must be buried deep. Which means it's big."

"Keep at it." I looked across at Knocker. "Come on, we've got a plane to catch."

"You want us to come with, Reaper?" Hunt asked.

"No, stay with Holly and Slick. If they find the scientist or the train containing the engines while we're preoccupied, you might need to run them down."

"Roger that."

————

It took us an hour and a half to reach the airport. The weather was becoming increasingly clearer and there was a real chance that we were going to miss the plane. What I didn't know at the time was that the flight had been postponed until the next morning.

On arrival, we parked behind a large hangar. Knocker and I grabbed the SCARs and walked toward where the plane was to be.

It sat on the apron, enveloped in darkness. We could see no one nor hear them. "It looks deserted," Knocker said.

I was thinking the same thing. "Slick, it looks like we've come up empty here. There is no one at the plane."

"Wait one, Reaper. I'll see if there is a flight plan adjustment."

Knocker and I stayed in the shadows out of the cold wind. Overhead, the clouds had mostly blown away, but the night was still very cold.

"Okay, Reaper, the flight has been delayed until morning."

"Then where are they?"

"I don't—"

CRACK!

"Sniper!" Knocker exclaimed, dragging me back into cover.

"Where is he?"

"On top of the hangar across the way."

I thought for a moment. The sniper had set up in a good

position. There was no way to get to him without crossing a substantial stretch of open ground.

I said, "Fall back. Let's get out of here."

Safely back at our ride, we climbed in.

I said over my comms. "We're pulling back. No point being here if the target isn't."

"Roger that," Holly replied. "Give us a moment and we'll see what we can come up with."

"So that was it, your mission was a bust," Holland commented.

"At that time, it didn't look good," I replied.

"You destroyed half of Berlin for nothing."

"We got the woman and child back safely," I pointed out.

"A Russian woman and child."

My eyebrows shot up and I shook my head. "Really?"

Holly placed her hand on my arm to calm me. The last thing she wanted to see was me going across the table to punch this asshole in the mouth.

She said, "I'm sure, Mr. Holland, if that was your wife and child, you would want us to do all we could to render them safe, yes?"

"They'd probably pay us extra to take them to a nonextradition country to keep away from this prick," I growled.

"I beg your pardon?" Holland blustered.

"You fucking heard me." I saw Newman grinning in the corner. *"What are you smiling at?"*

"You, burying yourself, hero."

"Don't worry, pal, we haven't got to you yet. Just wait until we do."

It was his turn to get mad. He leaped to his feet, but the harsh voice of Christine Ryan put a stop to current proceedings. "Enough! We shall take a break."

"I'm fine," I snarled.

Her eyes narrowed and her voice was even. "We shall take a break, and when we return, we shall continue."

So, we took a break.

Thirty minutes later we were back, and I was in the same mood as before. I hated dealing with idiots.

We were up against a stone wall, so to speak. We had no intel about the generals, the engines, the scientist, or the chips. So we waited.

Then, at eight the following morning, we received the required intel.

The cloud had lifted, and the snow was being cleared from the streets. Berlin was coming alive, and we were in the middle of it. "Reaper, copy?"

"Got you, Slick."

"We're in business. Archangel just surfaced."

"Great, let's go. Where is she?"

"Driving to the airfield. I'm currently tracking her on street cams," Slick informed us.

"Can you put us on a course to intercept?"

"Roger that."

He gave us directions and Knocker started the vehicle. Ten minutes later, we were parked up at an intersection, waiting for her to arrive. "Slick, can you change the lights to red when they get here?"

"Roger that."

I took out my Glock and checked it over as I always did. Knocker did the same.

"We going to carjack her, Reaper?"

"No, I am. You follow behind, for if I get into trouble."

"Roger that. Just watch your ass, Reaper."

"Reaper, here they come."

The adrenaline in my blood made my heart rate increase, the anticipation of what was to come running through my brain. Once more, I was on the verge of harm's way and God only knew what was on the other side.

I saw the lights change to red and then the dark SUV appeared. Climbing out, I hurried across the intersection on the crossing. As I reached the blacked-out SUV, I changed direction and made a beeline for the rear passenger door.

Jerking it open, Glock in hand, I climbed in. Natalia

gasped in surprise, but I ignored her at first, bringing the handgun up and shooting the man in the front passenger seat through the rear of his head.

Blood painted the inside of the windshield. I switched my aim to Natalia. "Driver, drive," I snarled.

He trod on the gas and the SUV shot forward, wheels spinning. My gaze diverted to Natalia and the case on the seat between us. "Hello, Natalia."

"Who are you?" she demanded, having mostly recovered from the interruption of sudden violence that had seen her bodyguard killed.

"My friends call me Reaper."

"You are American. CIA?"

"Not hardly. Let's just say I freelance for whoever needs me."

"Mercenary." The words were spat in disgust.

"Much like you, really."

"I am a businesswoman."

"If you say so," I said. "Slick, where are we going?"

"I'll just program their GPS. Tell the driver to follow it."

"Roger that. Driver, follow the directions the GPS gives you. Try anything and you'll join your friend. I'm quite able to drive should the need arise."

"What do you want with me?" Natalia demanded.

I patted the case between us. "The contents in this case are vital to stopping a disaster from happening."

"What do you think is in the case?" she asked.

"Microchips to help facilitate the launch of R-12 Cold War ballistic missiles."

A fleeting look of surprise crossed her face, but she managed to regain her composure. Obviously, she held no knowledge of what she was carrying.

"Morozov didn't tell you?"

"Who is Morozov?" Natalia asked.

"Gennady Morozov. The man you met with at the hotel."

She stared at me. I nodded knowingly. "What name did he give you, Natalia?"

"Boris."

"Very original."

In the background, I could hear the monotone of the GPS giving directions. Natalia stared at me. "Who is Gennady Morozov?"

"He's part of a group of Russians called The Gods of War."

She snorted derisively. "They are a myth. Such a thing does not exist."

"Neither does Stalin's Spear, huh?"

That got her attention. Then she went silent.

Our destination was an abandoned brickworks, and we rolled to a stop inside a large warehouse to find the others waiting for us. Knocker pulled in behind our SUV and climbed out.

"Holly, where do you find these places?"

"Don't blame me, it was Slick."

I helped Natalia out and noticed for the first time that the briefcase was handcuffed to her wrist.

"You want me to find an axe, Reaper?" Hawk asked.

"Just wait," Natalia growled. "I have a key."

Unlocking the stainless-steel cuffs, she passed the case across to Holly. Natalia frowned. "Have we met before?"

"No, but I wish we had." Holly placed the case on the hood of the SUV. "I need a combination."

"Three-five-nine-nine-six-nine-one-eight."

"It better not fuck things up or I'll have Reaper put a bullet in your head like he did Reuben." Holly was drawing on the intel gained regarding Natalia's bodyguard.

"There was no need for him to do that," Natalia said wanly.

"And there was no need for you to kill all of those that you have."

Holly put the combination in, and the case clicked open. She slowly lifted the lid and her expression changed visibly from one of hopeful anticipation to rage.

"Motherfucker. That motherfucker has bloody outsmarted us."

Natalia looked at the case and saw what the contentious issue was. The case was empty. Holly whirled on her. "You knew it was empty."

"No, I did not."

"You had to. It's your case."

"No, he gave it to me. I had to commit the combination to my memory."

Holly let out a roar of rage and threw the case onto the floor. "I'm sick of chasing my fucking tail. Just once I'd like a break."

"We got her off the streets, boss," I said, nodding toward Natalia. "The head shed will be happy to interrogate her."

"Fine, we'll hand her over to the embassy and she can be transported back to London."

"*Stop,*" *Newman interrupted.* "*You have Archangel in your custody?*"

"*We do,*" *Christine Ryan replied.*

"*Why weren't we told?*"

"*Like you tell us every time you take someone off the board and put them in a deep dark hole,*" *she replied.*

"*What have you learned from her?*"

Christine Ryan grinned mirthlessly. "*We have learned you're not as squeaky clean as you would have your bosses think. Shall we continue?*"

"We have to adjust our focus," I said finally. "Slick, the train or the scientist. I'm thinking that if we can locate Morozov, then we locate the scientist. I'd bet my left nut that he's riding herd on him."

"We need to get out of the city," Holly said. "There is an estate used by MI6 fifty kilometers to the north. I will give you coordinates. We should meet there."

"Shouldn't we stay in Berlin?" I asked her.

"No. They're gone by now. With the weather lifting like it is."

"Okay. We'll see you there."

She turned to Hunt and Hawk. "Also, gentlemen, as much as I would like to keep you around, I'm afraid your services are no longer required."

"You firing us?' Hunt asked incredulously.

"Story of my life," Hawk said. "Although Ilse will be glad to have me back in one piece."

"I hope that is okay?" Holly said.

"Just shout if you need us," Hunt said. "Watch your six, Reaper."

"Thanks for your help, Bord. Jake."

Knocker and I climbed back into our vehicle and headed north out of the city.

"What do you think, Reaper?" Knocker asked as we drove away from the dusty brickworks.

"I think we're pushing shit uphill once again, buddy. And it's a slippery slope."

"Yeah, my thoughts exactly."

———

The estate was deserted. Had been for the past few months. When Knocker and I got there, we found the grounds covered in white and a large fireplace that needed to be lit. Gathering wood and some kindling, we soon had a flame going, and the trusty nose of our resident alcohol connoisseur found a bar with drinkable whiskey, or scotch as it was called in the colonial country.

We sat and talked, discussing what we'd been subjected to so far.

"Reaper, I had a thought."

"Lay your wisdom on me," I replied, saluting him with my glass.

"What if Goodall wasn't Melinoe?"

"Shit, she was caught red-handed."

"I know, but something doesn't strike me as right."

"Like what?"

"The Russians are still getting information about our

movements. They set that trap for us at the museum. They still have someone inside. It's not Goodall, I tell you."

"You still haven't convinced me."

"It's a feeling. Even if she was bad, they still have someone else inside. They've been doing this too long not to have."

"Okay. Maybe they have."

"Then there is Dolos."

I nodded. "That has to be a deep cover. But again, we don't know where."

"I know one thing," Knocker said. "Being here gets me out of the shitstorm political freakshow election coming up in the next couple of weeks back home. Hard choice picking between the knob that is in and the one who wants to embrace the new world order, as he calls it."

"Can't help you, there, I'm sorry."

It was midafternoon when Holly and Slick arrived back with supplies and intel. Well, not much intel, but the food was welcomed. Knocker cooked. He decided a good old English stew was the order of the day and spent several hours in the kitchen preparing and getting it into the oven. The result wasn't half bad. For a novice, that is.

Sitting back, relaxing after our filling meal, we shot the shit for a couple hours while Slick continued working. I swear the boy is more machine than man. By the time we retired for the night, he was still hard at it.

And I was still asleep when he came to wake me at three in the morning. "Reaper, you awake?"

I groaned. "I am now."

"I found the train."

"What?"

"I found the train. It's on its way to Kiel."

"Get the others up."

Ten minutes later, bleary eyed, we were drinking coffee, trying to put together the intel Slick was feeding to us.

"Speak, Slick," I said. "But for shit sake, make it comprehensible. It's too bloody early in the morning."

"The train must have been laying up somewhere while the weather cleared. It is on its way to Kiel to meet a ship called the North Star."

"Where is it headed?"

"I don't know. I do know it sails within twenty-four hours."

"So we need to hit the train before it gets to Kiel," Knocker suggested.

"Yes."

"We're going to need a helicopter and some rappelling gear."

"How big is the train?"

"It looks to be a freight train."

"All right, we need a skilled pilot capable of putting us down on it. Or above it, anyway."

"You know that train is going to be heavily defended, right?" Holly asked.

"More than likely. But they won't be expecting us."

Knocker chuckled. "I love your confidence."

"Can you get us a helicopter or not?"

"Yes, I'll talk to Whitehall."

I nodded. "What's the ETA on the train?"

Slick said, "We have time, providing we can get it done before noon."

"Then let's do it."

CHAPTER 14

FOR OUR INTENDED ACTIONS, THE BERLIN AUTHORITIES NEEDED to be informed. Which meant informing the Bundesnachrichtendienst. Germany's Federal Intelligence Service. Who in turn drew on the services of the KSK. Or German Special Forces Command.

Drawing on their resources, they dispatched a team of six operators to assist. We created two groups of three that Knocker and I would lead in the assault on the train. They had their own helicopters, which we seconded. They also supplied us with all the combat gear and weapons we needed. We just didn't tell them we'd already been fighting in their city.

The KSK provided us with MP5SDs. Since it was going to be a daylight raid, there would be no need for night vision capabilities. Planning was simple and done on the run. We would assault both ends of the train, with Knocker taking the front. Two of his people would secure the locomotive while he and his second would methodically begin clearing the rest of the train. Myself and the other three KSK operators would do the same from the rear.

The sky was clear, and the landscape was blanketed in white. From where we were on the Eurocopter AS532

Cougar, it was a wonderous and blinding sight. Not that we could contemplate it for too long. There was work to do.

"Two minutes." The call came from the pilot.

We all pulled down our masks and prepared our weapons. I looked at the team and gave them a thumbs up, which was returned in kind. I felt the helicopter slow and begin to match the train's pace. When the time came, the doors were opened, and we deployed.

Knocker and his people moved toward the front of the train. My team went in the opposite direction, toward the rear. There were ten freight cars. For a moment we must have looked like actors starring in an action movie, but this was the real thing. And it was dangerous. Upon reaching the rear freight car, the four of us split up. Arne Frings, one of the KSK leaders, took the front of the car with another operator while I closed on the rear door with my soldier.

Climbing down, we breached at the same time. Erratic gunfire erupted, which I returned in kind with the MP5SD. There were two shooters inside the freight car, and both died swiftly. With the car secured, we had the chance to assess the cargo. One of the engines was there. So I figured, ten freight cars, one engine in each.

Moving on to the second car, we were surprised to find it empty. I frowned. Maybe there were more in the others. They would fit more than one per car.

As the team and I made to breach the next freight car we came under fire again. Frings grabbed a flashbang, pulled the pin, and deployed it. We waited for the detonation and one of the other operators led the charge through the door.

I heard the discharge of the MP5, then the call of clear. I entered and we found another motor. Just one.

"Knocker, copy?"

Nothing. Maybe he was busy.

"Knocker, copy?"

"Copy, Reaper."

"How many packages have you found?"

"One, and we're on our third freight car. How about you?"

"We've got two from three."

He said, "That leaves seven unaccounted for and four freight cars remaining to find them in."

"Roger that. Resistance?"

"Fuck all."

"Copy. Out."

I looked at Fring. "Something isn't right."

Progressing onto the next car, we discovered it too was empty, while the following one contained a single motor. Knocker had found one more.

I got on the comms and said, "Holly, copy?"

"Copy, John."

"We have a problem. We've got five packages, I say again, we only have five packages."

"How can that be?" Holly asked.

"They're smarter than we thought. Not placing all their eggs in one basket."

There was a moment of silence before Holly said. "John, continue to Kiel and check the ship. Maybe we'll get lucky there."

"Roger that."

I turned to Fring. "Sergeant, we're continuing on to Kiel."

"Yes, sir."

Knocker said, "There were never ten of them on this train, Reaper."

I nodded. "Highly fucking likely."

"It would seem to me that you and your team, Miss Smith, were lacking somewhat in all facets of the operation," German said scathingly.

"You have to remember that these people had been planning this for years, sir. They had every contingency covered. They were not your average terrorists."

"So that is what they were? Terrorists."

"If you wish to call them that."

"No, that's what you called them."

"No, sir, I said they weren't your average terrorists. At the time of the train operation, Shatov and Morozov were already implementing other phases of the operation."

"How could we forget?"

"The fucking ship is gone," Knocker said as we stood on the dock bathed in silvery moonlight.

"Christ. Holly, the ship is gone. We need to find it before it disappears for good. It can't be too far away."

"I'll get Slick onto it."

So they searched while we waited. It took an hour before Slick found the ship. It was in the Baltic, headed toward Russia.

"We found it, Reaper," Holly said. "It's in the Baltic. A helicopter is being organized to transfer you out there."

After a few calls, acquiring the equipment we needed, twenty minutes later, we were airborne.

The Baltic churned relentlessly beneath us as the helicopter skimmed perilously close to the wave crests. Across the vast expanse, the pilots discerned the *North Star*, a steadfast beacon on the distant horizon. Their warning came, advising that we were nearing our destination.

As we descended toward the ship, our attention shifted from the sea to the ship below us. The moon, a silvery sentinel, bathed the sky in ethereal light, but we failed to appreciate its beauty. Our focus was drawn to the stillness— the gentle breeze, almost imperceptible, a harbinger of favorable conditions for our mission.

Anticipation hung thick in the air as we prepared to board. The ship's deck, an enigma awaiting our arrival, held secrets we had yet to uncover. Our only certainty: uncertainty. Without intelligence on what awaited us, we stepped into the unknown, guided by the *North Star* and the moon's luminous path.

"One minute," came the pilot over the internal comms.

We gave our gear one last check and moved into position.

As the helicopter hovered above the ship, an odd sensation washed over me. Despite our continued movement, it felt as though we were suspended in time. The doors swung open, revealing our position directly above the stern.

Once the team hit the deck, it would secure the ship and then look for the cargo. Knocker and I were the first ones out. Once down, we held our position and waited for the others.

Upon reaching the ship's deck, our partial team swiftly secured the vessel before turning our attention to locating the cargo. Knocker and I led the way, stepping out first. As we descended, we maintained our positions, patiently awaiting the arrival of our fellow team members. Once all eight of us were safely on deck, the helicopter pulled up and departed. I selected one man, and together, we proceeded to secure the bridge. Ascending an internal stairwell, we encountered the captain and his watch officers, poised and ready for our arrival.

The captain of the *North Star* was Dutch. His gray hair and lined face attested to many years of exposure to the salt air. "What is the meaning of this?" he demanded.

"I'm sorry for the inconvenience, Captain, but it is believed that your vessel is carrying contraband items destined for use in terrorist activities. I must ask you to shut the motors down."

"Ridiculous."

"You do it, Captain, or I will find somebody who can. We're here to look, once we're done, then we'll leave. Depending on what we find."

"It is damned piracy."

I looked at the man beside me. "Jurgen, find someone who can shut this fucking tin can down."

Soon after, the vibrations in the deck began to subside

and the ship began to slow as the huge engines were shut down. Eventually, everyone called in, the ship had been secured without any trouble.

"All right, let's see what we can find." I looked at the captain. "I need to see a manifest."

Three hours elapsed before we had our target containers narrowed down to five. As only one of those was accessible, it gave us the information we needed. Knocker positioned himself in front of this solitary container, its door already ajar by the time Fring and I arrived. Together, we gazed into the cavernous void before us. It was Knocker that broke the silence:

"Chasing our tail is becoming a habit with these bastards, Reaper."

"Yes, it is."

The container was empty. We assumed that the others would be the same.

————

Dejected at yet another failure, we flew back to Berlin, spending the following two days being debriefed. By then, the Russians were well and truly in the wind. All we had were the five packages recovered from the train. The scientist was gone, Morozov had vanished, along with the microchips.

Our situation was rather precarious, akin to having egg on our faces. What we craved was a victory, no matter how modest.

The four of us sat in a small sterile room, waiting to be questioned further when Lisa Goodall appeared. I straightened in my seat, and I heard Knocker say, "Be fucked."

"What are you doing here?" Holly snapped.

"I was cleared of any wrongdoing when the real culprit was found," she replied.

"Who might that have been?"

"That's need to know, and you don't," she said evasively. "What I want to know is where you are at."

The room hung heavy with apprehension, an understandable tension filling the air. Eventually, Holly cut through it all and revealed the truth.

"We have a substantial amount of work ahead. Any creative ideas?"

"I've been through everything I can lay my hands on," said Slick. "I am unable to trace them. They must have discovered how we've been tracking them through the security cameras and stopped disabling them. Now they're just avoiding them."

"You are committing your total resources to finding the packages and the scientist?"

"Yes."

"How about you look outside the box."

"Ma'am?"

"Switch your focus. I know you want to find the packages. Maybe you still can, just take another route."

I stared at Goodall, suspicious of her motivation of getting us to switch our focus deliberately, trying to throw us off the scent. "What do you suggest?"

"You still know of two others."

"Shatov and Noskov," Holly said.

"Yes, why not switch focus to them? I'm not saying all your focus, but run the searches side by side."

"You're forgetting one other name," Knocker said.

"What is that?" Goodall asked.

"Dolos."

The woman frowned. "What about it?"

Holly explained about Dolos. "So far we have nothing, but it has to be a deep cover."

"Are you thinking it might be another mole in MI6?"

"It could be anything, but we can't discount that possibility."

"All right, then stick with what you know."

Again, there was hesitation.

Goodall sighed. "Okay, I get it, you don't trust me, and I understand that. You don't have to. But you do have to follow my orders."

"All right, let's see where it leads," Holly said, taking the decision out of our hands. "Slick, time to get square eyes again."

"Yes, ma'am."

I said, "Knocker and I will go and have another talk with Willi Lehner. Maybe we can shake something loose this time around."

Goodall nodded. "Do it."

Leaving the team to their inquiries, Knocker and I proceeded through the streets to Lehner's residence. As we drew closer, the wide-open main gate signaled that something was amiss. Our car rolled into the driveway, and there it was—the front door gaping open. Instinctively, my senses were on high alert. Drawing our weapons, we entered the home.

Inside, a grim scene unfolded: the wife lay lifeless just beyond the threshold, her body sprawled on the cold tiled floor, surrounded by a pool of blood. Meanwhile, Lehner, master of this house, was bound and confined in his own library, a chair serving as his unwilling throne. The signs were unmistakable: he had suffered both torture and death. Perhaps the tormentors sought answers—details he might have shared with Holly and Groves. Whoever had performed this macabre act was no amateur, their expertise in the dark arts was chillingly evident.

Initially, Lehner had endured the gruesome removal of his fingernails and then his fingers. His tormentors didn't stop there. They also plucked one of his eyeballs and extracted several teeth. Ultimately, the fatal shot to his head mercifully ended his suffering.

"Poor bastard," Knocker said. "That'll teach him to get involved with the wrong crowd."

"It doesn't get us anywhere," I replied. "Have a look around. See if you can find anything useful."

We meticulously searched his office, thoroughly examining drawers, a filing cabinet, and even discovering a hidden safe concealed behind a painting.

"Old school," Knocker said.

"Be that as it may, are you able to open it?"

"Give me a few minutes."

As he toiled over the safe, I pressed on with my investigation. Amid the clutter on the desk, a solitary sheet of paper drew my attention. Initially, it seemed inconsequential —a mere scrap lost in the chaos. But on closer inspection, I discerned a series of cryptic serial numbers scrawled across its surface. Could this innocuous paper hold hidden significance? Perhaps it was a breadcrumb leading to answers, or was it another red herring? Regardless, I folded it and slipped it into my pocket.

My persistence yielded further results. Beneath the surface clutter, I unearthed a delivery schedule. As my eyes perused the lines, a furrow formed on my brow. My brain interpreted this seemingly mundane document.

"Knocker?"

"Yeah?"

"There were two shipments of microchips."

"You don't bloody say."

"They split the shipment just in case. The first went the day before the storm. The second when Holly and the others were here."

"Where to?"

I flicked through the papers, looking. "Shit, where is it?"

Eventually, I found what I sought. "Amsterdam. I have an address."

Reaching for my cell, I called Holly. "Listen, they're all dead here. But there were two shipments of microchips. The first was dispatched to Amsterdam prior to the storm. I have an address."

"I'll get onto it right away, Reaper. Anything else?"

"Not yet. We'll get out of here shortly. We're searching for any additional intel."

"Got it," Knocker's voice was triumphant.

I ended the call and crossed the room to him. "What have you got?"

"Some cash, passports, a few hard drives."

"Pocket the hard drives and let's get out of here."

———

"They tortured and killed him," I told Holly. "Probably to ensure he hadn't told you anything he shouldn't have. His wife got the better part of the deal. Her death was quick and merciful."

"Have you passed the intel on to Slick?"

"Yeah."

"Do you remember the address in Amsterdam?"

Providing her with the particulars, she went to work while I watched. "The premises at that address belong to a shell company. North Sea Shipping."

"As most shady things do," I replied.

"The owner is Louis Van der Elst. Millionaire—no, multi-millionaire who ships freight globally. Apparently, he is on Interpol's watch list."

"Anything else?"

"No."

"Fine. Can you book me a flight?"

"To Amsterdam?"

"No, Lyon, I have a friend there who may be able to assist."

"I'll have you one by midafternoon."

Holly was as good as her word. With the kill order having been rescinded with the demise of the fake MI6 team, I was free to travel and was on a flight to Lyon by two and in a cab two hours after that. The taxi dropped me outside the headquarters of Interpol. I was there to meet Camille Franco, and as I entered the lobby, she met me there.

"Hello, John."

"Hello, Camille. You look good."

"Even with my clothes on?" she asked cheekily.

"No one wears a pantsuit like you do, Camille."

"You are such a shocker, John. Smooth though. What can I do for you?"

"Louis Van der Elst."

Nodding slowly, she said, "I think we'd better go somewhere for a drink so we can talk."

"That would be good," I agreed. "How about some dinner to go with it?"

Her dark eyes sparkled as she gave me a warm smile. "Are you trying to get me into bed already?"

I pictured her dark hair hanging down past her naked shoulders and her lithe form squirming against mine. "Sorry, as tempting as that sounds, not this time."

Camille took my hand as we walked. "Such a shame. Anyway, let's find a restaurant."

Twenty minutes later, she stopped and said, "This will do."

We stood beneath a sign perpendicular to the restaurant. "A steakhouse?"

"You don't approve?"

"No, no. I approve."

Seated comfortably, we placed our orders: steak, fries, and a refreshing beer. As we waited for our meals to arrive, we engaged in light conversation. However, once the food was served, our focus shifted to more serious matters—business. The clinking of cutlery and the aroma of the sizzling steak provided the backdrop to our strategic discussions.

"What is it you wish to know about Louis?"

"Whatever you can tell me," I replied.

She pointed one of her fries at me. "That doesn't sound good, John. Are you going to interfere with one of our ongoing investigations?"

"Not interfere as such," I replied.

"No, then maybe I should say blow it out of the water."

"He shipped something we were chasing from Berlin. I just need to know where it went."

"Something?"

"Microchips."

Camille drank some of her beer. "What kind of microchips?"

"The kind that will make an R-12 missile system operable."

She frowned. "I don't think I know what an R-12 is. New?"

"No, quite the opposite." I filled her in. "If they manage to get the new motors in, paired with the chips, who knows what they will do?"

Another drink. "All right. Louis is what you might consider multifunctional. A lot of his business is legitimate—the rest is performed from the shadows. We've had him under observation primarily for goods he ships into and out of Africa."

"Weapons?" I asked.

"Weapons, diamonds, slaves."

"And he's still walking around free," I noted.

"He's clever at what he does."

I nodded. "I'm going to need to talk to him."

"Then I will go with you. Tomorrow night."

"Why tomorrow night?" I asked.

"He has a date at the theater here in Lyon. It will likely be the only opportunity you'll have to get close enough to him," Camille said.

I was surprised by the news. "Fine, but what am I going to do until then?"

She gave me a coy look. "I'm sure we can think of something."

———

In the elegant lobby, I stood clad in a well-tailored black suit—it's fit neither too snug nor overly loose. Beside me, Camille radiated sophistication in a dress that perfectly complemented my attire. The gown, a matching ensemble, featured a daring cutaway back and a neckline that plunged with audacity. As the chandelier's glow danced upon her dangling earrings, they sparkled like captured stardust. Her arm, gracefully linked through mine, drew me closer, and in a hushed tone, she whispered, "Two o'clock."

Amid the bustling crows, adorned in their finest attire, I scanned the assembly and spotted our target. By his side stood an equally enchanting lady, their elegance complementary.

Camille said, "That isn't his wife."

"Being a naughty boy?"

"Always."

Entering the grand gallery, we settled into our seats, positioned just a few rows apart from Louis and his companion. The house lights dimmed, and the stage curtains were bathed in a spotlight glow. The orchestra, poised and ready, commenced their enchanting rendition of the overture from "Fiddler on the Roof." Anticipation hung in the air, building the excitement of the surrounding audience.

The show had a decent start, and up until intermission, it held its own. Perhaps you should consider noting it down in your diary for future viewing. However, during the intermission, Louis stood up to take a break.

Seeing him on the move, we followed at a distance, moving into the lobby and then along a corridor to where one of several bathrooms was located. Then we waited for him.

When he reemerged, Camille stepped in front of him. "Excuse me, sir, could you help me?"

Her French flowed like a silken stream, each word a delicate ripple of eloquence. The hours we shared together blurred the lines, and I almost forgot she was truly French.

Stepping in behind Louis, I poked the barrel of a P30 into his back and said, "You'll have to catch another viewing. Head for the door."

He remained transfixed. "Who are you?"

"Someone who just wants to ask you a few questions. That's all."

"You will not use that gun in here, my friend," he said confidently.

"Maybe not, but the knife I have will cut your heart out a lot quieter."

Louis had a change of heart, prompting us to guide him outdoors and into our waiting SUV. Camille took the wheel while I settled into the back seat alongside him.

I said, "Let's establish this first. I do not care about your everyday dealings. What I'm interested in is a shipment that arrived recently."

"What shipment?"

"One that was set up by this man," I said, holding up my cell and showing a picture of Shatov.

"I have never seen him before in my life."

I flicked the screen and Morozov came up. "Him?"

"No."

I had one more up my sleeve. "What about him?"

Louis hesitated. "No."

"Now I know you're lying, Louis. When did Noskov come and see you?"

"I've never seen him before."

"Camille?"

"Yes?"

"Do you have a good detailer?"

"One of the best, why?"

I took the P30 and pressed the muzzle against Louis's leg. "You're going to need them."

"No, wait!" he exclaimed. "Okay, I know him."

"When?"

"He came to me two weeks ago. He, along with two others. They appeared to be his bodyguards. I was hired to ship a package. Once it arrived, I was to forward it on."

"Where to?" I asked.

"These aren't people whose business you discuss," Louis said to me. "Even without him saying so, I knew."

"I'm interested in what you were or were not told. Where did they go?"

Louis hesitated. "Wrangel Island."

"Shit." Wrangel Island was in the Arctic. "What do they have there?"

"I don't know."

"You must know something?"

"No. My instructions were simply to deliver it there."

"How?"

"How what?"

I pressed the gun harder against his leg. "How were they being delivered?"

"By plane. I assume they made it."

"What do you mean?"

"The plane nor the crew ever returned. I was remunerated, so like I said, I assume that they made it."

"That's the last you'll see of your plane and crew," I informed him. "It's how *they* operate. If I were you, I'd be watching my back."

"What?"

"They don't like loose ends."

Pulling the vehicle to the curb, we let Louis out. After the door closed, Camille turned and looked at me. "Did you get everything you required?"

With a nod, I said, "I'm thinking a little more than what I bargained for."

CHAPTER 15

"WHY HAVEN'T WE HEARD OF WRANGEL ISLAND?" GERMAN asked. "It wasn't in the reports."

"Because we chose to omit those details," I replied.

"Why would you do that?"

I looked at Newman, the CIA Director. "We thought it best. Considering what we found there."

The answer only piqued his interest. "What did you find?"

"Remember what I said about the missiles that were removed from Cuba?"

Returning to London, we regrouped and began to plan our next move. The course had already been set, fate having scripted our journey. Goodall stood alongside us in the hushed confines of the meeting room. "Okay, let's get started. I believe Mr. Swift found out several items of interest."

Slick nodded. "I believe that the serial numbers were for the chips."

"For the ones we're chasing?" Knocker asked.

"Maybe."

"Anything else?"

"I found footage of Noskov in Amsterdam and of the plane that was used to transport the first batch of microchips. I'm assuming that it is still on Wrangel because there is no record of its return flight."

"That's what Louis said," I explained. "He was paid for the job, so he thinks that they got the chips."

"That figures," Knocker said. "The crew would have been witness to things they shouldn't have seen. Can't have that getting out."

I looked at Goodall. "Can we get a recon flight over the island? Reroute a satellite or something?"

"It might take a couple of days," she replied.

"I'm not going in there blind. We'll also need infil and exfil."

"I'll see what the RN has by way of vessels in the area," Holly said.

"Dolos," I said. "What do we have?"

"Still nothing," Slick said.

"Missiles? Engines? Scientist?"

"Nothing."

"Okay, let's think this through. Start with the microchips. What do we know?"

"There were two shipments," Holly said.

"Yes."

"Means there must be two sites," Knocker said. "Has to be."

"All right," said Goodall. "Let's say your theory is accurate. They have the missiles, etc. But two sites? Remember, they only have five engines."

"Wait," Holly said excitedly. "What if, like the chips, an early shipment was sent?"

"It's possible," I agreed. "But that would mean double everything."

"Including scientists," Knocker said in a low voice.

I turned to Slick. Words were not necessary. He nodded and said, "I'm on it."

"Two sites," Goodall reminded us. "Where?"

"We can assume Wrangel Island," I said. "That leaves just one more."

"But where?"

"What about the original site?" Knocker asked. "Seems to be as good a place as any."

"Cuba?"

"Why not?"

"Getting intel from there will be tough. We might need boots on the ground," Goodall said.

"Can we do that?" I asked.

"I'm sure we'll have someone in the region."

It was then that Christine Ryan entered the room.

"So, what do we have?" she asked as she sat down.

"Possibly two of everything," I replied.

She stared at me. "Well, if it isn't our friendly neighborhood murderer."

"Have you watched the video?"

"I have. That is the only reason you are free."

"Then you'd be reassured in the knowledge that had it been you in that seat, it would have been the same outcome."

She stared at me and was about to say something when the door opened again. As one, our heads swiveled, taking in the two men at the door.

"Sorry, sir, we can't use this one."

A statuesque, dark-haired gentleman in a well-fitted suit strode into the room. His eyes swept across our gathering at the table, and he offered a polite, apologetic smile.

"Forgive me," he said, his voice smooth and measured. "I hope I'm not disrupting anything?"

Christine Ryan got to her feet. "No, sir, we were just having a debrief."

He smiled. "Sorry, I'll leave you to it."

With the departure of the two men, the door was closed.

Knocker said, "What the fuck is he doing here?"

"Who was that?" I asked.

"Fergus Pridham," Christine Ryan said. "He is running for Prime Minister. He's just looking around while he's on the campaign trail."

"He's the wanker I was telling you about, Reaper," Knocker said.

"I see."

"Shall we get back to the matter at hand?" Christine Ryan said, redirecting the conversation.

We discussed the conclusions we'd already come to. Once we were done, Christine Ryan said, "A man in Cuba we can do, but an operation of that scale to Wrangel Island, that is something else."

"That is where the microchips were sent," I told her. "We're not asking for a full-blown operation just yet. Only a reconnaissance flight to see if there is anything there worth looking at."

"All right, we'll do it."

———

The initial step involved obtaining a satellite image of the island. However, this seemingly routine task showed some anomalies. Consequently, a decision was made to dispatch a Boeing P-8 Poseidon aircraft, which required in-flight refueling. Aboard this aircraft were two skilled pilots and a mission crew of seven.

At precisely 08:00 local time, the pilot radioed in to confirm their position directly over the target area. Yet, by 08:07, all communication had abruptly ceased. The Royal Air Force, RAF, and Royal Navy, RN, expressed a desire to initiate a search operation for the missing plane and its crew. Regrettably, this request was denied, grounded in the belief that any such action might inadvertently alert the Russians. It was a difficult decision, but the stakes were high: if the plane had indeed crashed into the sea, there would be no chance of recovery. The same grim reality held true if the aircraft had met its fate over land. The delicate balance between urgency and secrecy hung heavily in the air.

We convened at headquarters, where we received a comprehensive briefing on the event.

Knocker said, "That should tell you all you need to know."

Goodall nodded. "I concur. That's precisely why the operation has received clearance. You will be inserted, and subsequent extraction will be facilitated by a submarine team. *HMS Animus* will have the honor of overseeing this task. Your mission parameters are strictly observational, unless unforeseen circumstances dictate otherwise."

"So, pack explosives?" Knocker said.

"Prepare your gear accordingly. There won't be a QRF, Quick Reaction Force, available. In case you're compromised, your sole support will come from a UCAV, Unmanned Combat Aerial Vehicle, specifically an MQ-1C Gray Eagle stationed in Fairbanks, Alaska. They owe us a favor and have committed to providing assistance."

Slick said, "I'm still trying to work out how the Russians could do anything on the island without anyone knowing about it. A good number of nature studies have been done there. Surely, they would have reported anything suspicious."

"Some parts of the island are restricted and have been that way for years."

"What is the weather forecast?" I asked.

"You will have a small window of good weather before a chilly cold front sweeps in, putting a damper on things for most of the upcoming week."

"Sounds like fun," Knocker said. "Just like Arctic Warfare training."

"I hated that shit," I said quietly.

"Look at it this way, Reaper. No snakes."

"Except the two-legged kind. When do we leave?"

"Just as soon as you get organized."

"Bulldog One and Two are on the ground and Charlie Mike," I said in a low voice.

"Copy, Bulldog One. Read you Lima Charlie. Target is five klicks northwest. Good luck. Call if you need help."

"Roger that. Out."

Commencing our mission, we retrieved our gear and set out toward the designated target area. The biting cold gnawed at us, and the ground lay blanketed in a pristine layer of snow. In this unforgiving environment, we faced three formidable adversaries: the merciless weather, the ever-watchful Russians, and the polar bears. Wrangel Island, notorious for its polar bear population, was our destination.

Armed and vigilant, we carried C8 carbines and Glock handguns, our eyes shielded by NVGs, night vision goggles. Our attire consisted of thick layers of winter gear, a necessary defense against the elements. Within our packs, we bore spare ammunition and explosives, each item meticulously accounted for. Knocker held the detonators while I carried the prized cargo–the *good stuff*.

Our breaths crystallized in the frigid air as we pressed forward through the darkness, the weight of our mission heavy upon us, yet grateful that the weather had held. Wrangel Island awaited, harboring secrets and dangers that would test our mettle. We were soldiers of circumstance, bound by duty and the stark reality of survival in this frozen wilderness.

"Hey, Reaper?"

"Yeah?"

"You figure that their base is going to be underground?"

I'd tossed the idea around in my head some and came up with an opinion. "Yeah, it's possible."

"If it is, it's going to be a tough nut to crack."

"We've cracked a few before," I reminded him.

"Yeah. We've been in some tight spots as well."

"One thing at a time, my friend, one thing at a time."

Two kilometers away from our intended target, we stumbled upon the initial signs of activity: a sealed airstrip. Its length was sufficient to accommodate large military transports. Adjacent to it stood a control tower and an aircraft, an

A400 Atlas transport, once belonging to the French military. The entire scene was blanketed in snow.

From our vantage point atop a low snow-covered hill, we surveyed the ground using binoculars. After twenty minutes of patient observation, we confirmed that the area was devoid of any threats. Satisfied, we granted ourselves the green light to proceed.

"Eagle Six-Four, copy?"

"Roger, One. Read you, Lima Charlie."

"Bulldog is moving in to have a closer look. Out."

We descended from the hill to the airstrip, our boots crunching on the snow-covered gravel. Our priority was to secure the control tower. This two-story structure stood tall, its upper level encased in glass that offered panoramic views. A circular viewing platform wrapped around the tower's exterior, granting us a vantage point to survey the surroundings. "This place is all clear, Reaper."

"Yeah, I'd say they only use it when a plane comes in."

We headed downstairs and out into the snow once more. I looked at the Atlas. "Let's have a look."

We trudged across the fifty or so meters to the transport, discovering an open door. The interior of the aircraft was frigid. Knocker and I stumbled upon two lifeless figures clad in flight suits sprawled on the cargo bay floor. Their eyes stared vacantly into the abyss. As we ventured further, we encountered the pilots in the cockpit. Their lifeless bodies slumped over the controls, each bearing a single fatal gunshot wound to the side of the head—a grim execution in the cold silence of the aircraft.

"Well, we know what happened to Louis's fly guys," I said.

"Yeah, let's go."

After leaving the aircraft, we advanced toward the designated target zone. There we positioned ourselves atop a gentle, undulating ridge and established an observation post, OP.

"You were right, Knocker," I said. "Below ground."

"See the road, Reaper. It goes around that hill but nowhere else. Are you thinking what I'm thinking?"

"Could be, let's go and take a look."

We traced the perimeter of the target area, our footsteps cautious against the rugged terrain. Our eyes scanned the horizon, seeking a vantage point from which to glimpse the hidden side of the hill. To the casual observer, it remained concealed—a secret etched into the landscape. But we were not casual. We were seekers intent on unraveling the mystery. And so, with determination, we discovered what lay beyond.

"That's a big fucking door."

I nodded. "All we have to do now is find a way in."

"Look to your left. About ten o'clock."

Initially, my eyes failed to detect it, as it skillfully blended into its surroundings due to its camouflage. However, after a few seconds of observation, I managed to discern what he was seeing.

"A vent."

"Yes, it might be our way into whatever is down there."

"Let's check it out."

As we approached the vent, we found a substantial cylinder protruding from the earth. I guessed its simplicity: a straightforward conduit descending to the depths, expelling stagnant air while drawing fresh air from an alternate source.

"Rope, Knocker."

Knocker sifted through his backpack, fingers grazing the rugged fabric. His calloused hands emerged, cradling a coil of sturdy rope. He swung the vent cover open, revealing the dark abyss below. The steel rim provided an anchor and he secured the rope with practiced knots. Without hesitation, he lowered it into the vent, the coil disappearing into the unknown depths.

I said, "I'll go first."

Removing my pack, I said, "When I'm down, withdraw the rope up and lower the packs. It's the only way we'll fit."

"Roger that."

I cautiously slung my C8 rifle over my shoulder and descended into the narrow vent. The passage maintained a consistent width and started down the vent. Luckily it remained a consistent width throughout, which was a relief. As I reached the bottom, the dim light revealed a sprawling machinery room. I unhooked from the rope and dropped to a knee, silently unslinging the suppressed carbine. The air hummed with the distant whir of gears, and I knew we were in for a tense encounter.

"I'm down, Knocker."

The rope was withdrawn into the inky darkness above, and while I waited, I performed a 360-degree security sweep. Once the packs were down, I awaited the arrival of Knocker. Minutes later, when he was partially through the vent, I heard movement.

"Hold," I whispered urgently. "Pull the rope."

Maintaining his position, Knocker retracted the rope. Hoisting our packs, I took up position behind a large piece of machinery. I unslung the C8 and silently placed it on the floor. Then I palmed my suppressed Glock and waited.

Footsteps.

As they grew closer, the footfalls reverberated through the enclosed space. My own breaths took on new volume, seeming to echo off the walls. Was it mere illusion, or could the stranger hear my heartbeat as clearly as I did? Abruptly, the footsteps ceased, leaving a lingering tension in the air. Had they sensed my presence? The corridor held its breath. And then, as if dismissing my fears, the stranger resumed their journey, fading away into the distance.

My breathing came back to normal as the footsteps disappeared gradually into silence.

"Okay, Knocker, come on down."

The rope slithered from the ceiling, and Knocker completed his descent. As he touched the ground, he uttered, "Lend me a hand, Reaper."

I hoisted him onto my shoulders, standing tall. With

nimble fingers, he secured the rope back into the vent, concealing it from view.

"Right, where to?" he asked after I lowered him to the floor.

"That, my dear Watson, is the million-dollar question. Follow me."

The facility sprawled like a labyrinth, its corridors winding through rooms, subterranean passages, and vast storage areas. Our footsteps echoed in the dimness as we moved forward stealthily. Our objective: the elusive R-12 missile.

After an hour of navigating hushed hallways, we stumbled upon it—a colossal warhead resting in a cavernous room. Technicians had dissected its engine, tools scattered around. The clock read one in the morning, and the facility lay deserted, its secrets hiding in the silence.

We stood there, our breaths held, aware that this moment could alter the course of history. The R-12 missile, a silent sentinel, awaited its destiny—an instrument of power and destruction, dormant yet full of potential.

"Is that what I think it is?" Knocker asked.

"It sure looks like it. Get some pictures."

While Knocker used his phone to take photos, I moved closer to examine what the Russians were up to. "It looks like they're doing something to the engines. Maybe over-hauling them or cleaning them up."

I ran a hand along the exterior of the missile, and it came away with a thick coating of dust. "These have been here a long time," I said. "Look at the writing on them."

"Be fucked," Knocker said. "Do you figure..."

"I don't know. Get a picture of the number."

"Copy that."

"Alpha Two, this is Bulldog One, copy?"

"Copy, Bulldog One. You're a bit garbled but I can under-stand you."

"Two is going to send you some pictures. I need you to

run the number on the missile. Get back to me on what you discover."

"Copy, One. Send it."

"Knocker, send the photos."

"Copy."

In the dim light, I reached into my pack and retrieved a bundle of pre-prepared explosives. These devices had two paths to destruction: the first, if we chose to detonate them deliberately, and the second, a silent countdown set for twenty-four hours hence. With care, I concealed them deep within the recesses of the housing, ensuring they remained unseen by prying eyes.

We didn't need to place many, just in some strategic positions throughout the facility.

"All right, let's keep moving."

We continued silently through the complex. Then, like a revelation, we came across an ancient control room, a relic from a bygone era. The room, once sealed, yielded to our determination as we pried open its stubborn door. Our flashlight beams danced across the walls, revealing a spectacle frozen in time. There they were: the old control panels, keys worn but still proud. Banks of television screens, their picture tubes dimmed, yet still whispering secrets.

Knocker's voice broke the stillness. "I've just stepped onto the set of a sixties Apollo movie," he murmured.

And indeed, it felt that way—the room a time capsule of history.

Nodding slowly, I said, "You're right. This place has been around a long time."

"Since the sixties?"

"At least."

"Bulldog One, copy?"

"Go ahead, Alpha One."

"You're never going to believe this. The serial number on that missile dates back to—"

"The sixties. I'm going to say it was last seen in Cuba."

"Horseshit," Newman blurted out. "The missiles—all the missiles—from Cuba went back to Russia."

I stared at him. "Now, you know that isn't true. The Russians made a deal with the US government to put them there on Wrangel. In return, the US retained some missiles in Italy. The issue of them being left in Cuba was to prevent any dictator of the time flipping out and trying to impress his masters. That was the compromise."

"That isn't true."

I reached across the table and grabbed the file in front of Christine Ryan. Opening it, I found what I wanted, one of the missile photos that Knocker had taken. I threw it at Newman. "Then fucking explain that."

Newman bent and picked it up. His eyes flicked across it. "Then how—"

"You will get your chance to ask more questions, Mr. Newman," German said. "Just not right now. Continue, Mr. Kane."

"How did you work that out?" Slick asked, surprised.

"Wild guess," I replied. "Is Alpha there with you?"

"I'm here, One."

"What are your orders, ma'am?"

"I'm assuming you've already figured that out and started the process. Try and get a prisoner we can talk to."

"Yes, ma'am." I looked at Knocker. "Come on, Watson, we're Charlie Mike."

Following a road that curved further underground, we came to another room. This one was as large as the last, a pair of tall vertical blast doors off to one side.

Knocker said, "I bet I know what's in there."

We hurried across to a smaller door in the center of the blast doors. Knocker opened it and we slipped inside.

It took but a few heartbeats to figure out what we were seeing.

"I'll watch the door, Knocker. Plant a present."

Five minutes later, just as we were about to leave the silo, the appearance of two roving guards had us holding our collective breath. They were walking together, engaged in an indecipherable conversation. Silently, we pulled back into the missile silo, leaving the door slightly ajar. Although the doorway wasn't visible from their position, the opening must have acted like a beacon, and they headed directly toward it.

I could hear their voices gaining in volume as they drew closer, talking as they walked, no sense of urgency detectable. I looked at Knocker, who had already lowered his C8 and brought up his P226. I did the same. It was highly probable that they would stop and walk away before reaching the doors. But when they didn't, we were forced to take action.

Their faces showed complete shock as they came face to face with an armed man in the doorway. Fighting to unsling their weapons, the pair were pitifully slow. I shot both in the head with my suppressed handgun before they were able to slip the strap down their arms.

"Grab the other guy," I whispered urgently.

Dragging the pair back through the door, we left them on the floor of the silo, the closing door sealing their crypt.

Knocker said, "Reaper, we need to find a central position and bring it all down."

He had a point. "Let's keep going."

Progressing through the facility, we located an additional two silos, placing explosives strategically, trying our best to avoid more guards—something we were able to do. Traversing more corridors and cavernous rooms, we finally reached the central hub for the complex. It was modern and well-equipped, having superseded the outdated control room we'd found earlier. It was also unmanned.

"Knocker, this'll do. Plant three charges here and we'll get out."

In a matter of minutes, we had the charges placed, but then our judgment faltered. We hesitated, and that hesitation proved costly.

The control room erupted in chaos as bullets tore through

the air, obliterating circuit boards. The shooter, whoever they were, had left their mark, and their superiors would undoubtedly be displeased at the havoc wreaked. The blame rested squarely on our shoulders—we'd been caught up, too absorbed in gathering intelligence to make a swift exit. Knocker and I found ourselves caught in the crossfire, our priorities skewed, and escape plans forgotten amid the chaos.

Taking refuge behind a panel, we waited for our assailants to reload.

Knocker said, "I thought you were watching."

"I thought you were."

"Oh, nice."

I rose, firing at the shooter. His weapon hitting the floor made a clatter that echoed, and he fell backward, vanishing from our sightline, several rounds in his chest.

"Come on."

Leaving the control room just as the alarm went off, we knew that somewhere within the complex, soldiers were tumbling from their bunks, intent on neutralizing the threat, but until they were on deck, we had the guards to deal with.

"Contact front," Knocker called as we entered the hallway outside the control room. He opened fire as I ducked into a doorway opposite our position.

After firing a short burst, Knocker found a doorway across from the one I'd gone through. More bullets hammered along the hallway, ricocheting off concrete walls.

"We can't stay pinned down," I called over to Knocker.

"I can fix it."

Before I could say no, he took out a grenade, pulled the pin, and sent it skidding along the corridor toward the shooters. "Frag out."

The corridor trembled under the force of the explosion, its walls echoing with the anguished cries of the wounded. As I emerged from the room, I was met with a grim scene: two assailants lay on the floor, their lifeblood seeping onto the cold tiles.

"Reaper?"

"Yeah?"

"Which fucking way is out?"

I fired through the fog of dust at another figure. "Next question."

"Fuck it, let me lead," Knocker growled.

"Be my guest."

Knocker forged a treacherous path, each step a battle against the unforgiving enemy. We clung to every inch of ground gained, our resolve unwavering. But as our ammunition dwindled, hope seemed to fade. Then, like a beacon in the white expanse, we discovered an escape—a narrow passage leading out onto the snow-blanketed landscape. The cold air bit at our faces, but freedom lay ahead, urging us onward.

"Blow that fucking thing," I growled.

Knocker took out the trigger and depressed the button.

Beneath the frozen tundra, a low, ominous rumble emanated. The very earth beneath our feet quivered, as if awakening from a long slumber.

"Shit, we're too close."

We pivoted and sprinted, hearts pounding. Behind us, fiery orange geysers erupted from the heart of the island, their molten plumes shooting skyward. The deafening roar of the explosions reverberated across the rugged landscape, its relentless pursuit that matched our frantic pace. In a desperate bid for survival, we flung ourselves to the ground, the earth trembling beneath us.

The island, once serene, now churned with primal fury. Our breaths came in ragged gasps as we clung to the snow, eyes wide, waiting for the eruption to pass.

And then, as abruptly as it had begun, the tempest subsided. The geysers receded, their fiery dance extinguished. We lay there, hearts still racing, bodies bruised and dirt-streaked.

Rolling onto my back, I drew several more deep breaths, staring up at the darkened sky. Knocker loomed over me.

"Come on, Reaper, let's get out of here before we start to glow."

He put out his hand and pulled me to my feet, and we began trudging toward the coast.

I said, "You know we just fucked up a world heritage nature reserve?"

"I won't tell if you don't."

For the next few hours, we kept up a steady pace until the coast came into view. When we stepped onto the beach, we were hailed by a couple of the crew waiting beside an inflatable. The silhouette of the submarine was a welcome sight, and when we reached below decks, we were offered coffee and food.

The XO showed us to a couple of racks and we were grateful for the chance to grab some sleep. Then, two hours later, we were both shaken awake by the captain. A soft-spoken man by the name of Bentley. "I'm afraid I have some bad news for you."

CHAPTER 16

THIRTY-SIX HOURS LATER, WE WERE GREETED BY SLICK WHEN our flight touched down at RAF Brize Norton. He began to brief us on the unfolding events.

"They hit her Rover and dragged her out. Then they just vanished."

"You have no idea where she is?" I asked him.

Shaking his head, Slick retrieved his laptop from the front seat and placed it on the hood of the SUV. Opening the lid, he hit a few keys.

"All we have is this."

I watched the CCTV feed of four men and a woman walking toward a small jet.

"Where is this?"

"Tanner Field outside of London."

"Are we sure that's her?"

"Yes. But look at this. I managed to clean an image up."

The image changed. Knocker and I stared at it in silence. There on the screen in front of us was Lazar Noskov. Knocker spat on the tarmac.

"Fucking asshole. It's time to put him in the ground."

"We have to find him first," I pointed out. "It's interesting, though."

"What is?"

"Why they would want Goodall."

"Do you think it is a revenge kidnapping for Wrangel?" Slick asked.

I shook my head. "No, far too early. This was planned. I have a feeling we'll be hearing from them very soon."

As we walked into HQ, we found Holly busy working the problem. She looked up as we entered the ops room and said, "Good mission, chaps. Have you been checked over?"

"Yes," I replied.

"We won't start growing our second heads just yet, boss," Knocker added. "What's news?"

"We tried to track the plane but no joy on that. I'm surprised that Noskov bobbed up here in London."

"How come Goodall didn't have a team on her?" I asked.

"After what happened, I wanted to, but it wasn't cleared by the higher-ups. She wouldn't have it."

"Shit. All right. Boss, what do you want us to do?"

"I'd appreciate it if you could go to the airfield and speak with the owner. It's privately owned. A shady character named Kraft."

"Harry Kraft?" Knocker asked.

"That's him."

I stared at Knocker. "Why do I get the feeling that you know this guy and he's some kind of criminal mastermind?"

"No, no."

"Okay."

"He's worse."

"Fuck," I muttered with a shake of my head.

"I need to have a word to a friend at MI5 on the way."

"Why?"

Knocker grinned. "Just in case."

I looked at Holly, whose face held a puzzled expression.

She shrugged. "Fine, do whatever, but our top priority is to get Goodall back in one piece."

"Ma'am."

"Boss."

After climbing into our SUV, I asked Knocker, "What are you up to?"

"MI5 have Melinoe."

"So?"

"I want to know what the hell is going on, Reaper. Something doesn't add up."

I nodded. "All right, let's scratch your itch."

At Thames House, our journey paused, and we stepped inside. There, Knocker met with Gail Hurst—a woman whose presence defied expectations. Unlike his past romantic escapades, Gail, in her sixties, held a position of authority within the intelligence agency. Her seasoned experience elevated her to the ranks of the agency's leadership.

"Hello, Raymond, what brings you here?"

"Thought I'd come by and see my favorite bird," he replied cheekily.

"Get away with you," Gail said, playing along. "I'm still too much woman for you. Now, tell me the truth, Raymond."

"You have someone in a deep, dark hole. Melinoe. We need to talk to them."

Gail frowned at Knocker. "You know I can't do that, Raymond."

"Gail, one of our people has been taken. This might be the only chance we get to find them."

"Raymond, I—"

"Just listen for a moment, Gail. Just until I explain."

He spent the next few minutes painting broad brush-strokes over what we'd been mixed up in. Gail nodded slowly.

"I don't know, Ray, it's not the done thing."

"I wouldn't be here if we were not desperate for your help."

"Okay, come with me."

"They're here?"

"In the hole. Follow me."

The hole was a basement inside a basement. It was a place to hide secrets beyond prying eyes.

We trailed behind Gail, our footsteps echoing down dimly lit corridors. The air grew colder as we descended into the heart of the clandestine facility. An elevator swallowed us whole, hurtling downward like a descent into the unknown. The walls seemed to close in, suffocating yet strangely comforting.

And then, with a soft chime, the doors slid open. We stepped out into a sterile hallway, its fluorescent lights casting harsh shadows. Gail led us to an unmarked door—a portal to revelations.

"Interrogation room," she said, her voice devoid of emotion.

The room was stark: a table, two chairs, and a one-way mirror. We took our seats, waiting for our guest.

Minutes stretched like taffy. And then, with a precision that bespoke military training, they brought Melinoe in.

Armed guards flanked the prisoner, their eyes vigilant. Melinoe's gaze swept the room, assessing us.

Gail leaned forward, her gaze unwavering. "Melinoe," she said. "These gentlemen have questions. And you will answer."

As anticipated, it was one of the men who had accompanied Goodall in Berlin. His appearance spoke volumes: fatigued, weathered, and unmistakably fractured.

Knocker said, "What's your name. Your real name?"

"Patrick."

"Okay, Patrick, talk to us."

"What do you want to know?"

"Who is your boss?"

"What?"

"Okay, let's start with something simple. Where do you live?"

"Here in London."

"Good. By yourself?"

"Yes."

"Pets?"

"No—yes. A cat."

"Parents?"

He went quiet.

"Do you have parents still alive?" Knocker asked again.

"No, they died."

The guy was talkative for a mole. Maybe he was playing.

I said, "How long have you worked with Lisa Goodall?"

"One month."

"Why do they think you are Melinoe?" Knocker asked.

"Fingerprints."

"Fingerprints?"

"On the cell. It had my fingerprints on it."

"How?" I asked.

"I don't know."

"Did you handle the cell?" I asked.

"No."

"Come on, man, you must have handled it. How else would your fucking prints get on it?"

Patrick started to fidget.

"The only way you would handle the phone is if you are Melinoe," Knocker said.

He fidgeted again.

"Are you Melinoe?"

"No."

"I think you are."

"No."

"Yeah, you look too bloody nervous not to be."

"Fine, I'm Melinoe. There, satisfied?"

I wasn't. Not by a long shot. He was talking too easily. "Who is your boss?"

"No one."

"Is it Shatov?"

He went quiet.

"How about Morozov?"

Again, no indication, not even a flicker.

"Noskov?"

Nothing.

I glanced at Knocker who was looking at me. His gaze said it all. This prick wasn't Melinoe. He was a blind. Someone had something over him. "Patrick, I don't believe you."

"Why?" He was demanding that we did.

"You're not Melinoe."

"I am. I told you I was."

Now there was panic in his eyes.

Knocker looked at Gail. "Does he have any other family?"

"A sister."

"Where does she live?"

"Here in London. We sent some people to pick her up, but she wasn't home."

I stared hard at the man. "Does someone have your sister, Patrick?"

Again, he went quiet.

"Patrick, talk to me. Tell us what is going on. If they have your sister, we can help."

"Can someone tell me what's going on?" Gail asked.

Knocker said, "He's not Melinoe, Gail. Not as long as his asshole points to the ground."

"How can you tell, Raymond?"

"It's a feeling."

I said, "Patrick, if you want to see your sister alive again, you need to tell us."

He opened his mouth to speak. Hesitated, then words came out. "They'll kill her."

"Who? Who will kill her?"

"Whoever has her. They called to say they had Francis. They said if I didn't go along with what they wanted me to do, they would kill her."

"Damn it," Gail hissed.

"How did your fingerprints get on the phone, Patrick?" Knocker asked.

"She made me touch it. She must have known something

wasn't right. She wiped it down before I did."

"Who, Patrick? Tell us who," I said.

"Lisa Goodall."

"Damn it," I growled, reaching for my cell.

"It won't work down here," Gail said.

Looking at Knocker, I said, "We have to go. Thanks for your help, Gail."

"You will help, won't you?" Patrick pleaded.

I nodded. "You might have to stay here a while longer, Patrick, while we do it. If they find out that we know, then they'll kill your sister. Can you do that?"

"Yes."

I looked at Gail. She nodded. "I'll take care of it."

———

Once back on the street, I grabbed my cell and dialed Holly. "She's part of it."

"What?"

"Goodall. She's been part of it all along." I told her what we had found out.

"Oh, God. We need to find her. This can't be allowed to happen."

"There is a good chance the sister is already dead," I pointed out.

"Yes. But we'll do what we can. Our priority remains locating Lisa Goodall. She'll have intel that we can use. Where are you now?"

"On our way to the airfield."

"Okay. I'll brief Slick. Good luck."

———

Tanner Field, encircled by a substantial chain-link fence, stood as a bastion against unwelcome visitors. Privately owned, it witnessed only exclusive comings and goings. To gain access, one had to be either affluent or, like its proprietor, Harry Kraft, a criminal.

We pulled up at the gates in our SUV. Knocker's window slid down, and a security guard walked over. I could see the bulge under his coat indicating that he was carrying a firearm. "What can I do for you gents?"

His voice was deep, much like the character Onslow's from the TV series *Keeping Up Appearances*. "We're here to see Harry," Knocker replied. "Tell him Ray Jensen wants to talk."

"Mr. Kraft is busy."

"The only way Kraft would be busy is if he's counting his money or banging one of his bits on the side. Just tell him, mate."

The guard hesitated then walked over to his small security hut. After making a call he returned to our vehicle. "Go in. He's in the second hangar on the right."

"Thanks."

The SUV jolted forward, its tires gripping the narrow road as we traced our path toward the apron and the imposing hangars. Coming to a halt, we disembarked. The massive double doors, though only partially ajar, beckoned us. We slipped through the gap, stepping into the vast expanse beyond.

"Hey, Kraft, where the fuck are you?" Knocker called out.

"Didn't anyone tell you it's rude to talk that way to your betters?" a cockney voice called back.

We turned to our left and saw him approaching us, a slim woman in a short dress beside him, along with his two bodyguards. Knocker shook his head. "I bet the silly cow is cold."

"Who are you calling a fucking cow?" she demanded.

"No, I could be wrong. With a mouth like that, maybe not."

Kraft grinned. "This is Rosie. She's a...friend."

"She suck your dick with that mouth?" Knocker asked.

"Now, Ray, be nice."

"Fine."

"Who is your friend?"

"John Kane," Knocker told him. "We call him The Reaper. You can guess why."

He nodded toward me. "Mr. Kane."

"Kraft."

"What do I owe the visit, Ray. The only time I see you is when you want something."

"Private jet. Russians and a British lass."

"No ideas," he lied.

"Come on, Harry. We know they were here," Knocker said.

"You know I can't break privacy about clients, Ray," Kraft said sternly.

"It's important, Harry. Life and death kind of shit."

"Tell them to fuck off, Harry," Rosie growled. "Let's get back to what we were doing."

Knocker's eyes narrowed. "Shut the fuck up."

"You can't talk to me like that," she almost screeched. "Harry, tell him."

He turned to her. "Go back to the office. I'll be with you in a moment."

She huffed, giving Knocker a glare. Then whirled about and walked away, swinging her hips.

Kraft said, "You're wasting your time, Ray."

"We've been friends a long time, Harry. Don't make me push it. There's too much at stake."

Kraft stared at him. "Is there something you're not telling me?"

"Can't tell you, Harry. Just that if I don't find these people, a lot of others could die."

Just when I thought he was going to give us something, he said, "Sorry, Ray, I can't do it."

Then he turned and walked away, headed back to his office to take up with Rosie.

I should have anticipated it, but I was caught off guard. Suddenly, a Glock materialized in Knocker's hand, and he fired a shot into Kraft's leg. Kraft crumpled to the ground, and his bodyguards swiftly drew their own weapons. Instinctively, I reached for mine, and in that tense moment, we found ourselves locked in our own unique version of a Mexican standoff.

"What the fuck, Knocker?" I growled.

"Don't have time for this shit, Reaper. You boys put your weapons down."

The bodyguards didn't move.

"Harry, tell them I'm not fucking around."

"Christ, Ray, you bloody shot me."

"Sorry, Harry, but I warned you."

Kraft rolled over onto his back and struggled to sit up. "Do it. Put them away."

The bodyguards hesitated, looking at their boss before doing as they were told.

"The Russians, Harry?" Knocker said.

"What about them?"

"They come through much?"

"Yeah, frequent flyers."

"That explains why he's still alive," I said to Knocker.

"What?" Kraft said through the pain.

Knocker said, "They kill most people they come into contact with, Harry. You must be valuable to them for the time being."

"Where were they going?" I asked him.

"Berlin."

"They would."

Knocker walked over to Kraft. "Thanks for your help, Harry."

Kraft shook his head. "We're done, Ray. Anything we had is gone."

"I understand, Harry. Be seeing you around, Mucker."

"Fuck off."

CHAPTER 17

MI6 WAS ABUZZ WITH ACTIVITY. THE REVELATION ABOUT Goodall's betrayal and the desperate hunt for Patrick's abducted sister had ignited a sense of urgency among all the operatives.

Holly was in her office on the phone when I got there. Meanwhile, Slick was buried in his computer work, making steady progress. When I approached him, he was meticulously analyzing a live feed from a street camera, his focus unwavering.

"Talk to me, oh great spirit of the digital highway," I said as I stood beside him.

"This is Francis Thurgood getting snatched," he said as the picture rolled. "Three men and a van. We assume she's still alive because they need the brother's cooperation. Which means we have a good chance of getting her back."

I shook my head. "No, she's already dead."

"Hundred?"

"What?"

"I want to bet you a hundred that she's still alive. You see, I aim to collect."

I shook my head. "No, Slick, it's not a bet I want to win. What else do you have?"

"I tried again to track the plane, but have nothing."

"Look in Berlin."

He raised his eyebrows.

"Harry Kraft came through."

"Fine. Good stuff."

"And keep looking for Francis," I encouraged him.

The sun was going down when he finally came through. Slick had located the van driving out of London to the north. It seemed that after avoiding as many cameras as possible, the kidnappers had screwed up. An image was captured. From then on, it was a matter of deduction and good luck.

"We've got them, Reaper. The day she was kidnapped, they took Francis north out of London and stashed her in a farmhouse. We've now got a location."

"Do you have eyes on it?" I asked.

"We have a UAV getting airborne as we speak."

"All right, we'll gear up and get out there."

"Watch your six, Reaper."

"Always do."

I found Knocker just out of the shower. "What are you doing?"

"I, my friend, have a hot date with a lass from the Middle East desk."

Shaking my head, I said, "Not tonight."

"Ah, shit, Reaper, can't we have a night off?"

"Sorry, old chap, we've got a lass to rescue."

"You found her?" Knocker asked.

"Slick did."

"Where?"

"Farm, north of London."

"Then what are we waiting for?"

"You to put some clothes on."

Under the cover of darkness, we arrived at the farm. The undulating hills in the distance a barely visible backdrop for the sturdy stone farmhouse. Nearby, the barn and stables, also constructed from the same stone, stood sentinel in the outer yard.

Knocker and I used the barn as concealment during our approach. We scaled a stone wall, our movements muffled by the dampness of the lush field, still saturated from the earlier evening rain.

On the other side, we crouched down, our suppressed C8 carbines ready for use. I said into my comms, "Bulldog Team in position."

"Copy, Bulldog. Standby."

We waited for Slick to come back to us while we crouched in the shadow. "Bulldog, copy?"

"Copy, Alpha Two."

"Confirm six tangos on site. Two of them are patrolling the perimeter."

"Roger that. Bulldog moving."

Emerging from the shelter of the barn, we trudged through the muck of the yard. A sizable puddle obstructed our way, but we plowed through it, water spraying in all directions. Ahead, a shadow materialized in the eerie green glow of our night vision goggles. Without missing a beat, I squeezed the trigger of my C8 rifle, and he crumpled where he stood.

The impact could be felt through the damp ground, mud splattering outward from the force. I halted beside him while Knocker swiftly dragged the lifeless body away, concealing it from view. The night swallowed our actions, leaving no trace of our grim task.

"Alpha One, I need an update for the other tango."

"He's near the stables, Bulldog."

"Roger that."

Knocker and I moved to the right, our boots squelching through the mud-caked yard. We passed through a rusted steel gate, the ground changing from muck to thick grass.

But the respite was short-lived, the grass gave way once again to the cloying mud. It clung to our boots like shit-filled glue, each step a struggle against its relentless grip.

We halted in the shadow of a sizable shed, taking cover in its dark silhouette. I leaned cautiously, peering toward the stable. Initially, my gaze revealed nothing—a stillness that hung in the air. But then, a subtle shift of movement materialized. The guard stepped into view, framed by the stable's entrance. He hesitated there, lingering just inside, reluctant to venture farther.

And there it was—the reason for his reluctance, the faint glow of a cigarette tip betraying his presence. The night held its breath, and I watched, finger poised, ready to act.

Behind me, Knocker touched my shoulder and my waiting finger curled, the C8 slamming back against my shoulder. The guard dropped. Another one down.

"Alpha, tango down, we're Charlie Mike."

"Copy, continuing mission," Holly replied.

The farmhouse was two floors, the front coated in a mask of ivy. Woodsmoke rose from the chimney and dissipated in the cold, clear night sky. Knocker and I crept through the yard gate and turned left to go to the rear of the house itself. We ducked down as we walked past a window, the light from within illuminating its own patch of wet ground.

Our mission demanded silence. Any sound could spell the death of the young woman inside, provided she was still alive. We pressed on, the night enfolding us in its secrets.

Once we circled the farmhouse, we closed in on the back door—a threshold that would take us into the heart of the kitchen. The anticipation hung heavy in the air, our senses listening for every creak, every breath.

I reached out and touched the doorknob. It turned, and the door snicked open with a barely audible sound. My gaze shifted to Knocker, who had now lifted his NVGs, and his gloved hand held his suppressed Glock, raised and ready to fire.

We took a moment before crossing the threshold before

us. There was likely danger, secrets, and the promise of action. Once we crossed it, we were into the unknown.

"Go."

As the word hung in the air, I pushed the door with sufficient pressure. It went swinging open with a silent whoosh of air, without any sudden crash that might betray our presence to anyone within earshot.

Knocker stepped through the opening, sweeping the kitchen, making sure it was clear. I followed him in, my Glock in my hand. Using hand signals, Knocker indicated he was going to move toward the doorway.

I trailed him as he vanished through the narrow opening. He veered left into a spacious dining room dominated by a round table suitable for six. Yet, in that moment, it played host to only one occupant. A Russian man meticulously cleaning his disassembled firearm. Oil stained the wooden surface.

The Russian's jaw hung agape, his eyes widening as he noticed the unexpected figure before him. In an instant, the suppressed Glock discharged, and the man's head jerked backward, a mask of astonishment etched across his features. Gradually, he tilted to the right, collapsing onto the cold tiled floor. Crimson pooled around him, a stark testament to the violence that had unfolded.

Guided by Knocker's silent gestures, we navigated the dimly lit farmhouse once more. Exiting the dining room, we stepped into the living area. The room's focal point was a large television mounted on the wall, its glow casting eerie shadows. There, on the worn sofa, sat two figures, their attention riveted to the screen.

In this private theater, violence ensued once again. Our synchronized shots thudded, shattering the tranquility of their viewing experience. The television flickered, its glow now illuminating lifeless bodies sprawled across the sofa.

"Should be one left, Reaper," Knocker whispered.

I looked at the low-hanging ceiling above us. "Upstairs."

"I was thinking that."

I advanced along the dimly lit hallway before beginning my ascent up the stairs. My boots, still caked with mud from earlier, met each step with deliberate care. With every placement of my foot, I half expected a tortured squeak to echo from the wooden structure beneath me. The Glock in my hand remained steady, its cold metal a reassuring weight. I aimed it at the landing above, ready for any threat that might materialize. As I reached the head of the stairs, the silence enveloped me.

I approached the first doorway leading to a dimly lit bedroom. My hand reached out and grasped the knob, but before I could turn it fully, a hail of bullets erupted from within, tearing through the flimsy wood at its center. Instinctively, I jerked back, pressing myself against the wall, hoping it was sturdier than the door.

"Fuck," I muttered, adrenaline surging as the relentless gunfire showed no sign of stopping. Then, mercifully, it ceased. The shooter reloading. Knocker stepped forward, his boot connecting with the door. The jamb splintered, and the door flew open, crashing against the wall.

I held a flashbang in my fist, pin pulled and ready. With a swift motion, I hurled it into the room, then retreated. Knocker crouched on the other side of the doorway, head down, shielding himself from the impending blast.

The flashbang detonated, its blinding light and ear-piercing sound shattering the room within. We entered on the heels of the blast and found the shooter hunched, hands over his ears. Knocker pointed his Glock at him and fired twice. The man dropped to the floor, his blood soaking the carpet beneath him.

"That should be it," I said.

"Hopefully," Knocker replied. "Let's clear the rest of the rooms."

It took us five more minutes to do it and we found nothing more. I said into my comms, "Alpha, the target is clear. No sign of the package."

"Are you sure, Bulldog?" Holly asked.

"Affirmative. Unless she's somewhere we don't know about."

"Did you check the cellar, Bulldog?" Slick asked.

"What cellar?" I felt a surge of anger. This was something that should have been covered in the permission briefing. "We're moving to the cellar. Out."

We went back down the stairs and found a doorway that led into the cellar. I flicked on the flashlight fixed to the C8 and brought it up to my shoulder. I took the stairs cautiously. There was no telling if there was anyone else down there or if the stairs themselves were boobytrapped.

The moment the floor rose to meet my boots I stopped. Slowly I panned the light, taking it all in until it settled on the scared young woman backed into a corner. "Easy, girl. Are you Francis?"

She tried to back up further, making herself smaller. She made a scared mewling sound which was only just coherent.

"Take it easy, girl. We're here to help. You need to tell me. Are you Francis?"

She nodded vigorously. "Y-yes."

"That's good." I remained where I was and held out my hand. "Come to me, Francis. We'll take you out of here."

Behind me, I heard Knocker say into his comms. "Alpha, we have the package. I say again, we have the package. Need a medivac our pos."

The voice startled Francis and her eyes darted into the darkness. "It's okay," I said softly. "That's Ray. My name is John. He just sent for a helicopter to get us out."

Francis's eyes widened. "Patrick? Where is he?"

"He's fine."

She climbed shakily to her feet, reached out, and took my hand. "That's it, let's go."

————

Francis underwent debriefing and was subsequently permitted to return home alongside her brother. A thorough medical examination revealed that her most urgent issue was psychological trauma. Unfortunately, this was the only positive aspect of our situation. Despite our best efforts, we had yet to pinpoint Goodall's location—the scientist remained elusive. Additionally, the remaining microchips and rocket engines were still unaccounted for. Furthermore, our MI6 asset in Cuba had not yielded any significant leads.

"Why would they go back to Berlin?" I asked Knocker, hoping that his brain was tuned in to the same station. "Tell me that?"

"Because that is where it started," Knocker said. "Maybe they want us back there."

"To continue the war?"

"Who knows?"

We were relaxing in the recreation room when the door opened and Holly walked in, her visage a mask of concern. "You need to see this. You won't bloody believe it."

We followed her into the ops room, where Slick awaited us. Once we were ready, he brought up a video feed on the big screen. "This was sent to MI6 thirty minutes ago," Holly said.

Our eyes remained fixed on the screen, anticipation hanging in the air. Abruptly, an image materialized—a vacant chair, its emptiness echoing through the room. But the stillness was short-lived. Within moments, two shadowy figures emerged, their movements deliberate. Clad in ski masks, they positioned a hooded form into the chair, their actions precise and purposeful. The hood was lifted, revealing a face we hadn't expected: Lisa Goodall, her features etched with a mix of vulnerability and defiance. Our collective gaze lingered, questions swirling. What secrets did she harbor? What role had she unwittingly stepped into? The room held its breath, suspended between revelation and mystery.

Another person appeared behind her. He too wore a mask, but we could tell who it was. The attempt to conceal himself was pathetic. It was Lazar Noskov. He stared at the camera and said, "By now you know who the true Melinoe is, so we have no use for her anymore. And you are aware what happens when we have no further use for our assets. However, over the time she was embedded, Melinoe was able to obtain much valuable intelligence regarding your agencies. By the time I finish this sentence, a malicious virus has infiltrated your mainframe, initiating a cascade of shut-down procedures."

"Slick?"

"Oh boy, this is bad," Slick said as he started typing fran-tically. "It's a stealth virus. It's not even triggering anything. It'll just corrupt everything until the place goes dark."

"Can you save anything?" Holly asked.

"I'm trying. But whoever wrote it was brilliant."

I looked at the screen. "Didn't you watch this?"

"No, we waited for you," Holly said.

"Don't try to stop it," Noskov said. "It is impossible. You should have just enough time to see me do this."

In a chilling instant, a gun materialized in his grip, its cold muzzle pressed against Lisa Goodall's temple. The trigger tightened, and in that fateful moment, darkness enveloped more than just her life.

"Motherfucker," Knocker growled.

"That was good," Slick said, slumping back in his seat. "Bad but good."

"Yeah, but not good enough," Knocker said. "She wasn't expecting to die. They crossed her."

"How can you tell?" Holly asked.

"The expression on her face and the tap of her right index finger."

"Slick, can we get another look?"

He shook his head. "No, it's fucked."

I turned to Knocker. "Come on, Watson, talk to me."

He closed his eyes, trying to picture what he'd seen. His lips moved, but no sound emerged. Then he said, "It was Morse. Dash, dot dot, dash dash dash, dot dash dot dot, dash dash dash, dot dot dot."

"What does that mean?" I asked.

"Wait, let me think. It's…Dolos."

"What about Dolos?"

"Give me a moment," he replied. "Dot dash dot dot, dash dash dash, dash dot dash, break, dot dash dash, dot dot, dash, dot dot dot dot, dot dot, dash dot. Look within."

"Look within?"

"Yes, she said Dolos, look within."

"Look within where?" Holly asked. "MI6? Is that what she meant?"

"No idea, boss."

"What I don't get is that she knew about the operation to Wrangel, but nothing was done to stop it."

I thought for a moment. "Maybe she didn't tell them and that's why they killed her."

"It makes no sense," Holly said.

"It does if she wanted to keep her cover, but they pulled her out unexpectedly."

The door to the ops room opened and Christine Ryan stuck her head through the opening. To say she was angry was an understatement. "What happened?"

Holly gave us a sidelong glance. "Wish me luck."

CHAPTER 18

WE RELOCATED OUR OPERATION TO MI5 WHILE A TEAM OF THE UK's top computer experts worked tirelessly to restore MI6. The catastrophic system crash had global ramifications, imperiling the lives of numerous covert agents.

Gail established a secondary operations room for us, where I monitored the BBC news feed. The headlines were grim, detailing a terrorist assault on our intelligence infrastructure. The perpetrators remained unidentified, shrouded in mystery and menace.

While the Prime Minister attempted to downplay the situation, his primary opponent, Fergus Pridham, fervently advocated for it, drumming up support with unwavering determination.

"...has faced not only external threats but has also faced internal challenges that have put our citizens' lives at risk. The question arises: Why did our security services not antici-pate and prevent these attacks? It is increasingly evident that our security apparatus lacks effectiveness in several critical areas. Rather than focusing solely on global affairs, our secu-rity services should prioritize safeguarding our homeland. The threats to our democracy are real, and we must address them head-on.

"As we look beyond outdated alliances, we propose a

new approach—one that prioritizes our national security over international commitments. Imagine if a bomb had detonated on the streets of London. The consequences would have been devastating. Fortunately, luck was on our side this time. However, relying on luck is not a sustainable strategy. Our current Prime Minister appears complacent, asleep at the wheel. But we offer an alternative—a vote for change.

"If elected, we pledge to redirect resources toward strengthening our domestic security. Let other nations worry about their own affairs, we will take care of our backyard. Our commitment to safeguarding our citizens and preserving our democratic way of life is unwavering. By God, change is coming, and it starts with your vote. Remember, as citizens, we have the power to shape our nation's future. Let's choose wisely and prioritize the safety and well-being of our people. Us."

I flicked the television off. Behind me, I heard Knocker say, "Fucking wanker."

"I bet the new Soviet Union is loving him."

"If the asshole ever gets elected, he'll be a threat to the whole of bloody Europe. I'll never understand why his party gets the support it does. I mean, if they pull out of Europe, America will be right behind them. The same way if the Yanks pulled out, the Brits would go. But if that happened, it might as well open the front door for Sergey Lash. He'll...be fucked, Reaper, that's it."

I frowned. "That's what?"

"The best way to defeat an enemy is from within."

"You think that's what Goodall meant?" I asked.

"It makes sense. If the UK pulls out of NATO, then America will follow. That will leave the door wide open for Lash to bring the countries he needs back into the fold."

"It would mean a war of sorts," I pointed out.

"Hence the oil and diamonds for financial backing. We need to find out where the missiles fit in."

"Stalin's Spear," I told him. "That's where they fit in.

Missiles pointed at America as a threat to keep them from interfering with what might happen."

"We have to check it out."

"Yes." I reached for my cell and dialed a number. "Slick, I need you."

He arrived a few minutes later. "What's up?"

"I need you to do a deep dive on Fergus Pridham."

"On whose authority did you take it upon yourself to launch an investigation into a sitting MP?" Holland asked.

"My own," I replied.

"That would be overstepping your bounds, Mr. Kane. Should you not have run it up the chain to someone in charge?"

"Up the chain was busy with other things," Holly pointed out.

"I'm not talking to you, Miss Smith."

Holly closed her mouth, her eyes blazing. I had the sudden urge to give him a spray but a warning glance from Christine Ryan made me hold my tongue.

"I'm waiting, Mr. Kane."

"Up the chain were busy with other things. Besides, the fewer people in the loop regarding it, the better."

"Really?"

"Put it this way. If you, Mr. Holland, had found out that we were investigating your boss, would you have told him?"

"Yes, I would."

"And that is why I wouldn't tell you. It's called being a security risk. You shouldn't even be on the committee."

He glared at me, and I looked at German. "Do you want me to continue?"

"Yes. We'll go for a little longer and then call it a day."

"Fergus Pridham?" Slick said, trying to confirm what I'd just told him.

"That's right. I want you to Mariana Trench him."

"That deep?"

"Yeah."

"Okay. What am I looking for?"

"Anything that doesn't add up."

Slick nodded. "Okay. But what if Holly asks about what I'm doing?"

"I'll clear it with her. Can you handle that and all the other stuff that's happening?"

He grinned at me. "Sure, I can."

He left and Knocker said, "What are you going to tell, Holly?"

"The truth."

"When?"

"Soon."

Holly's displeasure was palpable. I relayed the unfolding events, and her gaze bore into me before she uttered a word. "You are playing with fire, John. Not just fire, but a roaring fucking blaze."

"We need to know, Holly. If we find nothing, all well and good, but we can't not look into it."

She nodded. "All right, we'll look. In the meantime, we think we've found Noskov."

"Berlin?" I asked.

"No, he's in India. That's where we're going."

"What's in India?" I asked.

"Bearer bonds."

———

I scrunched my nose, the familiar yet unwelcome assault on my senses hitting me as I stepped onto the bustling streets of Mumbai. Despite my previous visits, the pungent blend of cooking spices and the acrid odor of decaying refuse still caught me off guard. The city was a cacophony of honking horns, shouting vendors, and jostling crowds—a chaotic symphony that seemed to echo the very pulse of India.

Our makeshift base was an abandoned oil refinery, its rusted machinery now repurposed for our covert operation. Inside the TOC, Tactical Operations Center, Holly, Slick, and the other specialists huddled over monitors, their eyes darting between surveillance feeds and encrypted communications. Knocker and I, the field agents, were the tip of the spear—our mission unauthorized, our resolve unwavering.

The stakes were high. Noskov, elusive and dangerous, had connections within the Indian government sympathetic to the Soviet cause. We couldn't risk exposure. The consequences would be dire. As much as I longed for a clean shot to end it all, we needed him alive. Information was our currency, and Noskov held the key to unraveling a web of intrigue that spanned continents.

So there we were, in the heart of Mumbai, navigating the tangle of allegiances and betrayals. The smog hung like a shroud, obscuring the sun and casting shadows on our uncertain path. The crib was set, the trap laid. Now it was a waiting game—a delicate balance between survival and betrayal, where every breath tasted of danger and every heartbeat echoed with the urgency of our mission. Alive or dead, Noskov would reveal his secrets. And in this murky underworld, secrets were worth more than gold.

But first, we had to find him.

Holly gathered us around a table and started with, "That went smoothly. Fourteen hours and we're on the ground and set up."

Knocker nodded. "I'm impressed."

"Okay, this is what we have. In seven hours, that's fifteen hundred hours today, Lazar Noskov has a meeting with a diamond buyer. We know when the meeting will take place, but not the where nor with whom. We believe the exchange will be for five hundred million in bearer bonds."

"Surely there's not that many dealers in India who could manage something like that?"

"Only a handful legally do it," Holly said. "There are a few black-market operators who also deal in the trade. At the moment a single Crore is worth six and a half million US dollars. Some of these guys are worth up to seven thousand Crore."

"That is a whole lot of money," Knocker said with a low whistle.

"Some of the illegal dealers are worth more and have security details to match. Which means you chaps will have to be on your toes."

"I assume you are going to give us a jumping-off point," I said to Holly.

She opened a folder and took out a photo. The man captured in the image possessed an air of mystery, his dark hair a mass of unruly curls. His beard, thick and untamed, mirrored the shadows that clung to his rugged features. He was standing in front of a Maserati surrounded by young women dressed in bikinis.

"Manvir Yadav. Makes his money as a go-between for high profile criminals. Manages to stay ahead of the police and armed forces by paying off the right people. If anyone knows where and when this meeting will take place, it's him."

"Where do we find him at this time of the day?" Knocker asked.

"His penthouse apartment suite, downtown. The clock is ticking, chaps. We need answers yesterday."

"Bodyguards?"

"He's got a handful. All watching the perimeter," Slick said. "Our main problem is getting you inside the suite."

I looked at the picture again and had an idea. "Boss, how do you look in a bikini?"

Her eyes widened as she held up a hand, palm facing out. "No, definitely not."

———

"I feel like I'm naked," Holly growled as we made our way toward the elevator. "A bloody G-string bikini. What was I thinking?"

"At least you're wearing a wrap," I pointed out. "Where is your weapon?"

"Shut up."

As we stood there, anticipation humming in the air,

Holly's gaze swept across the lobby. She was keenly aware of the curious glances that might be directed her way. Meanwhile, I was clad in a crisp, white suit, the fabric cool against my skin, with a coordinating T-shirt underneath. The elevator chimed, its doors sliding open like a secret portal. We stepped inside, fingers brushing against the polished buttons, and selected the highest floor. Upward we went, carried by the silent machinery, the piped music like something from a strip joint.

I heard Holly say, "Just great."

I hid my grin.

The elevator glided to a gradual halt, its doors parting silently. As we stepped into the dimly lit hallway, our path intersected with that of two vigilant armed guards. Their stern expressions and poised weapons sent a chill down our spines, emphasizing the gravity of our situation.

"What do you want?" one of them asked in halting English.

"We're here to see Manny baby," Holly replied, laying on a thick accent.

The man stared at her breasts. "Do you have an appointment?"

"I think he's expecting us," Holly replied with a sultry smile.

"You can't see him without—"

"Damn it," Holly growled as her wrap fell to the floor, revealing the rest of her lithe body. She turned away from the two guards and bent over to retrieve it.

Being the gentleman that I am, I stared at the wide-eyed guards who nervously glanced at me before returning their gazes to the vista before them.

Holly finished by straightening up, thrusting her shoulders back to emphasize her assets before replacing the wrap. "Sorry, what was it you were saying?"

The man swallowed hard. "I'm sure Mr. Yadav will see you. Please, follow us."

As Holly stepped past me to follow them, she said in a low voice, "Not one fucking word."

Holly and I trailed behind the guards into the suite and were ushered inside. As we waited, one of the guards rapped on a nearby door before stepping in. Through the wood, we caught faint, muffled voices, and then the bodyguard reemerged.

"If you wait here, Mr. Yadav will be with you shortly."

I nodded.

The bodyguards left us and returned to their positions in the hallway. I looked around. "Slick, can you hear me?"

"Roger, Reaper."

"Where are the other guards?"

"Two on the roof and the others are one floor down in bed."

"Roger that," I said and took out my Glock and screwed the suppressor onto it before tucking it into my pants. I glanced at Holly. "You got your weapon, boss?"

A spiteful glare was her only response.

The door opposite opened, and a young woman, clad only in a red G-string, appeared and cat-footed past us to the bathroom.

I said, "You're wearing more than she is."

"Can we just drop it about the clothing, John?"

"I wasn't the one dropping my clothing," I reminded her.

The door opened once more, this time allowing another young woman to exit. This one was wearing less. I grinned to myself but decided not to push it. She stopped in front of us and said to Holly, "If you're next, good luck."

Then she disappeared.

The next person through the doorway was Yadav himself. On noticing us, he stopped and stared. Bare-chested, he wore only loose-fitting shorts and a well-toned six-pack.

He stared at Holly and grinned. "Cool, white meat. Can I have the leg or the breast?"

His arrogance had blinded him to the impending danger. Swiftly, I advanced, retrieving the Glock from behind my back. Without hesitation, I thrust the cold metal into his gaping mouth, my other hand applying force to propel him backward into the dimly lit room.

"Now, Manny, maintain absolute silence. Our time is limited, and your insights regarding the matter we're pursuing would be immensely valuable. Do you comprehend?"

He said something garbled around the suppressor.

"Just nod, Manny."

He nodded.

"Okay," Holly said. "Let's get started. There is a substantial diamond buy going down today. Where?"

"Hmpf."

"Take the gun out of his mouth."

I did as I was told and a trickle of blood from a cut lip followed it. Holly moved in closer.

"The diamond buy?"

"I don't know of any diamond buy. Who the hell are you people?"

I clamped my hand over his mouth and shot him in the leg. Not low, but the meaty upper part of his thigh. He screeched against my palm. I leaned in close and shushed him. Holly sat beside him. "Oh, no, that looks painful."

He nodded vigorously.

"The meeting place?"

I removed my hand. There was no way he wasn't going to speak.

He said, "The ruins. Sanjay Gandhi National Park."

"Good, now we're getting somewhere. Who is the buyer?"

"Samir Khan," he replied, his visage a mask of pain and perspiration.

Holly traced a line down his face with a finger. "See, sweetie, that wasn't too bad, was it?"

He shook his head. "N—"

Unspoken words hung in the air, stifled by the swift impact of my Glock against his temple. His body crumpled, collapsing onto the sinisterly stained sheets of the bed.

As the door swung open, a naked figure stepped inside. Her eyes widened at the sight of Yadav's lifeless form and the crimson pool that surrounded him. Misjudgment flashed across her face, a conclusion drawn too hastily.

Then she screamed.

And screamed.

Holly rushed over to her and threw a right hook that would have done a boxer proud. The girl's eyes rolled back, and she was out before she hit the floor. But by then, the damage was done and the bodyguards from outside the door were moving.

"Shit, that's torn it," I growled.

"Reaper, the two guards in the hallway are headed toward the door."

"No shit. What about the others?"

"The ones on the roof are coming down. There is no movement from—"

The suite door burst open and my Glock leaped into action. Two suppressed shots sounded, striking the first man who charged through. He stiffened, then crumpled to the floor. Undeterred, the second guard stepped over his fallen comrade, weapon raised. I realigned my aim and fired two more rounds. Moments later, a look of shock etched across his face, he collapsed beside his friend. The room fell silent for just a moment.

"Grab a gun, Holly," I said to her.

Holly bent down and picked up a fallen Beretta Storm. She checked it to make sure there was a round in the chamber and then fell in behind me. "Let's go, John."

"Knocker, we're on our way down."

"Copy, Reaper. I'll be here."

We hurried out into the hallway, but suddenly...

"Contact right!"

I opened fire and charged back into the suite. Holly, positioned in the doorway, wielded her Beretta with precision.

Amid the chaos, an unexpected sight caught my attention: a sun-kissed woman in a daring G-string bikini, unflinchingly firing at her assailants. There's something uniquely captivating about strength and beauty converging in the heat of battle.

She blew off four shots before taking cover. Looking over at me, she noticed I was standing there staring at her.

She said, "You'd better be thinking of a way out of here."

"Of course, boss."

"Stop looking at my ass. You're as bad as Raymond."

"Yes, boss."

"Someone mention my name?"

"Fuck."

She opened fire again. This time, it elicited a cry of pain. Holly drew back and looked at me again. "You going to shoot or not?"

"You're doing just fine, boss."

"Just do it."

I leaned around her and fired at the remaining guard, who was standing too far out in the hallway, presenting me with an easy target. Both rounds from my Glock punched into his chest and he died where he fell. I grabbed Holly by the hand and said, "Come on."

Hastening from the suite toward the elevator, we brushed past the fire alarm. Without hesitation, I pressed it, and Holly and I continued on our way.

Once out on the street, Knocker was there to collect us. We climbed in and I said, "Go."

He floored the gas pedal on the Land Rover, and we pulled out into the chaos that was the Mumbai traffic.

Back at the crib, Holly moved swiftly to change into khaki cargo pants and a one-shade lighter T-shirt. "That's better," she said with a hint of relief. "Where are we at?"

Slick said, "I've gone over the map of the National Park

and located several suitable options of where the meet might be. I know that Yadav said the ruins, but I suggest that Reaper and Knocker follow the buyer to the meet."

Holly nodded slowly. "Where is Khan?"

"I think he's at his club?"

"You think?"

"It's hard. Mumbai's camera systems and electronics can be spotty. Mostly unreliable. It forces me to rely on satellite feed."

"Great," Holly grumped.

"What is a billionaire crook doing with a club?" Knocker asked.

"Laundering his money. He owns a lot of businesses specifically for that purpose."

"So, we pick him up at the clue, follow him to the meeting, and go from there."

"Yes."

"Do we have a photo of him, Slick?"

Slick handed over a photo from the crib printer. Khan had dark eyes, a thick, black beard, and wore a dastār.

I picked up the photo. "He's a Sikh."

"Yes."

"Security?" inquired Knocker.

"Formidable," came the reply. "He never ventures forth without his entourage of seven or eight. Ex-military, now operating in the shadows of the private sector—or perhaps the darker, illicit corners. Their menace is palpable."

"Any sign of Noskov?" I asked.

"No. I've been unable to locate him, but as I said, cameras in the city are not what we are used to in the UK."

"Okay. I guess we'd better get ready."

Holly stared at me. "John, my advice is to follow Noskov and hit him along his route. Don't try anything in Khan's presence. Let the numbers thin before you do anything."

"Yes, ma'am."

"One more thing. If you can't take him alive, then the kill order stands."

"Yes, ma'am."

The briefing broke up and Knocker and I went to the mobile armory. We equipped ourselves with C8 carbines underslung with grenade launchers, extra ammunition, Glock handguns, grenades, flashbangs, binoculars, and the usual body armor.

Our selections made, we dressed for the occasion: jeans, T-shirts, baseball caps. Then we placed everything into the Land Rover.

"We're ready to go," I said to Holly once we were done.

"Good luck, John. Watch your backs."

"Yes, ma'am."

CHAPTER 19

STALKING KHAN OUTSIDE THE CLUB, WE SHADOWED HIM TO THE rendezvous point—a challenging feat among the chaotic Mumbai traffic. The street teemed with a familiar sight: cars adorned with dents like badges of honor—testament to the relentless hustle of the city.

But it was the traffic snarl that truly tested our patience. Vehicles pressed bumper to bumper, their horns wailing in discord, and drivers' clenched fists punctuating the frustration walls of vehicles with horns blaring and fists shaking. Motorized beasts weaved and collided, creating a cacophony of confusion and impatience. Amid this symphony of vehicular discord, our pursuit continued, fueled by determination and adrenaline.

"Be fucked, Reaper. This is crazy shit," Knocker stated.

"Just don't lose them," I reminded him.

"Easier said than done," he replied.

Up ahead the black SUVs which transported Khan and his men began to change lanes.

"They're moving, Knocker."

"Yeah, I can see that. How about you tell that bloke beside us to piss off so we can do the same." He flicked the turning signal on and started to edge across. I heard a grating sound and then Knocker put his head out the window. "Motherfucker. Get out of the fucking way. I indicated, are you fucking blind?" Drawing his head back into the vehicle, he said, "Shit, Reaper."

"Are you done?"

The Land Rover shuddered. "Yeah, but I don't think these idiots are."

We managed to get across into the next lane while up ahead, the Khan convoy of three SUVs headed for an exit. "You're going to have to go again, Knocker."

"Bloody hell," he snapped as his turning signal came on again. "More dents."

After a couple more near misses, we made the exit and managed to keep Khan's convoy in sight. Trailing them at a safe distance, they eventually led us to the national park.

"Stop here, Knocker."

He pulled over. I said, "Talk to me, Slick."

"I've acquired line of sight from the satellite. It's not going to last long, maybe ten minutes. I'll have to find another after that."

"Just tell me where they are."

"Keep following them, Reaper. I'll guide you in."

Knocker pulled back onto the road, driving slowly over the rugged artery until Slick spoke, "Coming up on your left, there is a narrow track. Nose in there and proceed on foot. They have pulled over about two hundred meters further on."

Emerging from the vehicle, we retrieved our weapons from the cargo hold. The forest enveloped us, dappled light casting eerie shadows on the gravel and leaf-strewn ground.

My urgency grew. "I need to know what's happening, Slick. Is Noskov there?"

"Not yet, Reaper," came the terse reply.

We pressed onward, the trees thickening around us. To our left, a rise in the terrain beckoned. Knocker and I ascended cautiously, then just before reaching the crest, dropped low, crawling the final stretch. As the foliage thinned, we gained an unobstructed view of the meeting point. I raised my binoculars, scanning the area.

Khan stood outside the SUV he'd arrived in, his men forming a protective perimeter. Tension hung in the air. This was the moment we'd been waiting for. Our mission depended on what unfolded next. We were ready, hearts pounding, as the shadows lengthened and the forest held its breath.

"Slick, copy?"

"Copy, Reaper."

"What are you seeing?"

"Not a lot. I'm losing the satellite. I've found another but we won't have visual for another ten minutes."

"Shit. Roger that. What about comms?"

"Comms will be good."

"Copy."

The rumble of engines echoed through the forest, and suddenly, three sleek black SUVs materialized. Knocker's voice cut through the tension: "What's the deal with these jerks and their obsession with black SUVs?"

"What color do we have?"

"I'd put us in the same basket, Reaper."

Doors opened and people disembarked. They were heavily armed, and as the other guards had, they formed a protective perimeter. Then he got out.

Lazar Noskov. The man we were here for. He stood beside his SUV and waited.

We waited.

No one moved.

"Reaper, something is wrong," Knocker said.

I was thinking along those lines myself.

Laying a cautionary hand on my shoulder, Knocker nodded to our right when I looked at him. Turning my head, I saw the problem. Two shooters were creeping through the trees to take up a position overlooking the scene below. "Shit."

Looking about for any others, my eyes locked on two more to our left. "On your left."

Turning his head, he saw them. Glancing at me, he suggested, "A double cross?"

"Yes. Slick, can you hear me?"

"Copy, Reaper."

Beside me, Knocker brought his weapon around to his left to cover the two shooters.

"Slick, it appears as though Noskov is about to double-cross Khan. They're about to go loud. We need eyes in the sky."

"I'm working on it."

"John, what's happening?" Holly asked.

"Shit's about to go down and we're stuck in the middle of it. What do you want us to do?"

"Copy. Noskov is still the mission. Capture or kill."

"Roger that. We're Charlie Mike."

"This is going to be interesting, Reaper."

"And then some. You cover left, I'll cover right. When this kicks off, we hit them before they know what's happening. Then we make Noskov a priority."

Moments later, the shooters flanking us unleashed a storm of bullets, but they weren't the sole threat. Noskov's hidden forces lay in ambush on the far side, concealed among the trees.

Khan and his men fell, crumpling to the ground where they had stood. Beside me, Knocker responded swiftly, eliminating the two targets on his side.

As for me, I rolled into position, adrenaline surging. The two assailants designated as mine were dispatched efficiently, leaving us with a single objective: neutralize the remaining threats and apprehend Noskov.

Our weapons swung around, and we unleashed a storm of fire down the hill. I took aim, dropping one of Noskov's men while Knocker eliminated another. They soon realized they were under attack from our position and returned fire, taking refuge behind the SUVs. Khan and his team lay motionless, casualties of the chaos.

We were the last ones standing, the sole obstacles in Noskov's path. I spotted another shooter and squeezed the trigger, but he ducked out of sight. I waited, heart pounding, waiting for him to reappear. In that moment, a 5.56 round obliterated the top of his head and he vanished for good.

While this was happening, Noskov had taken cover on the far side of his own SUV, placing the protective density of the engine block between us. Knocker muttered a curse as he burned through a magazine too fast. "Loading," he called out as he dropped the spent magazine on the ground and replaced it with a fresh one.

Then he was back in the fight and his suppressed C8 sent more rounds down range. I saw a Russian shooter fall, wounded or dead.

Movement beyond the vehicles captured my attention and I saw shooters at the edge of the tree line. We were outnumbered before this had kicked off, but now even more so. Then my mind latched onto a crazy idea. I slid back behind the brow of the hill and rolled onto my back. "Slick, have you got eyes yet?"

"Not yet, Reaper. A few more minutes."

"Damn it. Knocker!"

He slid back to my position. "What's up?"

"We need to move. We still have no eyes and if these Russians have any kind of training, they'll be trying to flank us. Both sides."

"You're right." Knocker looked around. "Those rocks over there?"

I nodded. "Let's go."

Keeping our heads low, we sprinted stealthily toward the cluster of rocks. Knocker and I took cover, swiftly reloading our weapons. I clung to the hope that sometimes, progress required retracing our steps, moving backward to ultimately move forward. And there, amid the tension, Noskov remained our elusive quarry.

As we waited, figures materialized on both flanks, closing in with deliberate purpose. Knocker said, "Looks like you were right."

Loading a grenade into my underslung launcher, I waited until the figures were in position. I fired.

The resulting explosion shook the immediate vicinity and beyond, the force knocking down our intended targets. Behind me, our friendly neighborhood Womble did the same, reducing the number of our assailants to a more manageable level.

"For the uneducated, a Womble is—"

"We know what a Womble is, Mr. Kane," German growled.

"A Womble, Reaper?"

"I thought it added a nice touch."

"I like it. Which one?"

"Orinoco?"

"That'll do."

"Gentlemen, if you are quite finished?"

A sudden burst of gunfire erupted from our previous position on the brow of the hill. Returning fire, Knocker and I saw another Russian go down. Then the handful of assailants began to fall back.

"They're running," I said.

Knocker leaped to his feet. "We need to stop Noskov."

Standing tall, I followed him. As he topped the rise he stopped and opened fire, standing like a true warrior against the heathen horde.

Sorry, a little over dramatic.

I reached his shoulder and saw the scene below. The Russians were scrambling for their SUVs, Noskov climbing into the second one. Loading another grenade, I fired at the lead SUV. In a massive ball of orange flame, it exploded, spraying flaming debris into the trees.

"Great work. I hope it doesn't start a forest fire," Knocker said as he concentrated his fire on the last vehicle in line.

Loading his own grenade, he sent it forth to do its thing.

The vehicle exploded like the first one, leaving Noskov a sitting duck within his.

Tires spinning, the SUV began to move.

I said, "Shoot the tires."

We changed aim and opened fire at the tires. Dirt and debris kicked up around the vehicle as it started to speed away. I started down the slope, firing at the remaining shooters as I went. "Come on, we need to get after him."

Having dispatched the three remaining Russians, we ran to the nearest of Khan's SUVs. Knocker jumped into the driver's seat.

I slammed the door behind me and said into my comms, "Slick, Noskov is on the move."

"Roger that. I've got eyes on him."

Knocker spun the SUV around and floored the gas pedal. The Range Rover V8 shot forward, the tires kicking up a rooster tail of dirt and gravel. Pressing the button to wind down the window, I prepared to fire.

A large cloud of dust emanated from the vehicle in front, but upon reaching the blacktop, the dust soon disappeared.

Knocker put his foot down, closing the distance between our vehicles. Leaning from the window, I opened fire at the SUV's tires, missing. The Range Rover lurched suddenly, and I was forced back inside.

Glancing at Knocker, I growled, "Can't you keep it steady?"

"I thought you could shoot straight?"

We sped on, weaving left and right. A figure emerged from a rear window and opened fire at us. Bullets ricocheted off our appropriated vehicle, causing Knocker to swerve even more.

Then the SUV vanished. It had turned a corner and disappeared. "Slick, where the fuck did he go?"

"Turn left, Reaper, turn left."

"But there is nothing there."

"Trust me, do it."

Knocker swung violently left and the Range Rover

crashed through some brush. There it was, speeding away from us on another road. Another gravel snake with sharper turns, seemingly forgotten about by my Formula One driver as he straight-lined them.

The Range Rover reared violently, its front leaping into the air. My head hit the roof and I felt my neck concertina. "Shit a brick, Knocker. I think I'm safer with fucking Noskov."

"Do you want to catch the prick or not?"

"Just don't kill us doing it."

The gas pedal went down once more, and the Range Rover surged as its power boosted. As we cleared the last brush, we were out on the street, headed back toward the heart of Mumbai.

We were soon back among the traffic, weaving in and out, trying not to kill ourselves or anyone else. Noskov's SUV made a hard right turn ahead of us down a narrow alley.

Stomping on the brakes, Knocker swung the wheel. As the nose of the SUV straightened, I could see Noskov's ride in front of us hammering along the alley, pedestrians scattering like barnyard chickens being chased like a coyote.

Mayhem ensued, but we were still able to negotiate it with Nigel Mansell behind the wheel. It was a close-run thing, but we managed to get through unscathed.

The SUV in front disappeared once more as it turned right out of the alley. Knocker followed, and before we knew what was happening, we were flying through a crowded street market with stalls already smashed from the passage of Noskov's ride.

"Be fucking careful," I called out.

"Shut up, I'm trying not to kill anyone."

"Really?"

"Do you want to drive?"

"I think I should," I replied.

"Well, you bloody can't."

He swerved around a smashed stand and then a couple

of Indian sellers. Before we could blink, we were free of the carnage but had lost ground and a visual on Noskov. "Slick, we need you again."

"Turn left up ahead."

Knocker braked hard once more and made the turn. In the distance, we saw Noskov's vehicle again. I have to say, the guy driving certainly knew his business. We were closing on him, but when he turned the next corner, he came to an abrupt halt like he'd been shot. The infamous Mumbai traffic had foiled his escape.

As we executed the turn, they swiftly exited the SUV. Noskov sprinted ahead, guided by a bodyguard who urged him through the congested traffic. Meanwhile, the two steadfast bodyguards held their ground, anticipating our arrival. The moment we emerged, they unleashed a hail of bullets.

Throwing ourselves from the Range Rover to avoid a face full of bullets and glass, Knocker and I searched for cover. I rolled away from the SUV and stopped behind a parked car. I pressed myself against a wheel as bullets hammered a staccato tattoo as they embedded themselves in the thin exterior.

"Knocker, are you all right?"

"Still kicking, Reaper."

"I'm going to draw their fire. Can you pot them both?"

"SAS, mate, SAS."

"Don't damn well miss."

Rising on my feet, I sent a fusillade hurtling, remaining in the open to draw their attention. The two Russians turned and began shooting. Bullets shredded the air around me. Then the low sounds of Knocker's suppressed C8 became audible. The two shooters dropped after a quick spasm, joining the detritus of the Mumbai street.

"Moving!" I called out. "Slick, where is Noskov?"

"He ran into an apartment building along the street on your left. A word of warning, the Mumbai police are on their way. You've got maybe five mikes until they arrive. You can thank the traffic jam."

"Roger that." I looked over at Knocker and pointed at the apartment building. He nodded and we scrambled between vehicles toward it.

Walking up the twisted driveway, Knocker growled, "It'll be like trying to find fucking Bugs Bunny in here."

As I opened the building's front door, Knocker stepped inside without hesitation. I followed him through, the body of a dead security guard on the white-tiled floor grabbing my attention. Having sustained two shots, his blood was pooling around his prone form. Knocker bent and checked for a pulse.

"He's done, Reaper."

I remained vigilant, covering him and watching three possible avenues of attack. When Knocker came to his feet, he said, "Where the bloody hell do we go?"

"Guess?"

"No time for bloody games, Reaper."

"It's no game, mate. I have no idea."

The sound of gunfire emanated from higher within the building. Knocker and I looked at each other and, at the same time, said, "Up."

Stepping past Knocker I started toward the stairs. He fell in behind me and we hurried to find Noskov before he escaped.

"Reaper, you have three mikes until the hammer falls. Estimate thirty Indian forces inbound."

"Fuck," I growled. "Roger that."

As we took the stairs two at a time, we were met by three oncoming civilians intent on escape. I grabbed one by the arm.

"Where are they?" I asked, hoping they spoke English.

"Second floor. Second floor."

I let him go. "Okay, get out of here."

Climbing to the second-floor landing, we found another security guard. He'd sustained a nasty gash to the head from being hit and was leaning against the wall, trying to stanch the bleeding.

As Knocker and I brushed past him, I heard him say, "Up the stairs."

Hearing gunfire rattling in the stairwell, we started up the next flight, pressing ourselves against the walls, trying to avoid ricochets.

Knocker grunted. "Fuck."

"You okay?"

"Caught a round in my plate."

I turned and dragged him up. "Come on."

Pushing harder until we came to a doorway, we stopped to catch our breath and focus. I looked to Knocker. "Ready?"

He nodded abruptly. "Hit it."

Turning the handle, I threw the door open violently. It crashed back against the wall, and I rushed through the opening, Knocker close behind. Intense gunfire rattled out, and bullets whipped past as we walked out onto the roof. Bringing my weapon around, I squeezed the trigger.

The shooter collapsed to the rooftop in an untidy heap, his weapon spilling from his grasp. Noskov, throwing a quick glance my way, lunged for the fallen gun, but a quick burst from my C8 stopped him short.

Knocker and I walked steadily toward him. "Hello, Lazar," I greeted him. My tone was almost friendly.

"Mr. Kane, we have a chance to talk at last."

"Reaper, police are in the building," Slick told me.

"John, get out," Holly said hurriedly.

"What is Stalin's Spear, Lazar?" I asked him.

He smiled. "I see you have worked out a little more of our plan. Stalin's Spear is part of a bigger picture."

"Are the R-12s part of it?"

He shrugged.

"What does Shatov have planned?"

"You keep thinking that Mikhail is the top ladder of the rung."

"You got that ass about, mate," Knocker said.

"Whatever."

"Is there someone above Shatov? Is that what you're saying?"

"There was always someone above," he stated.

"Dolos? Is Dolos the one issuing the orders?"

"No. Dolos is a completely different part of a bigger plan. Like Stalin's Spear, like Black Water, and Gorilla."

"Were they the operations in Syria and the DRC?"

"Yes, and you failed to stop them. Just like this time. It won't be long now, Mr. Kane. Everything will be over, and the Soviet Union will be restored to its former glory, and Mother Russia will be reinstated as the powerful nation it once was."

CRACK!

Noskov's head snapped back, a bullet entering his head. He collapsed to the rooftop, proud to the very end. I turned to see where the shot had come from. A lone figure stood on a rooftop across the street, a sniper rifle in his hands. He paused for a moment and then vanished. Noskov knew he was about to die and had faced it head-on.

The sounds of the Indian police echoed from the stairwell. I glanced at Knocker, and he nodded. We relieved ourselves of our weapons and got to our knees, interlocking our fingers behind our heads, and waited.

I said, "Holly, we're going to need some help."

CHAPTER 20

"WE SPENT A COUPLE OF DAYS IN AN INDIAN JAIL BEFORE OUR release was secured. From there, we were put on a plane and flown back to London."

"So another mission, another failure," German stated.

I shook my head. "No. We knew that the Russians were making a big move to reunite their country. Familiar with the names of the operators, except that of the fifth general, we were about to blow open the identity of Dolos and where the missiles were headed. We also saved the lives of two women and a child."

"But you didn't know," Holland pointed out.

"It was only a matter of hours," Holly pointed out.

"If it had been up to me, I would have pulled you from the field immediately."

"Overall, what we had accomplished was quite remarkable. We had uncovered a plot which, if successful, would bring the world to the brink of a nuclear war."

"I think you exaggerate to deflect attention from your screw-ups," Holland scoffed. "You lost a scientist, you lost microchips and rocket motors to bring nuclear missiles online, you had one of the main players in your hands and yet he slipped through your fingers—"

"Some fucker shot him," Knocker said.

"You had a spy working among you and things were about to

get worse. In all, you were responsible for letting things spiral out of control."

Newman seemed to be enjoying what he was hearing. I fixed my iron-hard stare on him and said, "Enjoy it while you can. Tomorrow will be your turn. Then the truth will be revealed."

"Shall we summarize and move on?" Christine Ryan asked.

"Fine."

After our return to MI6 headquarters, Knocker, Holly, Slick, and I were gathered in a briefing room. While we talked, Slick was busy doing his thing. Holly stood in front of a whiteboard, making notes and drawing diagrams.

She said, "This is where we're at. We know what they want with the oil and the diamonds. The Indian police could find no trace of either the bearer bonds or diamonds anywhere."

"Which means someone took them," I said. "Maybe he left them in the SUV, and someone retrieved them from there."

"That would make sense," Slick said. "Noskov made a call while he was being chased."

"Who to?"

"No idea."

Holly nodded. "Okay, so we put the base on Wrangel out of action, but we lost the second scientist and the chips along with the rocket engines. We have an idea where they're headed but have no confirmation as yet."

I looked at Slick. "Anything on Fergus Pridham?"

"I'm still digging," he replied.

Holly said, "I was going over what Noskov said before he died. Are we convinced that Shatov isn't the top of the tree?"

"Noskov was," Knocker said.

"Does that mean Lash is?"

Nodding, I said, "It would make sense."

"If he is, then we've got this all ass about. We were of the opinion that this was all planned and implemented by Shatov. How does Lash fit into that?"

"I think I've just found out how," Slick said. "Lash's father was made Marshal of the Soviet Union. But his grandfather, he was a war hero. After the war, he was involved in the intelligence side of things. He headed up a think tank to plan scenarios to implement in the event of such situations as the Nazi invasion."

"The Gods of War?" I asked.

Slick nodded. "I would guess in its earliest form. They would have refined it since then, but Lash's grandfather was the founder."

"Good work," Holly said. "However, we now have two divergent paths: the missiles and Dolos."

"Then we split out resources," I said. "I'll take the missiles, and Knocker can handle Dolos."

Holly frowned. "I don't like it, John."

"There is no other way," I replied. "I still have contacts throughout the intelligence community who can assist. You back up, Knocker. If I learn anything big, I'll read you in."

"But where are you going to start?"

My cell rang. I answered, listened, talked, and then hung up. "I just got a lead on Morozov. I'll start there."

"Where is he?"

"South Korea. An old friend followed him there from Prague."

"I'll get you a flight. Do whatever it takes to stop him, John."

"Yes, ma'am."

Glancing up at the large screen on the wall, the BBC news service rolling, my attention was drawn by the headline. A plane had crashed into the Atlantic. They were calling it a ghost flight. No one knew how long it had been missing for or its destination. Nor its origins. The whole thing was a mystery.

Staring at the screen, I frowned, my mind ticking over. "Son of a bitch."

Everyone fixed their eyes on me.

"Care to share?" Holly asked.

"I know why he's in South Korea."

"Why?"

"Microchips." I nodded at the screen. "They lost them. Now they need replacing."

"The ghost flight?"

"Yes. It fits."

"You get another chance, John. Take it."

————

"That will do for today," Christine Ryan said. "We will pick it up again tomorrow. Shall we say the same time?"

We all agreed and then I looked at Newman. "You'll get your chance tomorrow."

"Good. I look forward to dismissing your lies."

"If you say so."

Rising from our seats at the table, we turned and stretched, making to leave the room. Christine Ryan called out to me. "Mr. Kane, I think we will only need you tomorrow. Should the others be required, we'll call them in."

"Yes, ma'am."

As we exited the room, Holly moved in beside me once we were out of earshot and asked, "Why didn't you tell them the other thing?"

————

While we made plans, Shatov was holding another briefing with his two remaining generals. Morozov, on screen, appeared exhausted. "I'm sorry, sir."

"It wasn't your fault, Gennady, planes crash. Sometimes it's what they do. Have you found a new supplier?"

"Yes, I have set up a buy in a couple of days. Once we have the chips, we can proceed."

"What about the missiles?" Shatov asked.

"The rocket motors should arrive soon. They can be fitted once we have the chips."

"Good, good. I will let our illustrious leader know."

"There is something else," Morozov said.

"Yes, Gennady?"

"Kane and his friends. They have a knack of appearing when and where we least want them to."

"Yes, I'm afraid I have underestimated him and his team. It is time to initiate a new plan where they are concerned. We must bring in Grigori and his team."

"I agree. They are specialist manhunters. If anyone can kill Kane, it will be them."

"Then we are agreed. Good luck, Gennady."

"Thank you, sir."

The video call ended and Shatov turned to the only other general in the room. "I want you to go to England. You will oversee the operation there."

"You are worried?"

"I am...concerned that they have a way of causing us inconvenience. Take a double-sized team with you. Should there be any trouble, you need to deal with it. The ultimate power you hold is that your identity is unknown."

"Yes, Comrade."

Leaving Shatov on his own in the room, the general departed. But not for long. After a knock at the door, another man entered, moving across to stand beside the table.

Shatov greeted him, "It is good to see you. Are you ready?"

The man nodded. "I am."

"Good. We are relying on you to provide security for the packages. The presence of our people must be kept to a minimum or it will trigger alarm bells."

"There will not be a problem," the man said. "If there is, I shall deal with it the way I deal with all issues."

"Thank you."

"Was there anything else?"

"No, I think that shall do—oh, yes. In the event of any trouble, I might need to insert a specialist team to take care of things."

"I'm sure my people can handle it," the man said, almost offended.

"I'm sure they can, but the team I have in mind is to be used only if necessary."

The man nodded. "Okay."

"Thank you."

When the man left, Shatov was once more alone. His mind wandered, recalling all the events that had brought them to this point, of how far they had come and what was left to do. The ringing of his cell drew him out of his reverie.

He answered, "Yes?"

"Kane is on his way to South Korea. I thought you should know."

The call ceased and Shatov nodded thoughtfully. They would be ready.

——————

"You should have said something about South Korea," Holly repeated.

"It'll come out tomorrow," I replied. "We'll discuss it then. Has there been any progress on it?"

Holly shook her head. "Not yet. I have Slick working on it."

"I know someone who will be able to tell us."

"He's still not talking."

"Let's go and see if he's changed his mind."

Heading to the SUV we'd been using, we clambered in, pulling away from the sidewalk. Two hours later, we stopped just outside a large stone-built house. A familiar face stepped out of the shadows. "Wasn't expecting you people tonight," said former Navy SEAL Borden Hunt. "To what do we owe the pleasure?"

"We need to talk to our friend. How is he?"

"The same as usual. Silent. Withdrawn."

"Any trouble? Anything suspicious?" I asked Hunt.

"No, nothing."

We went inside. "Hey, Reaper."

I turned my head and saw Slick. "You found anything yet?"

"No, whoever it is has covered their tracks really well."

"We need to find out who the mole is, Slick. Or we could all be in serious trouble. That is the whole idea of the inquest."

"Well, I can only do what I can do. Why don't you go and waterboard the prick we have locked away. Get him to tell you."

I nodded and headed for the stairs. Solid wooden steps led down into the old cellar. I stopped at the locked steel door and opened the hatch to look inside. The prisoner was facing away from me. "Hey," I said.

"What do you want?"

"Are you going to talk?" I asked.

"I am talking to you now."

"You know what I mean. Maybe if you help us, we can help you."

The man remained silent.

"Well?"

"What do you want?"

"We need you to tell us who Hecate is?"

"All right, I will tell you," he said. "But you must do something for me in return."

The capitulation was too easy. "What?"

He turned and stalked toward the window in the door, placing his face so close I could see into his dark, troubled eyes.

"You must kill me, John Kane, for I have nothing left to live for."

And, as I stared into the eyes of Sergey Lash, I knew it would be the only way to get him to talk.

"Okay."

A LOOK AT BOOK FOUR:
THE CUBAN GAMBIT

As the world edges closer to a new war, Cuba becomes a bloody battleground...

Kane, a relentless lone wolf, embarks on a high-stakes mission to dismantle a sinister missile operation hidden deep in the Cuban jungle. His perilous journey begins in the ruthless underworld of South Korea, where violence knows no bounds. From there, Kane heads to the heart of Cuba with one goal: to destroy the missiles before they can ignite global chaos.

But formidable enemies stand in his way—General Gennady Morozov, mercenary leader Grigori Igoshin, and Cuban cartel boss Julio Garcia. As Kane navigates a web of treachery and danger, the lush green jungle is about to be drenched in blood.

Will Kane succeed in his mission, or will the world plunge into war? Dive into this explosive adventure now and join Kane on his relentless quest.

AVAILABLE SEPTEMBER 2024

ABOUT THE AUTHOR

A relative newcomer to the world of writing, Brent Towns self-published his first book in 2015. Last Stand in Sanctuary took him two years to write. His first hardcover book, a Black Horse Western, was published the following year.

Since then, he has written twenty-six western stories, including some in collaboration with British western author, Ben Bridges; several action adventure novels, such as his bestselling Team Reaper series; the novelization to the 2019 movie, Bill Tilghman and the Outlaws; as well as scripted a handful of Commando Comics. Not bad for an Australian author, he thinks.

Often up until the small hours of the night, bashing away at his tortured keyboard in Queensland, Australia, Brent loves to lose himself in the world of fiction. If you're interested in sharing your thoughts in more detail, scan the QR code below! Your feedback is invaluable to him—and often helps shape his future writing endeavors.

www.ingramcontent.com/pod-product-compliance
Lightning Source LLC
Chambersburg PA
CBHW010729250626
47155CB00011B/3622